Scribe Publications
VIENNESE ROMANCE

David Vogel was born in 1891 in Satanov, Podolia (now Ukraine), and when World War I broke out he was living in Vienna, where he was arrested as an enemy alien. He emigrated to Tel Aviv in 1929, but left for Berlin after a year, and later settled in Paris. After the outbreak of World War II, he was imprisoned by the French as an Austrian citizen, and later by the Nazis as a Jew. In 1944, he was deported to Auschwitz, where he perished.

VIENNESE ROMANCE

DAVID VOGEL

Translated by Dalya Bilu

SCRIBE

Melbourne • London

Scribe Publications Pty Ltd

18–20 Edward St, Brunswick, Victoria 3056, Australia
50A Kingsway Place, Sans Walk, London, EC1R 0LU, United Kingdom

Published by Scribe 2013

Typeset in 11.5/15.5 pt Dante MT by the publishers
Printed and bound in China by 1010 Printing

A Cataloguing-in-Publication data record is available from the
National Library of Australia

scribepublications.com.au
scribepublications.co.uk

CONTENTS

FOREWORD

Lilach Nethanel

I

The untitled manuscript published here for the first time as *Viennese Romance* was discovered in 2010 among the literary effects of David Vogel, preserved in the Gnazim archive in Tel Aviv. Once I had deciphered the manuscript, I realised that before me was a complete and unknown work by Vogel. On fifteen large sheets of paper, darkened by the coating of ink, Vogel concealed no fewer than 75,000 words, written in minuscule script. This is an early Viennese novel, and at its centre is the figure of Michael Rost, who shares some characteristics with Vogel himself, and some aspects of his biography too, as a young subtenant in a bourgeois household who becomes entangled in affairs with the mistress of the house and with her sixteen-year-old daughter.

Around one hundred years after Vogel started writing it, in all probability in the 1920s, and after being buried for some fifty years in the literary archive, the tangle of letters has been unravelled to reveal a full-length novel written in his youth, preserved as a kind of historical document from the early twentieth century and as a coded biographical account of the young Vogel's life in Vienna. *Viennese Romance* completes Vogel's literary canon, and proves that even before he burst into the consciousness of the Hebrew readers of his time with *Married Life* — his only Hebrew novel hitherto known — he already had in hand the drafts of another novel, which he subsequently worked on and left in manuscript form, undated and untitled.

Apart from episodes taking place in Paris at the time of the Paris World Exposition, after World War I, the essence of *Viennese Romance* is located in the early years of the century in Vienna, capital of the Austro-Hungarian Empire before its collapse. Gypsies, Russian-Jewish émigrés, Austrian army officers, bourgeois bureaucrats and patriarchs, stage actors and cabaret singers — these are the people who populate the cafés or sit in the tavern and eat cold cuts washed down with copious quantities of liquor, stroll in the public park to the strains of an orchestra, or bet on cards in smoke-filled back rooms. In a manuscript littered with corrections and erasures, Vogel introduces an eclectic mix of marginal characters, from wealthy heirs to hardworking artisans, including Peter Dean, who has made a fortune from various dubious projects and becomes an industrialist and a man of property as well as Rost's patron; Fritz Anker, the dissolute aristocrat; and a group of Jewish émigrés frequenting Stock's restaurant — all of these and others enter and exit the novel as if through a revolving door. Sometimes they are given a broader role in the development of the plot, taking the lead in substantial episodes; sometimes they are left as a gallery of types; and sometimes it is just the dust of their daily lives that filters through the window of the room where Rost is sitting, such as the singing of the rustic maidservant shaking the sheets outside the window, or the face of the old woman staring into the avenue, or the dull thuds heard from the apartment where Glekner the blacksmith is beating his son, or the pleas of a prostitute trying to wheedle an extra crown from her client. These are the hedonistic men and women of Vienna, seeking in vain for satisfaction in cabaret shows, in pointless military parades, in the beds of prostitutes, and starting to doubt the point of their mundane existence, with a burgeoning and corrosive doubt that will break out in its full horror in the killing fields and the destruction of the impending world war.

Against this background is sketched the story of Michael Rost, a young Jew of Russian–Polish extraction who has emigrated to Vienna alone. A number of extracts from the young Vogel's personal diary, written in Vienna in the years 1912–1922, are given fictional expression here in the form of Michael Rost and others. Like Vogel himself, Rost arrives in Vienna penniless, and first lives in the house of a sterile old woman who keeps a canary in a cage, and like Vogel, who in his diary tells the story of the triangular love affair that he conducted with a woman older than himself and with her daughter, Rost too becomes involved in an affair with his landlady, Gertrude, and her daughter, Erna. This autobiographical episode, which is given dramatic development in the novel, is one of the most fascinating treasures of Vogel's corpus, and it features again in one of his early, hidden poems, which describes two women, mother and daughter, with the poet trapped between them: 'And I am caught between two women / Both one and the other, long-tongued / She allures with her scarlet passion / And she with her white innocence.'[1]

II

In the middle of the last century, the Gnazim archive was established to preserve the literary legacy of Hebrew writers, in the shadow of reports of the Jewish Holocaust in Europe. Among the materials committed to this archive was a substantial portion of Vogel's literary estate, all trace of which had disappeared a few years before. Since then, and to this day, other parts of the corpus have been located in New York, in France, and in Tel Aviv, and these too have been transferred to the same archive, in the file numbered 231 and labelled 'David Vogel'.

The file contains pages of script of varying size, some of them ready for sending to the printer and others riddled with erasures and corrections; there are also notebooks containing poems, lists, a German one-year diary dating from 1917, a school exercise book, letters, and stamped postcards.

These faded scraps of manuscript, which long ago lost any spark of relevance to the outside world, include letters destined for people who have long since left their homes, and probably left this world as well, and urgent reminders, long since expired, of debts owed in antiquated currency. Like a key to a door that is no longer locked, we can now read in one of the notebooks a railway schedule ('Public train to Salzburg at 9.30 p.m.'), the hurried draft of a letter sent by

Vogel to Yosef Aharonowitz in Jaffa ('Dear Aharonowitz, my friend Wilansky wrote to tell me that he consulted you about my [immigration visa], and you very kindly promised to take this up with the authorities'), a memorandum scrawled on a scrap of paper ('1. about the pictures 2. to the dentist 3. buy new shirt'), or a few words written on one of the pages of the one-year diary ('Spring day today; wonderful, cool weather'). And in another place, in round script, in a hand not used to writing Hebrew: 'And he fell silent and gave me a look of sorrow such as I had never seen before on his face. I took out his cigarettes and put one between his lips.'

Some 120 years after Vogel's birth, an unknown work has been discovered in his literary legacy. In fact, during his lifetime, only a tiny proportion of Vogel's work was released from the seclusion of the writing desk, from the pocket of the dressing-gown, from the pages of a notebook or an exercise book, and printed as complete works. In the past sixty years, since Abraham Broides and Dan Pagis began working on the literary archive, and with the material having also been examined by Menahem Peri and Aharon Komem, original and unknown chapters from Vogel's work have been found, including his last several poems from the 1940s, his personal diary dating back to World War I, and his second book of poetry, which was thought to be lost. There is also a Hebrew translation by Peri of a novella that Vogel wrote in Yiddish during World War II. Peri has also re-edited the whole of Vogel's known prose corpus — the novellas *In the Sanatorium* (1927) and *Facing the Sea* (1934), and the novel *Married Life* (1929–1930) — on the basis of the manuscripts in the archive. This project, most of it carried out in the 1980s and 1990s, restored Vogel's prose to its rightful place on Israel's literary bookshelf. It was Peri who first placed Vogel at the centre of the modern Hebrew literary map, not only as a poet but also — and especially — as a novelist, whose work may be read alongside the classic works of modern literature, both in their original language and in translation.[2]

It is likely that before the veteran Vogel scholars set about examining his literary legacy, the fifteen pages comprising the manuscript of the concealed novel from his youth had come to light on several occasions but had not yet been fully deciphered or identified as independent work. The pages on which the novel is written are crammed with tiny letters that fill all the space on the paper, without margins and without any division between chapters and paragraphs, and at first sight I too took this to be a haphazard collection of untitled drafts. Furthermore, when I deciphered one page selected at random from the collection of sheets, I thought that this was no new discovery but an unknown draft of the novella *Facing the Sea* — admittedly a partial and very early draft, but clearly evoked in it was the summer landscape characterising that erotic novella, set in a resort village in the south of France. I even recognised the familiar names of the holidaymakers in this first reading, by the morning light filtering in through the large, darkened windows of the reading room in the Gnazim archive.

It was only on one of the subsequent pages, likewise plucked at random from the collection of papers, that all at once the sunny, indulgent atmosphere of the novella changed into a description of an urban environment: instead of the long stretches of sand of the French coast, suddenly a tram laden with passengers passed close by a canal, the pink lights of a cabaret flickered, a uniformed police officer patrolled the Ringstrasse. There was no need to read any further — I knew that this was Vienna, Vogel's home from 1912 to 1925.

The collection of papers scattered over my desk thus comprised, besides the draft of *Facing the Sea*, another unknown manuscript, similar and almost identical to it in appearance. After some time, following the decipherment and arrangement of all fifteen sheets, I realised that this was an early novel that Vogel had encoded in tiny and cramped handwriting, and then buried among the other manuscripts — either for storage or for further revision at some time in the future, a time that was never to come.

III

As a young poet beginning to publish his poetry in Hebrew periodicals, Vogel wandered between the capital cities of western Europe. In 1912, after an initial itinerant period, he chose to make his home in the city of Vienna. Vogel's routine in Vienna was typical of the civilian experience of his times, in the early twentieth century: the inferno of World War I; the urban avenues and the bustling tramcars; the conversations in cafés; the mutual loans of a few coppers for a meal, to mail a letter, or to go towards the rent owing to a stern and rapacious landlady.

In 1925, some years after publishing the collection of poems *Before the Dark Gate* in Vienna, the first and only such collection to be published in his lifetime, Vogel made his way to Paris. Following an abortive attempt at emigration to Palestine, and a brief sojourn in Berlin, Paris was his home until World War II. In Paris, too, Vogel lived the life of an émigré poet, roaming the streets, harassed by the burden of writing, and worried for his physical and economic survival. His friend Moshe Ben-Menachem said of him:

> For two hours and more he would drag his weary feet from his apartment in the southern suburbs of Paris to arrive in time at his café, the Coupole, and here he stood by the door hoping that today he would be lucky and meet someone, preferably someone with five francs to spare for him, or even less. For five francs you could buy your whole world — bread to eat and cigarettes to smoke, even a few pages for writing on.[3]

After Vogel's death, these pages were buried with the rest of his literary remains, sent from France to the USA, and ultimately to the Gnazim archive in Tel Aviv.

The peripatetic course of this literary heritage until the time of its gradual consolidation in the Gnazim archive is the result of an unclear and sometimes bizarre sequence of events, associated for many years with the question of Vogel's ultimate fate during the war. In 1944 he disappeared without a trace; and after the war, reports of his disappearance began to feature in the Israeli press, and various accounts of his death were circulated. Hillel Bavli wrote that he heard about Vogel's last moments from his daughter Tamar Vogel-Mizrahi, who emigrated to the USA after the war: 'In 1944 he was about to be deported from Paris to Poland, to one of the extermination camps, and before the train left the station he escaped from the hands of the murderers — and collapsed and died of a heart attack.'[4] Another account, according to which he was shot while attempting to escape from the railway wagon, was taken up and expanded in poetic style in a tribute composed for him by Moshe Ben-Menachem:

> And suddenly the sound of gunfire fractured the white silence, and a man, resembling a child lost in the forest of the world, fell to the ground in the white field; he sank down slowly, quivered a few times like a dying bird, and a small pool of blood gathered slowly beneath him, and spread until the white snow all around him was stained bright red.[5]

It was only years later, in 2005, that Dan Laor discovered Vogel had in fact been murdered in Auschwitz. Laor found a list of prisoners sent on 7 March 1944 from the internment camp at Drancy to Auschwitz, and Vogel's name was included. 'The rumours that circulated formerly, according to which Vogel escaped at the last moment from the death-train in Paris and died of a heart attack, or was shot, were unreliable from the outset', Laor declared when his findings were published.[6]

But leaving aside the solution to the riddle of Vogel's disappearance during the war, a question remains: how the manuscripts he left behind came to be found and how they arrived in the Gnazim archive.

From indirect testimony it emerges that before his arrest by the Gestapo, Vogel had time to bury his writings in the garden of a guesthouse in the township of Hauteville in south-eastern France, where he lived during the war years.

According to the literary historian Shimon Halkin, after the war the painter Avraham Goldberg, a family friend, excavated the garden of the guesthouse, found the cache, and handed it over to him. At the end of the 1940s, Halkin passed on all the papers in his possession to Asher Barash, later to be the founder of the Gnazim archive.[7]

But how did Avraham Goldberg succeed from the outset in locating Vogel's literary legacy in the garden of that guesthouse? And was it really there that the cache was found? Is it likely that Vogel, in a hurry to leave Paris with his young daughter, would have risked travelling by the crowded and chaotic wartime trains, carrying a suitcase crammed full of his precious manuscripts? Perhaps the material, or some of it at least, was left in Paris, his principal residence for the last fifteen years of his life, the same city where Goldberg himself was based for long periods of time.

If, in spite of all this, Vogel chose to move his writings to Hauteville and bury them there, as Halkin said, in the garden of the guesthouse, lest they be destroyed or lost, he would have needed to keep his papers in a sealed box to prevent damage by moisture or soil contamination, and he would have had to bury them in a deep enough hole. He would have needed to dig in secret, perhaps in the night, to avoid arousing suspicion, and then mark the site and find some way of conveying this information to Goldberg, who was himself forced to go into hiding during the war. Communication between the two of them would have certainly been sporadic and unreliable. After the war Goldberg would have had to locate the manuscripts according to the agreed clues, dig with pick and shovel to the estimated depth, scratch with his fingernails and forcibly take hold of the object revealed (safe? wooden box? cardboard wrapping? parcel swaddled in sheets?), and draw it out of the wet ground, soaked by the rains of summer or winter.

In the years 2008–2010, when I sat in the old reading room of the Gnazim archive, then located in the Saul Tchernichovsky house, the contents of the Vogel file seemed smooth and orderly, and even the large pages of the hitherto-unknown novel had not been folded or creased, or stained or torn, and were just a little frayed at the edges. Through the footsteps of time, through the dusty degeneration of the paper, it was still possible to decipher the script of a youthful novel, unripe at times, like the record of the beating of an anxious heart.

IV

Viennese Romance is, for the most part, the product of an early period of writing in the Vogel corpus, and the style sometimes shows signs of immaturity by comparison with his style in the book of poems *Before the Dark Gate* (1923), and in the novel *Married Life* (1929–1930). In fact, essential elements from the plot of *Married Life* are hinted at in this early work: for example, the story told by Misha the anarchist about his friend who was forced to bring up his child single-handedly, in the absence of its mother, with the child not surviving its first year; and the story of Max Karp, the writer and artist, and Malvina, his spouse, who are doomed to years of marriage, united by a bond of mutual antipathy. These vignettes and others like them are brief sparks prefiguring Vogel's future writing. Whether because of the undeveloped style in which some of the chapters are written, or on account of the content that recalled his own love affairs, Vogel decided to conceal the early drafts of what was to have been his first Viennese novel and to concentrate his efforts instead on the writing of *Married Life*, a more sophisticated Viennese novel, which he completed and published at the end of the 1920s.

It was only in the early 1930s, some five years after moving from Vienna to Paris, and more than ten years after hiding his first drafts, that Vogel in all probability returned to his earlier novel. At this juncture he added to the Viennese plot an opening set in Paris after World War I, and copied this into the manuscript that we hold. At about the same time, Vogel was writing the novella *Facing the Sea*, an early draft of which, as we have seen, became mixed up in the pages of the manuscript of *Viennese Romance*. In view of the graphic similarity between the two documents and, more significantly, on the basis of the letters that Vogel wrote during these years to his editor at the time, Asher Barash, it may be presumed that he worked on the two texts in parallel, or approximately so. Apparently, in November 1932 Vogel wrote to Barash, informing him that apart from his work on the novella, he was also busy writing a new novel: 'I am about to finish a long story. Besides that, I am also working on a big novel, which is still in the preliminary stages.'[8]

But this 'big' novel was never presented for publication, and *Facing the Sea* was the last prose work published in Vogel's lifetime. The fate of the manuscript of *Viennese Romance* was linked with the fate of the Yiddish novella that Vogel wrote during World War II, which remained a manuscript and was never copied into final form. Likewise, the extant manuscript of *Viennese Romance* cannot be considered the final form of the work: the cramped writing, the absence of paragraph divisions, and above all the ostentatious absence of a title — all of this shows that there was still a final revision to be done, and perhaps more.

Another document in the archive proves that Vogel intended to continue editing the manuscript. In this document we find the Viennese opening of the novel, describing the arrival of Michael Rost in Vienna and his early days in the city.[9] Contrary to the opinion expressed by Menahem Peri in his afterword to the collection *Extinguished Stations*, these are not the opening pages of a Hebrew novel that Vogel was planning to write in the early 1940s, but a revised version of the manuscript of a novel that had been written many years before, and was waiting as a part of Vogel's literary legacy for renewed editing.[10]

It is possible that work on the final version of *Viennese Romance* was interrupted in the late 1930s or the early 1940s; it is also possible that Vogel's internment at the beginning of the war (as an enemy-alien resident in France) caused him to neglect his early novel, and also at this point to stop writing in Hebrew, concentrating, upon his release from detention, on composing a chronicle of the war in Yiddish, the novella *They All Went Out to War*. Possibly, it was this historic upheaval that led Vogel to replace Michael Rost, his young and arrogant philanderer from Vienna, with the middle-aged artist Weichert, who has a daughter and a sick wife, and who, after numerous vicissitudes and spells of internment in various French prison camps, is finally put into a railway wagon and sent against his will to an unknown destination. One way or the other, apart from the political circumstances that influenced the course of his writing, we have no firm testimony other than this short document that contains the revised version of the opening of the novel and that ends with a blank page: at the top, Vogel has written only the heading 'Chapter Two' without any words underneath. Also surviving are the fifteen pages of the full manuscript of the Viennese novel, kept in Vogel's pocket, pending clarification of its ultimate fate.

V

In all of Vogel's work, this early text represents his most concentrated effort to write a novel with multiple focuses, a novel where the narrative structure seems to reflect the city described in it, the windows of its buildings, lit up and darkened in turns, hinting at the existence of close and parallel currents of life. In light of what Oded Menda-Levy and Shachar Pinsker have recently written regarding the link between Vogel's style and the urban landscapes in which he lived and wrote,[11] we should consider the note that Vogel jotted in the margin of a truncated manuscript found in his archive, declaring his intention 'to write a novel about Paris, about Montparnasse, entitled "The Bee-hive"'.[12] Despite his plans, Vogel never wrote a novel of this kind, and the evocation of the Paris World Exposition in *Viennese Romance* is the closest he came to writing 'The Bee-hive'. Inspired by the Exposition, Vogel worked on the first and the lost drafts of the novel with its Viennese plot, centred on the love triangle between Rost, the mother, and her daughter.

The teeming relationships between Rost and his women,

and between the other characters, male and female, who appear in the novel, lie at the very heart of Vogel's enquiry, in his work in general and in *Viennese Romance* in particular, into sex and sexuality. In the early twentieth century these topics were central to the thinking of distinguished Viennese writers, including Freud, Arthur Schnitzler, Joseph Roth, Robert Musil, and Otto Weininger. Vienna was described, in Schnitzler's words, as a city steeped in twilight, where the codes of morality and bourgeois restraint had been fractured, and the erotic and the criminal were revealed instead as the guiding principles of social and economic relations, far more potent than the legal system, family, or profession. In Vienna at the turn of the century, ropes were not infrequently suspended from attic beams, ready for the necks of young girls who had fallen pregnant and been thrown out of their fathers' houses. And in the suburbs of the city, in an old tenement recently converted into a hotel, was the room in which the brilliant but cursed young man Otto Weininger shot himself dead in October 1903.

The influence of the Weininger scandal and of his book, the pseudo-scientific tome *Sex and Character*,[13] is evident in *Viennese Romance*. Through the romantic triangle between Rost, his landlady, and her daughter, Vogel tried to offer a basis for a categorical characterisation of the male and female sexes, thus shifting this story from the realm of light erotic drama to that of sceptical investigation, in keeping with the spirit of the early twentieth century. In the sexual characterisation of the mother and daughter, and in the crude sketches of patriarchs, feminists, revolutionaries, anarchists, servants, and prostitutes, readers may have reservations about the sexual 'typecasting'. From this point of view *Viennese Romance* is an uncomfortable document, articulating the fear of the differences between the sexes. In this sense Vogel follows in the footsteps of his teacher Otto Weininger, who is explicitly mentioned in the novel:

> There was someone, a writer, who invented something new, a kind of instrument, if you will, to measure the male substance in a woman and the female substance in a man. No more and no less. So and so many grams of the female substance in a man — disqualified! An inferior specimen! Because according to him, needless to say, women are base creatures, afflicted by every shortcoming, incapable of genius. Genius! And after coming up with this invention, he killed himself. He went and killed himself!

The sexual chemistry between male and female 'substances' is presented in Weininger's book as a decisive factor in determining character; that is, the fixed and unchangeable foundation of all personality. At the basis of the study of character — alongside the science of physiognomy, of which Weininger was one of the first proponents — stands a stubborn refusal to admit the principle behind the Enlightenment, meaning the very ability to shape a person's social and personal values. From this perspective Weininger expresses the great change of awareness in turn-of-the-century Europe, from the idea of rational progress to Expressionism, which focuses on sensual human existence. The young Vogel read Weininger's theses with great interest and not uncritically; and by means of the amorous exploits of the foreign tenant in the respectable bourgeois household, he sought to express the political, social, and economic doubts of a society that was redefining its centres of power and its racial dynamics.

VI

Like his more familiar work, *Viennese Romance* again identifies Vogel as a European author writing in Hebrew. But as stated previously, the novel differs from his other writing in its unfinished state, and the writer's hand can be seen annotating and erasing, still unsure whether to leave on the page the references and the background information that he carefully excluded from his published work. These include such landmarks as his ancestral home, the town of his birth, and the emigration routes of the Jews at the beginning of the century; the Yiddish accents in the language of the customers at Stock's restaurant; the hoarse singing of the tenor turning up at Jewish weddings to perform for a few copper coins; the relocation of Michael Rost, Misha the anarchist, and Yasha the Odessan to the capital of the Austro-Hungarian empire — all these were drawn from the early life of Vogel, who roamed between the cities of Podolia and Galicia, first as a *yeshiva* student and then as a Hebrew teacher, before settling in Vienna. The description of the brightly lit and technologically advanced European city is often transformed into an evocation of his native town, with the dog in the garden of the priest's house, soldiers patronising the Jewish brothel, young revolutionaries rebelling against the conformist lifestyle of their mercantile parents, and the minuscule number of emigrants trying their luck in a desolate Oriental land. Similarly, the manuscript of

Vogel's hidden novel is a signpost guiding the reader from the illuminated avenues of western European capitals, the scenes of Vogel's restless meandering, to the haunts of his childhood in the east of the continent; and from the polished, edited versions of the body of work that he published in his lifetime to a bundle of erasures and corrections representing a preliminary stage in the process of drafting and crafting.

The final and essential assessment of the manuscript is this: Vogel's writing hand hovers over the page like the pendulum of a clock, like time. His hitherto-unseen novel throws new light on his familiar work, precisely because it is riddled with corrections and erasures that expose the living process of writing, the agonising and the rewriting. Here we find snippets of everyday life, simple and occasional notes from the young Vogel's life in Vienna and later in Paris, such as the names of stars of the silent cinema, Henny Porten and Adolphe Menjou, as well as popular tunes from the operettas of Jean Gilbert, the Hungarian March, and Yiddish wedding songs. There are also brand-names of various liquors, including slivovitz and Bénédictine, the smell of the printers' ink on the evening papers in the cafés, the sight of the avenues divided between lanes for riding and lanes for driving, electric bulbs illuminating apartments with bright lights that people at the turn of the century were not yet accustomed to. All these are snapshots of daily life in the European capitals of the early twentieth century, patterns that have long since withered and faded away — except in the literary legacy of David Vogel, File 231, Gnazim archive, Tel Aviv.

VII

My thanks to the Society of Hebrew Authors, and to the director and staff of the Gnazim archive, who put the Vogel literary legacy at my disposal on every one of my visits to the reading room. My tutor Professor Avidov Lipsker-Albeck from the Department of Hebrew Literature at Bar-Ilan University was a key collaborator in the initial stages, and there is not enough room on the page to express my gratitude to him. Merav Kane-Yosefi generously helped me with the documentation of the manuscript and arranging it in readiness for deciphering. Professor Yitskhok Niborski and Sharon Bar-Kochva kindly explained to me the Yiddish quotations in the text, and the Hebrew expressions borrowed from Yiddish; and Dr Claudia Rosenzweig translated for me a German song that turned up in the text, written in Vogel's unclear German hand. Thanks also to Am Oved Publishers, whose help with this sensitive project from beginning to end has been very professional and supportive. Most crucial and important of all has been my collaboration with Youval Shimoni, in the preparation and editing of the text, an experience that has been a pleasure and a privilege.

(Translated by Philip Simpson)

NOTES

1. David Vogel, 'Hidden Poems 1911–1913', from David Vogel, *Collected Poems* (ed. Aharon Komem), Hakibbutz Hameuchad, 1998.

[xxv]

2. The novella *Facing the Sea* was re-edited by Menahem Peri and published for the first time in book form by Siman Kriah in 1974. Since 1986, prose works of Vogel have been published under Peri's editorship in the New Library series for Hakibbutz Hameuchad: *Married Life* (1986), *Extinguished Stations: novella, novel, story, diary* (1990), *Facing the Sea* (2005), *In the Sanatorium* (2008).

3. Moshe Ben-Menachem, 'Beyond the Dark Gate: a tribute to the late David Vogel', in Yosef Arica, B. Mordecai, and Yitzhak Agen (eds), *Onyx: Forum for Literature Philosophy and Art*, Nisan 5714 (1954), p. 209.

4. Hillel Bavli, 'Three Authors: David Vogel', *Post*, issue A, Marheshvan 5710 (1950), p. 33.

5. Moshe Ben-Menachem, 'Beyond the Dark Gate', p. 215.

6. Dan Laor, 'Where Were the Prisoners Taken? A crucial chapter missing from the war-time chronicle of David Vogel', in *From Centres to Centre* (ed. Nurit Govrin), Tel Aviv University and Beth Shalom-Aleichem, 2005, p. 411.

7. In his introduction to an edition of *Beyond the Silence* (poems), Aharon Komem added a marginal note to the effect that he heard this himself from Shimon Halkin in Jerusalem, on 23 November 1980. See: Aharon Komem, 'The Travels of Vogel's Legacy', introduction to Aharon Komem (ed.), *Beyond the Silence*, Hakibbutz Hameuchad, 1983, p. 62, note 2. Menahem Peri repeats the story in an article for *Siman Kriah*, issue 18 (May 1986), on the publication of the short story 'The Lodger': 'After World War II, the painter Avraham Goldberg dug up the garden of an old woman with whom Vogel lived before he was sent to an extermination camp, and he found manuscripts of Vogel, among which this story was "hidden".' Ibid., p. 72.

8. Letter dated 3 November 1932, preserved in the Gnazim archive: File Vogel 231, C – 41861 – A.

9. Manuscript preserved in the Gnazim archive: File Vogel 231, C – 13455.

10. Menahem Peri, 'Vogel Lost Vogel', afterword to David Vogel, *Extinguished Stations*, Hakibbutz Hameuchad / Siman Kriah Books, 1990, p. 328.

11. Oded Menda-Levy, *Reading the City: the urban experience from the mid-19th century to the mid-20th century*, Hakibbutz Hameuchad, 2010. Shachar Pinsker, *Literary Passports: the making of modernist Hebrew fiction in Europe*, Stanford University Press, 2010.

12. Manuscript in Gnazim archive (see note 9).

13. Otto Weininger, *Sex and Character* (*Geschlecht und Charakter*), Braumuller, Vienna, 1903; tr. Ladislaus Lob, Indiana University Press, 2005.

VIENNESE
ROMANCE

PROLOGUE

Michael Rost glanced through the window at the fine threads of an autumn shower falling on the riverbank. 'Hmm,' he said, and left the room. It was about ten at night. A reddish-brown sky lay over the roofs; the pavement gleamed moistly. His tall body leaning forward with a slight stoop, he strolled at a leisurely pace along the gradually emptying streets, past the brightly lit display windows, past the prostitutes standing under the awnings. After a while he went into a café. He nodded briefly in the direction of a few acquaintances and sat down opposite the entrance at a small table whose occupants had just left. Emmy Vitler, her red hair cropped and her slim figure dressed in black, waved a slender, delicate hand, and gave him a friendly smile. Without waiting for an invitation she sat down next to him and lit a cigarette.

'I was at the cinema. I left in the middle. A boring film.'

'Did you go alone?'

'Yes, I sometimes do. By the way, lately Igon has been paying attention to the pretty little Pole. You know her. A real charmer.'

With pouting lips she took little sips of the steaming

coffee. Next, she took a gold compact out of her black hand-bag and powdered her face. From the whispering embers of the cigarette lying in her saucer, its tip stained red by her lipstick, a reddish-blue spiral of smoke rose, giving off a pungent, perfumed smell.

'And who is taking his place in the meantime?' Rost smiled.

'Impudence! But I'll tell you anyway. I'm taking a short break to explore philosophical questions about the meaning of life …' And she laughed an arch little laugh.

'Have you reached the right age? One usually begins such pursuits at the age of fifty and over. According to my estima-tion you have about twenty-five years to go.'

'Plain women start at any age.'

'Are you trying to fish for compliments? Do you really need them?'

'All women do. Even the most beautiful. Without them she grows ugly.'

'And the one who pays the most compliments wins the prize?'

'Maybe.'

'In that case … in that case all is not lost for men suffering from all kinds of deformities.'

Emmy immediately imagined a horribly disfigured crip-ple crouching over her body. A wave of revulsion rose in her throat. 'Please stop. You're making me think the most loathsome thoughts.'

Men and women of all ages, nationalities, and languages crowded round tables crammed closely together. They drank, talked, laughed loudly, smoked, gave themselves up completely to that spirit of revelry, real and artificial at once, in which the atmosphere of the city was steeped. Rost looked at the entrance, scanning the faces of the diverse crowd going in and out, blocking the way of the waiters, who were forced to raise their trays of drinks high above their heads. His bloodless, oval face wore a hard expression not devoid of cruelty. Again he was prey to that piercing boredom lying deep in the heart of a man, like some cancer of the soul, the inheritance of entire generations who had not denied themselves any of the pleasures of this world, and some of whom had put an end to their lives, sickened by satiety. He drank a little of the black coffee in front of him, which had already grown cold.

'Here's Gregor!' Emmy indicated a man in a cap and a shabby summer coat, excessively wide and too short to reach his knees, who was making his way straight to their table.

Emmy introduced him. He pulled up an unoccupied chair from another table and sat down. He turned straight to Rost, without any preliminaries: 'Where is your studio? You're a painter, aren't you?' As he spoke he exposed the stubs of a few isolated orange-brown teeth.

'I'm not a painter at all.'

'You're a sly customer!' His mouth twisted into a sound-less laugh.

He poked a short pipe into his mouth, and with his other hand he took off his cap and put it on his lap. His head was bald, round and gleaming, emphasising the stubble of his beard. 'And what philosopher are you reading now?'

'Not that either. You are completely mistaken.'

'In that case, you are even more worthy of buying me a cup of coffee or, rather, a glass of wine. You understand something about life, Herr Rost! With people of your ilk

Paul Gregor likes to waste words, hee-hee. Garcon, white wine!'

Emmy laughed.

'I'm not at all sure that I am worthy of the honour,' joked Rost.

'Indeed you are, sir! Don't be so modest. I lost my hair and my teeth to it, and I know what I'm talking about!' He sucked vigorously on his unlit pipe. 'However, if you happen to be a writer, you are entitled to study me and make use of me to your heart's content. In this you have been preceded by many another. These poor writers, apart from a few exceptional cases, lack imagination; and interesting people are so rare. And so they fall on me like hungry dogs. I have plenty — enough for everybody!'

'No, I'm not a writer either.'

'No? If so, you are a rare bird indeed.' He pressed his monocle, which was hanging from a black cord, into his right eye and made as if to examine his interlocutor, his pale, watery eyes twitching and his mouth twisted in laughter. Rost met his look with a mocking expression.

'No!' Gregor delivered his verdict. 'You won't find another dozen like you here, I bet. Not in this quarter — no!'

'And you yourself, for instance?'

'Me? A writer, of course; that first of all. A writer of letters begging public benefactors. What can I say — the Germans are uncivilised barbarians! They have no more understanding of painting than a monkey. Coarse, unmannerly brutes, stupid as oxen. And if you were unlucky enough to be born a German painter — you have no option but to become a "writer".' He took an angry gulp of his wine.

Emmy explained: 'Herr Gregor is no doubt in a gloomy

mood again, and so he takes it out on the poor Germans.'

'Quite right. And I've suffered a terrible tragedy too!' And he added: 'My cat committed suicide yesterday.'

'Committed suicide?'

'Threw himself off the third floor. Died on the spot. Lately he's been very depressed. It was obvious to anyone. And he didn't want to eat anything either. Maybe he was sick.' He blinked his little eyes and adjusted the monocle. 'I always bought two steaks for lunch, one for me and one for him. Today I only bought one.'

'He probably fell out of the window by accident,' said Rost.

'You think so?' Gregor brandished his pipe excitedly. 'In that case, my dear sir, you don't understand a thing. A cat, you should know, is never injured in a fall. He always falls on his feet and gets up again. Let me tell you: my cat *committed suicide*! Yes! Because he was depressed! He couldn't shoot himself in the head just so you would believe him!'

Rost stared at him for a moment, his dark green eyes penetrating.

'And apart from that, what have you been up to, Herr Gregor?' intervened Emmy.

'Painting pictures, as usual. All on the same canvas. For a whole year on the same canvas, hee-hee. I've already painted a hundred.'

'A hundred on the same canvas?'

'A hundred on one canvas?'

'Why not? I wipe out one and paint another in its place. The last one will contain them all; anyone who buys it will have to pay for all one hundred. Actually, I'm writing a new philosophy — the writing and the painting are one and the same. It will be the most profound and original work of its generation, I can guarantee.' He finished his wine and ordered another glass, saying, 'I assume you have no objections, Herr Rost!' After which he added, 'And what do you yourself do in this metropolis?'

'It's a secret.'

'Is that so? And the means? Keeping secrets requires means.'

'Sufficient for my needs.'

'Enough for a loan, for example?'

'To whom?'

'To me, of course.'

'Perhaps. How much?'

'Twenty and up. The sky's the limit.'

'Let's say twenty.' Rost laughed and handed him two folded notes.

Gregor took them between his thumb and forefinger and dropped them into his overcoat pocket. 'What will you drink, Herr Rost? Now that I'm rich again, I can afford to treat you. And you, madam? How about a Bénédictine?'

He pressed them until they agreed to order again. 'Why don't you drop in to visit me sometime,' he said to Rost as he tamped the tobacco in his pipe.

'Perhaps when I have the chance.'

'But I'm not always at home.'

'Do you want me to come?'

'Not really. I only said so to be polite. Sometimes, you see, I can even be polite, hee-hee. But one day, when the opportunity offers itself, I'll take you home with me. To see my painting. Don't forget that the man sitting opposite you is the greatest German painter of his generation! A fact known in London, although not in Berlin. What do the Germans understand about painting? Just a minute, sir —' He jumped up and went to meet a short paunchy man with a flushed face and bulging crossed-eyes, who had just emerged from the adjacent hall.

'An original character,' said Emmy, 'and far from a fool. I like listening to him talk and jump from one subject to another. Sometimes he says quite strange things.'

Rost gave her a light. 'Don't you think the time has come for us to have a little love affair, Emmy … without any obligations.'

She laughed; whether in agreement or refusal, it was hard to say.

'Come to me tomorrow. At about three o'clock.'

'Maybe I will.'

'I'll be expecting you,' said Rost firmly. Then he signalled to the waiter and paid.

Rost left the café and walked in the opposite direction to his hotel. Let Lucy wait for him as long as she liked! She was beginning to bore him. It had stopped raining in the meantime. A chill, penetrating wind blew in the streets. There was a smell of autumn in the air, of prostitutes, of sleeping citizens, of coal smoke from a passing train. On all sides, advertising slogans proclaimed their messages, blue and red, pink and purple, blinking on and off. Passing the gaping jaws of the metro you were assailed by the close, foul breath of human beings, preserved for decades and rising ceaselessly to the surface, sometimes accompanied by the muffled rumble of a train. People streamed out of the cinemas. Here and there a woman rocked a sleeping baby in her arms. Indeed, the desire to banish the dreary monotony of daily life with the help of Greta Garbo, Adolphe Menjou, and their like was very strong, but the moment you emerged from the cinema it seized hold of you again, grim and sordid, spreading weariness through your limbs and leaving a bitter dryness in your mouth.

Rost walked slowly along Rue du Bac, which wound its narrow, rainy way towards the Seine, and which was already completely given over to the stillness of the night, interrupted only rarely by a solitary bus. The roar of the city had already died down. He felt a growing desire to commit an act that would begin and end with the night, and would afterwards be confined to the depths of his soul as a closely guarded secret, the kind of act that embodies the future of a man like the seed inside a fruit. But he himself could not define the nature of this act. The flames of the gas lamps on both banks of the river were reflected in the dark water like two gently wavering, parallel rows of oil spots.

A man approached with hollow steps and stood next to Rost, who was leaning on the rail of the bridge and looking down.

'The water's freezing, my friend. This is not the season for swimming.'

'Nobody imagined it was.'

'You're wrong. Less than an hour ago I was here when a young girl threw herself off the bridge. From exactly the same place where you're standing now. I ran to stop her but I was too late.'

'Why did you want to stop her?'

'Out of pure human sympathy, my friend. Concern for my fellow man. It's clear to me that the next moment she would regret it, even as she fell.'

'But you didn't jump in after her. You saved your own skin.'

'That's a matter of temperament. I am not by nature an impulsive man, and I am not in the habit of offering myself up as a sacrifice. As long as my health isn't threatened, I'm at your service!'

'Very convenient, I must say.'

Rost moved away, accompanied by the stranger, a short, shrivelled man with a narrow face and a moustache. Without an overcoat, and with the collar of his jacket raised, he kept his hands in his trouser pockets.

'You should really buy me a drink. In return for the favour I did you.'

'For the favour you did me?'

'Certainly,' replied the stranger gravely, 'I prevented you from drowning ...'

Rost burst into loud laughter. 'You are insane, sir. I had no intention whatsoever of drowning myself.'

'Don't say that. You can never tell. I know something about it, believe me. When a man stands like that and looks down at the water, he is suddenly seized by the idea — that's how it is! It's already happened to me once, and it was only by the greatest effort that I succeeded in grabbing hold of the poor man's hair and pulling him away in the nick of time: before he could turn this way or that, he was grabbed from behind. In any case, I deserve a cognac.'

'You may deserve it. Perhaps everyone does. The question is whether I feel like paying.' And after a moment: 'By the way, is this your only possibility of getting hold of a cognac?'

'At the moment — yes.' He pushed a cigarette under his moustache and lit it with a lighter. 'You'll agree with me that nobody is under the obligation to be always capable of paying for his own drinks.'

They walked along the bank for a while and then turned into the street leading to Les Invalides, to the tangle of ancient winding alleys around the halls of the market. Here, there was already a bustle. Carts laden with produce trundled heavily towards the halls. On all sides people were busy preparing the daily bread of five million souls.

'And by tomorrow night,' pronounced the stranger, 'there won't be any trace of all these thousands of tonnes of food.'

'You'll get your cognac.'

'I thought so.'

'Indeed?'

'Stinginess is out of fashion.'

'Is saving souls your only occupation?'

'You're making fun of me. It's only my temporary occupation.'

'And the steady one?'

'The steady one ... I ... my sister ...'

'Ah, your sister!'

'We were ... I was an actor. I'm not lying.'

'An actor, of all things.'

'An actor in a small neighbourhood theatre.'

'And now?'

'I started to stutter.'

'But I haven't heard you stutter, on the contrary.'

'Not like this. Only on the stage. I was the avenger, you know; I had to wave my sword and stab the traitor with the words: "Die, villain!" But at the last minute an idea suddenly popped into my mind: if I were to stutter now, it would sound really ridiculous. And I immediately began to stutter. On no account could I get past the *d* and the *v*. And from then on, whenever I stepped onto the stage I immediately started to stutter. It was as if the words stuck to my mouth.'

'And your sister —'

'She's an orphan.'

Rost gave him a cigarette.

'I taught her dressmaking. She works in a clothing shop.'

'Hmm.'

'Her boss has taken a fancy to her. You yourself are a foreigner. A German, if I'm not mistaken.'

'Let's say an Austrian.'

'It makes no difference to me. I'm a cosmopolitan, you know; it's less tedious, don't you think? Let's go in here.' He indicated a small bar. 'They know me here.'

In the long narrow bar, where a few rowdy, rather suspicious-looking customers were seated, Rost ordered two cognacs. His companion emptied his glass in one swallow and wiped his moustache with the back of his hand. Rost studied the golden liquid in the round glass with its long, slender stem, and by an unconscious process of association he thought of Emmy. Yes, she would come. Definitely.

'Another one?' he said.

'If it's no trouble. You know, I was a prisoner of war in Germany. I was working in an alehouse in a small village. The owner's name was Martha. A very strong woman. Tall like you, with arms like two iron bars. She wrote long letters to her husband at the front and went to bed with me. What can I say — it was wartime! But she had a nineteen-year-old daughter, and I went to bed with her too. In the end the mother heard about it, and she slapped me on both cheeks and sent me back to the camp. The child, I heard later, was born to the mother, not the daughter.'

Rost paid.

'What, you're leaving already? Good. I won't keep you. But if you ever need me, you can always find me here. They know me well here; you only have to ask for the actor. I have certain connections, you understand' — he winked slyly and made an insinuating gesture with his hand — 'and a man like you …'

'A man like me?'

'A man like you will sometimes need a man like me.'

'You think so?'

'I know something about people.'

'No. A man like me does not need a man like you.'

'You never know. In any case, you'll find me here.'

Aimlessly he strolled through the crooked, deserted alleys, which seemed to be holding a secret and gave rise in him to an unconscious inner tension. From time to time an enormous rat raced over the dank asphalt and disappeared into the iron grating of the sewer. A dim, distant whisper, which seemed to lack any material existence, floated through the air, once in this direction, once in that, and then died down, leaving behind it a dense silence that united with the blind buildings in a frozen stillness. An unclear memory of a night like this, buried beneath the rubble of the years and their events, flickered inside him, and at the same time something pale and undefined hovered before his eyes, apparently related to, and perhaps even crucial to, that night in the past. But Rost did not like digging up the past. Every event in his life, once it had sunk into the depths of the past, lost its reality for him, as if it had never happened; whereas the present moment, this damp, round autumn night, simply bored him, unlike those of his peers who avidly pursued every passing moment and found everything of interest. Yes, it was time to make for the boulevards and take a taxi home.

The erect figure of a woman emerged from the shadows and made straight for him. He stood still in the middle of the pavement until she came close. The pale-orange light of a nearby lamp fell on a young face with strange, deeply shadowed eyes that looked at him with a certain hesitation. There was a tense, unusual charm about this face. A brief moment passed before she said: 'Please spend the rest of the night with me. I can't be by myself today.' And she added quickly: 'You don't have to pay. Not even for the hotel room.'

Rost deliberated for a moment, and then gave way to the inner impulse to go with her. For about ten minutes the two of them walked in silence through the streets, until she stopped in front of a small hotel with a sign announcing: 'Hotel Grenoble, every convenience provided.' Rost was taken up to a room on the third floor, pervaded by the lingering smell of women's cosmetics. It was a small room that gave off a sense of mournful solitude, the wallpaper patterned with red flowers on a blue background, the bronze bed taking up almost a third of the space. After removing her coat and hat and hanging them up, together with those of her guest, on a rack attached to the door, she brought a chair up to the table for him, and took a bottle of wine and glasses out of the cupboard.

'Your face is not unsympathetic,' she said as she sat down opposite him and crossed her legs. 'How fortunate for me that you were the one I happened to meet.' She poured the wine and took a sip. Her thick chestnut hair, with its occasional glints of gold, was rolled around her head, making her look a little like a mushroom. Not ugly, decided Rost.

'Today, I'm celebrating!' she said with a nasty smile. 'I'm celebrating my birthday. My parents, hee-hee, my parents made today a cause for celebration … Do you have parents too? But surely not like mine — mine are unique.'

Rost gave her a cigarette and lit it. 'Your parents?'

'Oh, so you want to know, do you? It interests you? And you imagine that I'm prepared to go into the details of my life with anyone off the street? Not so fast, my dear!' Her dark eyes suddenly flashed with tremendous hostility. 'Not a word! You won't get a single word out of me, you hear?' With an angry backward toss of her head she tried to flick away the wisps of hair that had fallen onto her forehead.

Rost took hold of her hand and said firmly: 'Listen here, little one, I didn't come here to argue with you, understand?'

'What then? You want to go to bed? Right away? You don't look like someone who's never seen a woman before, I can tell! And if you feel the urge — here goes!' She emptied her glass.

After a short pause, in a changed voice trembling with an undertone of sorrow, she said: 'People need an illusion, you know, even if only once … is life possible without it? The lover stole into his beloved's room in the dead of night, ha ha ha! Come on, drink a toast with me: here's to your beloved!' She stood up and took a few steps towards the bed, turned round, and came to stand next to him. Then she changed her mind and sat down on her chair again. With her head resting on her hand, she sat for a while without moving.

'This is all a little strange,' reflected Rost, looking at her as he smoked. 'How long have you been doing this job?'

She raised her eyes to him in bewilderment, as if surprised at his presence there. Then she spat out venomously: 'Four, five years — at your service, noble sir! Anything else you want to know? In the quarter they call me Ginger Janet, and a while ago my "husband" was sentenced to hard labour … Have you calmed down already? Everything's as usual, no?'

Rost rose to his feet. 'You want to drag me into a fight, is that it? Or a little rape perhaps? And what are you selling?'

At these words she jumped from her chair, blushing deeply. Frantically she began to strip off her orange dress, her pink silk slip, her suspender belt; throwing them one after the other onto the bed until she was left in her shoes and stockings. Her figure was very shapely. She came up to him and pointed at various parts of her body, boiling with rage: 'Here you are, sir, this is what I'm selling! … And this! … And this! … Inferior merchandise, is it? Spoiled goods?'

Rost burst into loud laughter. 'Not a bad introduction, I must say!' He sat down and pulled the naked woman onto his lap. 'Very well, my little one. I'm ready to celebrate your birthday with you!'

She sat there for a moment, her shoulders shuddering. In the end she stood up and wrapped herself in a dressing-gown that she took out of the cupboard. Tears glittered in her eyes. After resuming her previous seat, she poured herself a glass of wine and drank it. 'Please don't think I'm crazy or vicious. I know very well that you could get up at any moment and walk out of here, and then … I'm so afraid of that moment. I admit it. This bottle, the table, the bed — it all terrifies me, all of it. When you leave here I'll be left alone again. Do you know the feeling of a person on his own, left all alone in the whole wide world, who suddenly starts to feel afraid? Everything is apparently the same as always, but one fine day a drop of fear enters your soul, and that drop remains in you, and it spreads inside you until it takes over your whole being like a kind of blood poisoning ... and there's no escape. But why am I telling you all this? I'm selling my body — please help yourself! So you won't have taken the trouble for nothing!'

She sat still, her eyes fixed on her lap, and the whiteness of her body gleamed between the flaps of her gown. Her bosom rose and fell, and her breath sounded noisy and uneven. A pregnant night laid siege to the room and the two people who were strangers to each other. The night was host to multitudes of rats, scurrying about in secret without making a sound, and a mysterious murder was committed in it too. Far from here, or perhaps even very close, a shot split the darkness, and in its wake came a desperate scream. Apart from this, the seeds of love still sprouted here and there, on this night as on all other nights, from one end of the world to the other. But the woman here, on the chair, with her naked, abandoned body, seemed utterly desolate and full of dread and despair — and why couldn't he get up and softly stroke her hair, even once? He didn't do it. Only sat and smoked. Why should he? Was it his job in life to save shipwrecked women? He, Michael Rost, of all people? He didn't have the talent for it, not at all! And if she didn't stop this game of nerves quickly, his mind was made up ... but on the other hand, it would be interesting to see how all this ended.

At last the woman raised her head and looked at him. Her lips parted slightly, but she said nothing. She stood up abruptly, as if detaching herself, approached him and started to fawn on him, as if she had now completely recovered, stroking his head, pressing her breast to his cheek. She even sank to her knees before him, and as she rested her head in his lap she whispered something inaudible.

In the end he felt a little ridiculous. He picked her up and threw her onto the bed.

She jumped up. 'You think I need your pity? I spit on it, you hear, I spit on your pity! Pah!'

He sat at her feet. 'Why are you so hot-headed? I don't pity you at all. You are quite mistaken. I would advise you, on the contrary, to go ahead and kill yourself …'

She stared at him indignantly. 'Where do you get that from?'

Rost laughed soundlessly. He saw her round white calves next to him, trembling slightly, and felt a sudden spasm in his fingers. The woman started as if from a bad dream, and jumped onto his lap. Winding her arms around his neck she whispered, her breath hot on his face: 'My love, thank you for coming to me tonight! For not refusing to come … how can I reward you …' And after a split second: 'Tell me, do you really want me to kill myself?'

Rost laughed silently again and said nothing. A few moments slipped by.

'If only I could see the child,' she said to herself. 'He's seven now, and I don't know what he looks like; I'll never know what he looks like, never!' Her arm was still wound around Rost's neck, and her fingers unthinkingly fondled the lobe of his ear. From the corridor the sound of footsteps approached, muffled by the carpet. A door opened and closed again.

The woman spoke again. 'You know, I lied to you before. I have only been doing this for a few months — about three months. And none of the rest is true either. I have only been back from the south for a short time. My lame Dutchman became disgusting to me and I left him. But we're here to amuse ourselves, right? You still haven't touched your wine. Here you are.' She reached for the table and set his full glass to his lips.

Rost did as she wished and drank a little. Then he took the glass from her hand and returned it to the table.

'You're a nice girl,' he said, running his fingers through her hair.

'You think so? Hee-hee … but … you know what — no! Now I want to have some fun!' She lowered her head to him and bit him on the lips until they bled.

'Keep your hair on, little one! I'm a bit too big for you to swallow.'

She jumped off his lap and downed a glassful of wine. Then she took another bottle out of the cupboard and uncorked it expertly. 'Let's pretend your name is George and I've already been in love with you for a whole month, what do you say?'

'Why not!' Rost laughed.

'Just tell me that you wouldn't have behaved like that. I'll believe you. No, better yet, don't say anything.'

She went on standing next to the table without moving, the corkscrew with the cork in her right hand and the whiteness of her naked body thrown into relief by the frame of her black gown with its huge flame-coloured flowers.

'Don't look at me like that! Your eyes … don't think I'm afraid of your eyes. I'm not in the least afraid of them, you hear!' She put the corkscrew down on the table and sat next to him on the bed.

'Your perfume smells so good.'

She seemed not to have heard. After a moment she said, more to herself than to him: 'They showed up out of the blue, the son and his mother, a tall English matron dry as a stick, biting off her words as if she had a pipe in her mouth. I don't know how they found out where I lived; they explained that they wanted to take care of us. A destitute young girl, all alone in the world with a small baby … I was still exhausted after the pregnancy, the hunger, the hard work, misadventures, and ordeals, and after the birth, which nearly cost me my life. The baby was only six weeks old. And I believed them. I was still so young. What do you want — a girl of seventeen who less than a year ago was a high-school student! They gave me money to go out and buy various necessities. They would stay behind to look after the baby. After all, they had some connection to this baby, didn't they, and also to me, needless to say. When I came back half an hour later there was nobody there. An empty baby carriage and a letter on the table.'

'And there was nothing to be done.'

'There was nothing to be done. Where to look for them, if you knew nothing about them! Not even the name. The letter said that they were taking the child with them to England. It was his, and I didn't even know his name. That night I didn't know what was happening to me, I was so drunk. When I woke up in the morning, after the masked ball at school, I found myself in a strange hotel room with this Englishman, whom I had never seen before in my life. He drove me home in his car, and that was the end of it.'

'And you didn't see him again.'

'I met him once or twice by chance a few months later, after my parents had thrown me out of the house. He offered me money, but I spat in his face.'

She wrapped herself in her gown as if she felt cold. She stared straight ahead of her, as if through a wall at unknown distances. Perhaps she was looking inwards, into her very soul.

Rost put his hand on her. Through the fabric of her gown he felt the warmth of her soft, smooth body, which shuddered slightly at his sudden touch. She turned her face to him. It was very beautiful then, in its sad nobility. She came closer to him. As if seeking shelter she buried her head in his chest and lay still. Rost cupped her small breast in his hand. 'And afterwards?'

'Afterwards?' She drew back and sat up straight. A torrent of furious rage flooded her again, making her gasp for breath. Her whole body trembled with anger. With some effort she succeeded in opening her handbag, which was lying on the bed, to take out a handkerchief. She blew her nose noisily. 'Afterwards? I mistakenly believed that my parents' hearts would soften. I didn't ask them to take me back again, truly I didn't, only to help me find the baby, no more. Who else could I turn to? I overcame my pride and wrote to them. A week later I wrote again, you understand; I wrote to them twice.'

'And there was no answer.'

'As if I'd thrown the letters into the Seine. After six weeks had passed I stood outside the house and waited for my father to come home from the office. He pretended not to know me. He tried to ignore me as if I was some inanimate object. When I barred his way, he pushed me so hard that

I fell onto the pavement. I was overcome by an insane fit of rage. Everything I had suppressed inside me burst out. I fell on him, slapping, biting, scratching; I smashed his glasses; I reduced him to a pile of rubbish. If I'd had a gun I would have killed him. It took the combined efforts of the concierge and her son to drag me off him. She took me into her home and tried by various means to soothe my spirits, but I only sat and cried. I cried for a long time. Then I stood up and left. For a long time I wandered the streets aimlessly. Evening fell and I went on wandering; I'm surprised that I didn't put an end to my life there and then. I was probably too stupid to think of it. Later a strange man attached himself to me, walking next to me and talking to me. I didn't protest. I let him do what he wished with me. He led me to a restaurant. I ate mechanically and drank to intoxication. I stayed with him. After two weeks I left him. Why did I leave him? I don't know myself. He was a kind man. He surrounded me with love. Maybe that's the reason why. I couldn't take in so much goodness. Everything inside me had hardened, turned to stone. He was very sad when I left him.'

Rost took a sip of wine and lit a cigarette. The woman asked for one too. His watch said it was ten minutes to three. So he had only been here for an hour, and it seemed like three at least. He stood up and went to the window. The alley was deserted. The light of the electric lamps was wasted. It seemed that it was starting to drizzle again. In the town of his birth the street had been only dimly lit by a few solitary lamps, with a faint, slightly sweet smell of lilacs in the air, which was fanned with every gust of wind and mingled with the sounds of youthful laughter, free and ringing, without any jarring note. And from the nearby streets, where the houses with the red windows were, a different kind of laughter rose from time to time, drunken and hoarse and lewd, which was also absorbed by the quiet, comfortable darkness of his street. But he, Rost, was not there now. It was a long time since he had disappeared from that place.

He turned back to the room again. The woman smoked in silence. Rost observed her for a moment. All at once the whole scene rose before him: a stern official — for some reason he pictured him with a beard and moustache, a respectable citizen — returns home from his office one afternoon, and outside his front door, his wayward daughter, banished from home and memory, suddenly falls on him, slaps him, smashes his glasses, tears his tie, and makes a public scene in front of the neighbours and the concierge.

Rost laughed aloud, and the woman stared at him in bewilderment. 'Hmm ... yes,' he exclaimed, 'not bad!' He topped up the glasses and handed hers to her. 'Here's to your courage!'

'To my courage? ... Yes, why not? To my courage! Ha ha ... you think I haven't got enough courage to ... Come here to me. You're a man, aren't you?'

'I think so.'

'Do you fancy me?'

'Yes, I should say so.'

'Then why don't you kiss me? Go on, set me on fire! Kill me with a kiss.'

1

Twenty years ago Michael Rost showed up in one of the capitals of Europe, whose king was already old, rather stupid, and had whiskers growing on both sides of his clean-shaven chin. It was an ancient city, its spires and Gothic cathedrals looming out of medieval mists, with a river running through it. And Michael Rost was eighteen years old, a tall, blond youth, without a conscious purpose or money in his pocket. He was on his way to one of the lands of the Near East, a land left desolate and abandoned for thousands of years, which a handful of idealistic people with an attachment to the distant past were trying to revive by the hard work of their hands and the enthusiasm beating in their hearts. In his hometown he had left his teacher father, his mother, and a few sisters. He found the city where he had landed no worse than others, and in fact there was no reason for him to continue on his journey. He decided he might as well settle down here as anywhere else. From the five kronen he had left after his long journey, he paid for a week's lodging (including fleas and bedbugs) in the home of a Frau Shatzman, and ate a few lean meals in a soup kitchen.

After that Frau Shatzman announced, rubbing her thumb against her fingers: 'Money, young sir, money — here you pay in advance. Fly-by-night birds!' Rost didn't know exactly what kind of birds she was referring to. Instead of answering her, he blew his cigarette smoke into her face and picked up his bag.

The city was already getting ready for spring. The last blocks of ice were floating past in the river. But in Herr Stock's 'strictly kosher' eatery — a combination of a bar, restaurant, inn, and café — it was possible to drink a glass of tea for four pence and warm yourself all day for nothing in the fumes of cheap tobacco, pungent smells from the kitchen, and shouts and arguments. Here, Michael Rost sat at a big table, and his neighbours sipped steaming tea and nibbled raisin cake. A skinny Jew with a pointed beard finished drinking his tea and adjusted the pince-nez on his nose.

'Where to?' he asked Rost. 'America?'

'Possibly.'

'So the company cheated you too. May they burn in hell! They promised to take you straight from the border to Rotterdam, and left you here to eat up your last pennies — now go chase the agent! And you, young man, is it Boston or Philadelphia? Who do you have there?'

'I don't have anyone there.'

'All alone?'

'All alone.'

'And when does your ship sail?'

'It's already sailed.'

'Already sailed? Do you intend crossing the ocean by foot?'

'I have no intention of crossing the ocean.'

'So you're not going to America? So talk! Why this silence? Look at this impudent pup — you talk to him like a human being, and he answers you like an animal. What then? Are you trying to tell me that you're staying here?'

'You've hit the nail on the head,' said Rost with a laugh. 'I'm staying here.'

'So, he's staying here. You can sell your teeth right now; you won't need them there. This is a hard town! It isn't America, where anybody who wants to can get rich. Remember my words, I know what I'm talking about. Have you heard the name Yankel Marder? You haven't? Here he is' — he pointed to his chest — 'famous from Mohyliv to Odessa, all over Ukraine: when Yankel Marder says something, you can put your signature to it with your eyes closed!'

But Yankel Marder wasn't finished with him yet. 'And what, for instance, are you thinking of doing here?'

'For example, getting married …'

'Getting married? What do you say to him, Shefftel?' He turned to a tall fellow in a black Russian shirt with a wandering Adam's apple, who was concentrating on cutting his nails with a penknife. 'He's going to get married! And where are you going to find a wife, a pipsqueak like you?'

'Don't worry, I'll find one.'

'Forget that nonsense. A boy like you, you'll go to the dogs here. Take my advice and go to America. You won't be sorry. You'll see life there; you'll live like a prince, a king! You know what America is? Ask me and I'll tell you: the dollars are lying in the streets there; all you have to do is reach out and grab them. The stupid Yankees throw their money out of the windows, and you come and collect them — that's America!'

'How do you know? Have you been there?'

'What's that got to do with it? Who doesn't know about America? A babe in the cradle knows. Here, look.' He took a picture out of his coat pocket and waved it in front of Rost's eyes. 'You see that? My brother. My own flesh and blood, rich as a lord.' The picture displayed a fellow with a bowler hat on his head and a cigar in his mouth. 'He only arrived there three years ago, and now — he's a millionaire! He could buy you the Czar's palace if he wanted to.'

'What are you babbling to him there about America, mister?' intervened a man from the next table. He had three gold teeth, a bulbous nose, bulging fish eyes, a few days' growth of stubble on his face, and his voice was very hoarse. 'I was there, in your America — may the earth swallow it up! America, ha! He's going to America! Better to be buried in the ground than to go to that accursed land. Take my advice, mister. Go to the company and get back the money for your ticket, and go back to where you came from, without looking right or left. Run, I'm telling you, run to wherever your legs carry you and don't go to that country!'

'And what about my brother? My brother the millionaire? Here's the picture, look!'

'Your brother? A cock-and-bull story if ever I heard one.' The man waved his hand in a gesture of contempt without looking at the picture. 'Your brother a millionaire? A beggar, a miserable peddler! If he earns fifty cents a day it's a lot, yes sirree. Fifty cents a day and not a cent more, and works like a horse for it — that's your brother! If you want to know about America, ask me.'

'You must have had bad luck in America to run it down like that.'

'I had bad luck in America? Do you know who you're talking to, mister? You're looking at the famous singer Arnold Kroin! Note the name Arnold Kroin, known all over the world. A heroic tenor, the top singer in all the theatres of America! Arias from *Carmen*, *La Traviata,* and *Tosca* — I didn't succeed in America?'

The tall lad in the black Russian shirt finished paring his fingernails, folded his penknife, and said with a laugh: 'A heroic tenor, the lead singer — with a voice like that?'

'What do you know about voices? A new authority!'

'You're as hoarse as a crow! Arias, *Carmen*, *Tosca* — who do you think you're kidding, mister? If you were the top singer in America, I agree that it must be a lousy country.'

'Listen to the great expert. Where do you get off? Have you ever heard a real singer in your life? You're still wet behind the ears! You know what a heroic tenor means? *Do-re-mi-fa-sol* — just wait a few days until I get rid of this cold, and you'll hear Arnold Kroin.'

'I'm not interested.'

'Just as I said, you understand as much about singing as a frog understands philosophy.'

'You should give your heroic tenor as a gift to the museum: they've never come across such a strange phenomenon before.'

'A person might as well talk to a herring as waste words on you. You should be hung up to dry.'

'What do you say to him, Shefftel,' Yankel Marder came to his aid, 'a nothing like him a singer in America, where the greatest singers in the world come from! Who would be gullible enough to believe him?'

'And you, goat beard, wouldn't even be allowed to set foot

on the continent! They'll send you back on the same ship as you came on. Nobody's waiting for people like you there!'

'In my opinion you yourself haven't been there either. What do you say, Shefftel?'

'He hasn't,' the latter delivered his verdict.

'It's beneath my dignity talk to people like you. Arnold Kroin and wild animals like you!'

'No, no, don't speak! Save your tenor for your singing.'

Michael Rost still did not know where he would sleep that night, but his mind was not overly troubled by this question. It was clear to him that something would come up. The place was full of movement and noise. All three halls were packed with people of all ages, nationalities, and walks of life. Standing and sitting they conversed, argued, made shady deals, chatted idly; drank tea, beer, and brandy; and gave rise to a ceaseless din.

Behind the bar in a spotless blouse loomed Malvina, the owner Reb Chaim Stock's daughter, with a black velvet ribbon tied round her glossy black hair. Her almond eyes were black, she had a narrow hooked nose, and her thin, lipless mouth was tightly pursed. When she laughed she revealed small, pretty teeth, but when her mother appeared in the doorway to the kitchen, which led off one of the halls, it was immediately evident to all what the daughter would look like in forty years' time: squat and square, with a brown wig reaching right down to her eyebrows. Her face was broad as a dish and bony, eternally glistening with a sheen of cooking grease, and a few grey curls sprouted from her chin and jaws. She would station herself in the doorway, rattling the big bunch of keys on her broad hips like some terrible weapon, and call: 'Quiet, gentlemen, please! My ears are ringing!' For a moment a cowered silence fell. But as soon as she disappeared into the kitchen the clamour rose again. Afterwards her jarring tones would rise from the kitchen, where she imposed her authority on the cook and the servants by screaming and scolding in her Polish German, or she would appear in the doorway again and shout: 'Malvina, please go and see where your father has disappeared to!'

And the father, a respectable Jew with a magnificent long beard, would be busy in a dark corner of the corridor or one of the unoccupied guest rooms, pinching the bottom of one of the sturdy red-cheeked maids, whose resistance had been weakened with the help of a few coins. Occasionally Reb Chaim Stock would emerge from the corridor with one of his respectable cheeks slightly flushed from a modest slap, but apart from that his face showed nothing at all. Its composure and dignity were not in the least impaired. The yarmulke peeping out from underneath his hat was back in its place; the watery little eyes gazed cold and penetrating through the pince-nez, from which a narrow black cord descended to his jacket pocket; and the beard cascaded luxuriantly in all its glory. His movements were as measured and deliberate as always, and his speech was calm and quiet. Only Frau Stock, who knew her husband well, would whisper when nobody was listening, 'You old lecher!' without receiving a reply.

Thus time passed in this corner of the city, with the constant changing of the maids, due on one hand to the strictness of Frau Stock and on the other to the excessive friendliness of her husband. But Malvina, without leaving her place behind the bar, would whisper at length with

Max Karp, a young man from Galicia with a head as big and round as a pumpkin and a green plush hat with its brim lowered over his yellow curls. He would always turn up at mealtimes with a bulging briefcase under his arm. There was a secret understanding between Malvina and this blond youth, and she was waiting for the right opportunity to marry him. In the meantime she would feed him his favourite delicacies — stuffed intestines, roast chicken with groats, chopped goose liver — in a special room set aside for honoured guests. With a mouth full of adoration she would call the waiter from one end of the hall to the other: 'Alfred, a nice drumstick for Herr Karp, done to a turn!'

Max Karp was attending night classes and preparing in secret to take his matriculation exams. According to the testimony of his close friend, spoken with devout looks and in a lowered voice only to those worthy of it, Karp wrote wonderful poems and was destined for greatness. He had not yet published anything because the public was not yet ready for it, 'because, ah, I'll explain another time,' the friend would say discreetly in a reverential tone. The man destined for greatness wore slightly shabby patent-leather shoes and green socks. He would often stand at the bar and whisper to Malvina. She, with a beaming face and a coy smile, would eat him up with her eyes between pouring one glass of brandy and the next, while he stood there with a disdainful expression as if it were all beneath his dignity.

All was not lost for Michael Rost. Not at all. He received a positive reply to his question, and a free couch was found in the room shared by Shefftel and Yankel Marder on the first floor of Stock's restaurant-inn. He could stay with them for a few nights, as long as he took care that nobody saw him coming and going, and they even treated him to a cup of tea and a slice of cake, which were more than welcome.

In the meantime it was getting dark, and Yasha the Odessan appeared in a paint-stained white overall. Recently, for lack of any alternatives, Yasha had taken up house-painting and was doing well. In the evening, when the day's work was done, he would go to the cinema with fat Fritzi to lament the bitter fate of poor Henny Porten, seduced and abandoned with a swollen belly. Now he needed an assistant for a few days and could find no one better for the job than Michael Rost. They agreed he would start the next morning.

Yasha was a brave lad whose bony face bore an expression that was simultaneously arrogant and childish. All the bullies and ruffians of the neighbourhood were afraid of him. He had already spent more than one night in jail for breaking the bones of one of them. He had been living here for a few months, and his past was shrouded in mist. It was rumoured that in Odessa he had been the head of a gang of thieves and that he had a few murders to his credit. There was no clear proof for these rumours, and their veracity could be questioned, although judging by his character he might well have earned a reputation for such deeds. It was said of him too that during the pogroms he and six of his mates had routed the pogromists who broke into the Moldavanka quarter.

He had a soft spot for Rost and took him under his wing. On the following days Rost worked with Yasha. He cleaned, scraped walls and ceilings, mixed paints, carried heavy pails, learned how to hold a paintbrush, and pushed the hand-cart holding the ladder and the rest of the gear to and fro.

As he worked, Yasha sang *'Mein tata is a shmaravaznik'** and suchlike ditties, making the empty rooms echo.

Spring surged through the city, flowing into houses through their open windows. The maids and nannies in their white aprons gave off an intimate smell of work that brought to mind mothers and childhood homes; and life was open and transparent, attainable simply by reaching out your hand. Rost too began to sing without thinking *'Mein tata is a shmaravaznik'* and Yasha's other songs. Sitting with him and fat Fritzi one evening in the cinema, the latter reached for him with her hand. Rost stopped her. Getting involved with Yasha in such matters was not to be recommended.

He went on sleeping secretly on the sofa in Shefftel and Yankel Marder's room. Later the job with Yasha came to an end. Yankel Marder and Shefftel were finally able to continue their journey to Rotterdam. Rost now had a little money, and he rented a room with Berl Kanfer, a boy with a girl's face who earned his living from a crushed finger. For two months he had worked in a factory where he was lucky enough to have one of his fingers crushed. Ever since then he had been living off the company's sick fund, and waiting for the compensation from the factory owner for his crushed finger, in order to travel to Switzerland and try his luck at business. In the meantime Berl Kanfer spent his days at Stock's drinking tea and arguing with Marcus Schwartz the playwright-director, who was apparently thinking of using him as a character in one of his invisible dramas.

Marcus Schwartz was equipped with all the accessories

---

*   Yiddish: 'My father is a dirty working man'.

of his profession: a black hat with a brim as broad as a wheel, long hair, a short beard, horn-rimmed spectacles, a flying necktie, a velvet jacket and striped trousers, patent-leather shoes, a ring with a skull, a cane, a briefcase full of dramas, a black pencil and a red pencil, and a thick book on dramatic structure. He was in the habit of strolling in the park, the briefcase under his arm and the book open in his hand, reading as he walked and underlining sentences or inserting question marks or exclamation marks with the red pencil, according to whatever in his opinion raised questions or deserved attention. The names constantly on his lips were Sophocles, Aeschylus, Goethe's *Faust*, Shakespeare, Hauptmann's *The Weavers*, and so on; and he would introduce them into every conversation. His dramas had been almost staged on innumerable occasions — in various theatres in Berlin and here too, as he would tell anyone willing to listen — but the censors were always against him ... He and God were eternally at odds, and in his dramas, which none of his acquaintances had ever seen, he railed against the heavens at every opportunity, and the censors, of course, in these benighted countries ... It could be said that he owed his reputation as a dramatist exclusively to this hostile censorship, without which he would have had no excuse to have his plays unstaged. Only yesterday he had had an appointment with Furst, the director of the Volkstheater, who had promised him a staging in two months' time, no later, before the end of the season — just wait and see! He only hoped that this time the censor would let him be ... and so it went. Thanks to the enmity of the censors, he entered into relationships with the nannies next to the baby carriages in the parks, and with respectable matrons of a certain age, who were only too happy in the innocence of their hearts to spread their wings over the gifted young dramatist with a brilliant future, relentlessly persecuted by the censors.

Apart from this, Marcus Schwartz had a weakness (sometimes found among ignorant laymen) for heavy, difficult books in all branches of science, criticism, and philosophy, and he would buy them whenever the opportunity offered: precious volumes in splendid covers, and rare first-edition facsimiles no longer to be found in the market. He was already the proud possessor of a collection of hundreds of such volumes. It was doubtful whether he had ever read a single one of them from beginning to end, but almost all of them had scribbles in the margins to show that he had 'gone through' them. In any case, he would carry one of them with him whenever he went out, together with the briefcase of dramas, like a man who changes his collar every day.

He lived in a narrow room with a painter from Odessa. One half of the room was full of books on shelves, in boxes, and on the table; the other, crammed with paintings, sketches, frames, palettes, paintbrushes, an easel, and so on. So the two of them lived, each in his corner, and brewed tea together on the Primus stove.

And Michael Rost lived with Berl Kanfer of the crushed finger, known at Stock's as 'Berl the virgin'. Their room on the bottom floor was long and narrow as a knife, and the window at its end looked onto the small square of a high-walled courtyard in which a grey, bloodless, monotonous day was imprisoned, both summer and winter. This courtyard was pervaded by the smells of bed linen and diapers hanging out to dry, of cooking, of cats and dogs; by the sounds of babies crying, women shouting, quarrelling, gossiping from window to window, according to the hour of the day. In the morning the courtyard resounded with the beating of carpets and featherbeds, accompanied by clouds of dust and fleas; in the evening the young voice of a maidservant could sometimes be heard, singing of her youth and her green village. And nevertheless, despite the coming and going of the generations, time seemed to stand still in the courtyard; and the hustle and bustle of life, full of movement and change, seemed thousands of miles away, as if in another world. Michael Rost, sitting at the window from time to time in the afternoons to learn the language of the land, with his landlady's room full of old furniture, and with babies, yelling, and stinking smells besieging his door, would raise his eyes from his book and reflect, with an enjoyable sense of dedication, that his life, at any rate, would not suffer from the boredom of habit and settled routine. He already knew that no situation would hold any fears for him, that he was going to plumb every emotion and shade of emotion to the depths, and that this strong, supple body of his was going to experience every aspect of life, without exception.

As darkness fell, Berl Kanfer entered the room in a good mood. He had received his money from the sick fund today, and he invited Rost to partake of the feast he had brought with him: sausage, butter, and cheese. Berl's full cheeks were slightly flushed and he chewed with evident relish. 'I forgot to tell you,' he said with his mouth full, 'Raizel asked about you. She gave me a note for you.'

'Raizel?'

'The one from Stock's, with the auburn hair.'

Rost read in the badly written note that Raizel would wait for him at eight o'clock on a certain street corner.

'I won't go,' said Rost firmly.

'A top girl! I wish she'd invited me.'

'You can go instead of me if you like.'

'You're joking.'

'I'm not joking. Tell her that I'm busy this evening. You can tell her whatever you like, I don't care.'

Berl hastily finished his meal. He changed his tie, oiled his hair with its reddish glints, brushed his clothes and hat with a scrubbing brush, and his preparations were complete. Before he left, Rost managed to extract a handsome loan from him without asking for it directly, something he would certainly not have succeeded in doing in any other circumstances.

Berl's good mood lasted for another two days after this episode. After that, his face suddenly clouded, and he started to stagger with his legs wide apart like a sailor. He circled Rost a few times, as if he wanted to say something, until he burst out in the end: 'The dirty whore! She should be locked up in jail!'

Rost examined him for a moment in silence, and then laughed loudly. 'Nice work.'

'What are you laughing at, you beast! It's all your fault.'

'My fault? How come? I don't even know her. I've never spoken a single word to her in my life. Go to the doctor right away!'

'I've already been.'

'And?'

'It can be cured with two to three months' treatment.'

'So it's not so terrible. You should thank God for getting off so lightly!'

'Lightly, lightly!' Kanfer mimicked with twisted lips. 'I have to suffer for him. You were invited to a rendezvous — you should have gone! Why do you send others in your place?'

'Nobody forced you. A person has to pay for his pleasures.'

At this Berl Kanfer fell onto his bed, where he lay sulking in silence.

Yasha the Odessan told the story later at Stock's to a few of the regulars and fat Fritzi, and wrapped it up with his broad baritone laugh: 'What a bastard he is, that Rost! He'll end up on the gallows, ha ha ha!' Not long afterwards Raizel disappeared from among the maidservants at Stock's, and Reb Chaim Stock began to slip out at the same hour every afternoon. He was suffering from an 'intestinal disease' that required treatment for two to three months.

2

Spring was already in full bloom. The city and its people were spick and span. The women appeared more attractive, pretty in their mauve and violet dresses. The terraces of the cafés were full of fashionably dressed idlers, whose time was their own, morning, noon, and night, and whose lives had no room for others. Most of them belonged to that class of society who devoted themselves to their own empty existences, their well-being, and their pleasures. Everything was done for them, and they themselves did nothing. For the most part they were eaten up by a gnawing boredom they could not escape. What was permitted was already well known to them, as was a little of what was forbidden. And here they were, sitting on the café terraces on a spring afternoon, the band playing wistful, melancholy waltzes as a background to their boredom, as they wondered how to fill an empty evening with something new and stimulating.

Rost remembered the last days he spent in the street of his childhood, which was traversed from dawn to dusk by a long caravan of peasants' carts loaded with sugar beets for the sugar refinery on the outskirts of the town. The carts, harnessed to a pair of small horses, sweating and breathing heavily, and their strenuous creaking; the peasants walking calmly and deliberately at their sides, resigned to their fate, smoking pungent tobacco or chewing coarse bread smeared with pork fat or sponge cakes yellow-green with saffron — all this made an impression of the eternal, exhausting labour of man and beast, labour without end or purpose. Boys would lie in wait at the roadside to collect the long, dark-orange beets that fell from the carts. Some of the boys armed themselves with sticks studded with sharp nails to fish the beets off the cart itself. Sometimes, caught in the act, they would run into the courtyards and alleys and side streets under a barrage of curses from the peasants, who never succeeded in catching the light-footed lads. Thus the beet-laden carts would trundle past without a pause, day in and day out in a never-changing rhythm, dragged from remote fields to the refinery, whose whistle piercing the air divided the time for those townspeople who did not possess a clock, while the harnesses tattooed the chests and ribs of the horses, whose coats were already bald on both sides, rubbed bare by the ropes.

Rost strolled the streets of the city centre. It was evening. Lately he had been living in the single room of a seventy-five-year-old woman, whose white hair was sparse and whose mouth was empty. He slept on the sofa, the old woman on two joined beds made of heavy old wood with headrests round as wheels and piled with eiderdowns, and the canary in its cage between the two windows. The room was always permeated with a dull smell of rotten wood, cold coffee, and old age. The windows overlooked a big square on which stood a pump and a trough. Three mornings a week it was used as a produce market, and women walked through it with bags full of vegetables. But in the afternoons the square was empty: boys played football there, and a few pigeons pecked at the ground.

The old woman was getting ready to move into an old-age home. Today or tomorrow her son would come to make arrangements for the room and the furniture. In the meantime she made daily demands for rent from Rost, who put her off with promises that today or tomorrow he would get money from his parents in the mail. Sometimes she treated him to tasteless coffee that she brewed for a week at a time, and told him toothless, disconnected scraps of stories about her husband, who had died twenty years before, and about her life as a widow. At the same time she cast dim looks at the little bronze Jesus, hanging on his cross above the joined beds, with his skeletal head drooping on his shoulder. She said: 'Soon, my day too will arrive. These rotten bones are no longer good for anything. Everything is ready. It will be a fine funeral.'

Rost couldn't stand the smell of death, and spent as little time as possible in the room.

One day he lingered outside the window of a clothes shop and looked at a pale-grey suit on a wax doll with a foolish face. The suit was already faded and should have been changed.

'So which of these outfits do you prefer?' asked somebody next to him. Rost turned his head. A man with a moustache smiled at him.

'What's it to you?'

'I didn't mean to offend you. I simply think that such

things are not worth more than ten or fifteen minutes of a person's attention — to choose, try on, and buy.'

'Very clever,' said Rost sarcastically and looked at the stranger. His face was not unsympathetic. There was something winning, without being obtrusive, about his expression.

'I'm a practical man, if you'll excuse me,' said the stranger.

'And when a person has no money?'

'Ah, money! I suppose you think that money's the main thing when it comes to buying a suit.'

Rost moved off. The man accompanied him. The boulevard was crowded with people at this hour of the afternoon, army officers in starched uniforms and elegant women among them. The strains of wistful waltzes drifted out of the cafés and were swallowed up in the clamour of the streets.

'Do you smoke?' asked the man.

'When I have the wherewithal.'

'Would you like to go in here?' he said, indicating a luxurious café they happened to be passing by.

Rost drank hot chocolate and ate cakes. 'May I order another cake? I feel a little hungry.'

The stranger sat opposite Rost and watched him eating greedily. His face was intelligent, and his brow was hard and square, giving off a sense of vigour and perhaps a certain stubbornness. His thick hair, cut short and bristling above his brow, was already sprinkled with grey at the temples. He could have been about forty years old. 'And now, with regard to the suit,' said the man and appeared to hesitate.

Rost finished eating. A pleasant languor spread through his limbs. It was a long time since he had eaten so well. 'With regard to the suit?'

'You can, of course, acquire it. Nothing easier! You go in, try it on, and buy it.'

Rost looked at him questioningly. A strange person! Either he was insane or else he had hidden motives. In any case he should wait and see how things turned out. Rost was not a man to shrink from adventure. Wasn't it for this that he had left home in the first place?

'My proposal seems strange to you,' said the stranger, as if reading his thoughts, 'because it does not conform to convention. Admit it. Which is precisely the reason why! My actions cannot be measured by the usual criteria. I have different rules — my own rules.' He pushed his cigarette case towards Rost. 'You are not a fool, my young friend. This is evident at a glance. And you are here to make a new start. Which is difficult and easy at once — depending on the point of departure. I too once began, at your exact age, from nothing. How do you intend to begin, if I may ask?'

'I don't know yet. I'm waiting for a suitable opportunity.'

'Good. Let's say you change your external circumstances today. Beginning with a suit and ending with a nice room. A suitable opportunity, would you say?'

'I think so.'

'And in three days' time, on Thursday, we'll meet again. The same time and place.'

He introduced himself by the name of Peter Dean, called the waiter, and paid. When they emerged from the café the sun had already climbed high in the sky. They went from one store to another. Peter Dean did not stint on his purchases. He bought everything necessary, of the finest quality, and with the taste of a man of the world, not forgetting to add a handsome suitcase as well. Then he gave Rost a one-hundred-kronen note and took his leave. 'In the meantime, find your-self a nice room, and on Thursday we'll meet at the café as arranged.'

Rost got onto a tram and rode with his full suitcase to the old woman and the canary and the skeletal little Jesus. The next morning he informed her that he did not intend to wait for her to enter the old-age home. The old woman said that she was heartily sorry to hear it. She was already accustomed to him, and if he did not have the means to pay her what he owed at the moment, she would be happy to wait. It would not present an obstacle. Rost said excitedly: 'Goodbye, Frau Messerschmidt, I'm changing my skin!'

He travelled to a quiet quarter near the centre of town with respectable houses that were always closed and silent. One of those well-to-do bourgeois neighbourhoods whose entrances were usually free from the 'Room to let' notices so typical of poor neighbourhoods. He wandered through the sleepy streets, where the commotion of the city sounded muffled and far away. After viewing a few rooms not to his taste, he rang the bell of a second-storey apartment, where a bronze nameplate bore the name George Shtift. A woman of about thirty-five, not ugly, opened the door. 'The room belonged to my brother-in-law,' she said in an apologetic tone, 'who is now studying in Heidelberg.'

The room she showed him was spacious, tastefully furnished, and filled with the mild warmth of a summer afternoon. There was a very faint, distant scent of lavender in the air, more of an idea than an actual smell. The two windows overlooked the quiet street and boasted heavy wine-coloured curtains. The landlady followed his movements with a genial smile on her face. Hungarian or Italian, decided Rost. He took the room.

Frau Shtift said, 'Make yourself at home. If you like playing the piano, the drawing-room piano is at your disposal.'

That afternoon Rost moved his belongings. After sundry small expenses and the month's rent for the room, he had about twenty kronen left. Early in the evening he went out into the street and the city seemed transformed. It appeared more expansive: life was no longer contracted into one low point, into the food of a single meal, blurring the shapes of everything else until they lost their reality. Everything around him now flaunted its reality, demanding attention. A hidden weight was lifted from his heart. His gaze became freer, sharper. Dusk encroached little by little on the streets. The shutters descended on the display windows. The electric signs were already blinking in brightly lit letters; packed trams returned clerks and shop assistants from the city centre to the suburbs. Rost strolled at his leisure, renewed, open to absorb the evening through every pore of his body. The canal water grew darker as night approached.

In Stock's the tables were already set for dinner. Reb Chaim Stock once more moved from hall to hall at his deliberate, dignified pace, with his hands behind his back, and Malvina stood at the bar, pouring glasses of brandy and mugs of beer. Two waiters, with flat yarmulkes perched on their heads like little black patches, wearing white, almost clean, jackets, served a few early diners and called out in Hungarian accents to the kitchen: 'Stuffed derma, roast beef, grits!' and to Malvina: 'White wine with soda water!' and to the air at large: 'Careful, gravy!'

In the tea hall, divided from the main hall by a high opaque glass partition, the gang was gathered around a big table: Yasha the Odessan with fat Fritzi; Arnold Kroin the heroic tenor; Marcus Schwartz the dramatist; Berl the virgin, still living off his crushed finger; Misha the anarchist, who was in the habit of rejecting the arguments of his interlocutor with the words 'I spit on everything'; and a gnarled, sinewy fellow blind in one eye, whose seeing eye was small, black, and piercing as a needle. Rost now saw him for the first time.

Some of them had empty brandy glasses in front of them and they were in high spirits. 'Look who's here!' Yasha welcomed him in his strong baritone. 'We haven't seen you for ages.'

'What a dandy!' called Fritzi. 'What did you do, rob a bank?'

'Take a seat!' said Yasha, the main spokesman. 'What will you drink?'

'Not at all, today it's my turn. Alfred, slivovitz for everyone! And your finest pickled herring.'

'I told you he robbed a bank!'

Marcus Schwartz tossed back his hair, his tie flying in all directions like an exotic black bird. 'In two weeks it will be decided,' he said, turning to Berl Kanfer and Misha the anarchist, 'and when they stage *The Wheel of Fate* you'll all drink champagne with me! What a celebration it will be!'

'Don't tell me your tales!' Misha cut him off.

The one-eyed man drank in silence, his seeing eye darting from one person to another. For a moment it rested on Rost, examining, questioning, and giving rise to an uneasy feeling.

This fellow had showed up at Stock's a couple of weeks before. Nobody knew where he had come from, who he was, or what he did for a living. For some reason they called him Jan, without knowing if this was his real name. For the most part he kept quiet, without taking part in the conversation. When the opportunity offered he played dominoes or cards in the back room, which led off the corridor and had a window overlooking the courtyard. He almost always won. A kind of unspoken rivalry existed between Yasha and Jan, and Yasha was only waiting for a chance to break his bones. But Jan never gave it to him. He never reacted to his provocations. He pretended not to hear, while playing nonchalantly with the penknife he took out of his pocket.

The restaurant filled up with the clatter of tableware, talk, laughter, calls for the waiter. From outside, through the open windows, rose the voices of children at play, the barks of fighting dogs, the croak of a distant harmonica. Fat Fritzi sat opposite Rost and devoured him with her eyes. Rost pretended not to notice. Then she said: 'And when are you going to get married, little Rost?'

'Soon.' He laughed.

'A brunette?'

'Of course, a brunette like you.' Fritzi's hair was as yellow as the skin of an onion.

'First we have to find a wife for Berl the virgin,' said Yasha. 'He can't wait any longer.'

'He doesn't want a brunette.' Fritzi laughed. 'It's Raizel or nothing.'

Berl Kanfer blushed and held his tongue.

'Jan, you blind dog, why don't you sing us a song?' joked

Yasha to the laughter of his companions. 'Our famous tenor forgot his voice at home.'

Jan shot him a look like an arrow from his single eye and said nothing. They drank another glass, and Yasha suggested a game of blackjack. They moved into the back room and shut the window. Jan took a worn pack of cards out of his pocket.

'No, blind man,' said Yasha, 'we'll play with different cards.'

Berl Kanfer was sent to the waiter and returned after a moment with a new pack of cards. The four of them played: Jan, the tenor, Yasha, and Rost. The others sat behind them and watched. This time Jan lost. He dealt the cards in silence. From time to time he threw a malevolent look at Rost and the stack of silver coins growing in front of him.

'How much is left in the bank?' Rost counted. 'Seventeen, twenty-one — the lot. Give me a card.' Jan dealt him a ten. 'No more.' Jan took a card for himself, got an eight, and went over the limit. He had twenty-three, while Rost with his three cards had no more than fourteen, and he won. He collected the coins and dropped them into his pocket.

'You're not playing anymore?' asked Jan.

No, he didn't want to go on playing; perhaps another time. He parted from the gang and left. He had won about forty kronen.

Rost strolled along the dimly lit nocturnal alleys and thought about how easy it really was to acquire money, and how it lost its value once you had it in your possession. Only the day before yesterday he had been naked as a marble statue, with nothing to look forward to but Frau Messerschmidt's cold coffee, which gave off a smell of dilapidation and death, and now he had a fine room in the home of a good-looking young woman, elegant clothes, and money in his pocket.

After crossing the bridge over the canal, in whose dark water the flames of the lamps trembled like golden drops of milk, he turned into one of the streets in the city centre and heard hurried footsteps behind him. Someone seized him by the arm. He turned around and saw Jan with his lean, ugly face and his closed eye sunk into its socket.

Rost shook the alien hand off in revulsion. 'Well?'

'I lost about thirty kronen.'

'I suppose so.'

'You're going to give me that money back now,' said Jan quietly.

'Do you return money to people who lost to you?'

'No.'

'And you think I'm going to give you your money back?'

'I'm certain of it.'

'You're mistaken.'

They were standing on a street corner in front of a big bookshop. In its unshuttered display windows, large volumes were visible in the light of a street lamp. To the left was a dimly lit alley.

'You see this eye?' Jan pointed to the empty hollow in his face. 'The person who blinded it was found later, stabbed to death.'

Rost turned to leave.

'Wait, my friend! I'm not finished yet.' Jan held his arm in a vice-like grip.

'Let me go!'

'Give me back my money, you pup!'

'Let me go and I'll give it to you!' cried Rost, and with lightning speed he planted his fist with all his strength in Jan's only eye. He heard Jan groan and saw him clutch his face in both hands. Rost escaped into the alley. He ran for about twenty minutes from one deserted alley to another, and then he slowed down. There was nobody behind him.

'I taught him a lesson he won't forget!' he said to himself, and took a deep breath. He was not far from the Schottentor and set out for the Ringstrasse. He decided to walk. The mild spring evening seeped into his soul with the fragrance and warmth of sweet, heavy wine. His right hand still retained a vague sense of the contact with Jan's face. He felt a slight revulsion at having touched this unpleasant character, at the bodily contact with him. But the energy aroused by the incident had still not been completely exhausted, not by the blow nor by the running in its wake. He needed some outlet for this surplus energy, some liberating act.

First of all he went up to a policeman and asked for directions to some street or other without any intention of going there. The policeman described politely and in great detail, to which Rost paid no attention whatsoever, where the street was and how to get there. After that he went into a café and ate cold roast veal and drank beer. A made-up girl sitting alone at the next table sent him inviting looks and smiles. Rost did not respond. He paid and left the café. The street where he lived was not far off. He went on walking along the Ring, crossed the little garden of Karlsplatz, where young couples were making love on the shadowed benches, and came out behind the church looming up dreamily against the background of the dark sky. In front of his building he came across his landlady, Frau Shtift, with a tall, slender girl of about sixteen. Frau Shtift introduced her with a smile: 'My daughter, Erna.'

'Your daughter?' asked Rost in surprise. 'I would have thought her your sister.'

'As you see, I'm not so young anymore,' said Frau Shtift, not without coquetry.

'I don't see any evidence of that.'

The doorman rattled his keys and opened the door. The three of them went up to the second floor. When they switched on the light in the passage, Rost looked quickly at Erna, who did not give him so much as a single glance. She had wonderful blue eyes and pitch-black hair. Rost said, 'Sleep well,' and retired to his room. He was not unaware of the fact that Erna had not replied to his salutation, but only pulled a disdainful face.

It was almost eleven o'clock. Rost was not yet tired. He paced to and fro in the room, inspecting the various articles of furniture, the photographs showing women in nineteenth-century clothes and a moustachioed officer in the Hussars. Then he went up to the window and looked out for a while at the deserted street with the spring evening flowing silently through it. The sound of the city was muffled here, vague and insubstantial. In the opposite house the lights went off, and the blinds were drawn on the two windows. 'Time to go to bed,' said Rost to himself with a sigh of resignation. At that moment there was a knock on the door. Frau Shtift opened it and stood in the doorway, wearing an orange dressing-gown that clung to her shapely figure. 'I just wanted to ask if there was anything more you needed. The maid has already gone to bed,' she said, with an encouraging smile unrelated to the content of her words.

Rost was somewhat taken aback. 'If there was anything more … in other words …'

Frau Shtift remained standing next to the door, smiling. She gathered the dressing-gown around her body. Her feet were shod in high-heeled slippers.

Rost moved a chair away from the table. 'Perhaps you would like to sit down for a while.'

She came in and sat down on the sofa. 'Am I disturbing you? Did you want to go to bed already?'

'No, not at all. It's a pleasure — I'm not in the least sleepy.'

'When my husband is at home we always go to bed at eleven, except on special occasions. He likes order.'

'And where is he now, if I may ask?'

'He's gone to Klagenfurt on business for three weeks. Please sit down; why are you standing?'

Rost moved a chair up to the sofa and sat down facing her.

'And I, on the other hand, like to stay up late.' Frau Shtift smiled. As if accidentally, she straightened the gown on her thighs. Rost caught a glimpse of her gleaming white body, completely naked under the dressing-gown. A shiver ran down his spine. His lips twitched to say something, no doubt something idiotic and irrelevant, but the words stuck in his mouth. A hard lump rose in his throat and choked him. Frau Shtift's eyes, like two smouldering coals, burned into him as she went on smiling. The room suddenly became unbearably hot, and at the same time Rost felt so cold that his teeth began to chatter. The silence thickened. Nothing moved. Abruptly Rost uprooted himself from the oppressive silence, rose from the chair and stood up straight, took a step towards the middle of the room, and immediately changed his mind and returned to his place. In a voice that was choked for some reason, he exclaimed, 'Clearly!' The word hung loosely in the air, without being connected to anything. He realised how ridiculous he must seem, and he was filled with rage against himself.

'Madam is clearly from Hungary,' he said, more loudly than usual.

'Why there, of all places?'

'Oh, I don't know. I just thought so.'

'My parents were from Trieste.' She leaned back on the sofa. Rost's eyes were on her fleshy mouth, and the triangle of throat and cleavage exposed by the neck of her gown.

'How young you are!'

'Not so young. I'm nineteen,' he said, adding a year in the vague fear that she would despise him for his tender age.

'Come and sit here,' she said suddenly. 'On the sofa.' Rost did as she wished. She brought her face up close to his and looked deep into his eyes. 'My big boy!' she exclaimed in a rather hoarse voice, and in a passion of lust sank her full, wet, burning lips into Rost's mouth, a kiss that lasted an eternity and sucked the last drop of life from his body.

Frau Shtift was suddenly completely naked, the dressing-gown lying at the foot of the sofa. Thus she stood before him, large and naked, dazzling his eyes with her gleaming white flesh. Rost sank to his knees and buried his face in this white fire. At that moment he could have bellowed like a slaughtered bull; he could have murdered someone or killed himself. He climbed up her shuddering body, he covered the mound of her belly with kisses, he sucked on her nipples and thought that he would die, but Gertrude

Shtift tilted his head backwards and whispered, her mouth opposite his: 'Get undressed, my darling, my big boy.' She went up to the open window and closed the heavy curtains. Then she stretched out on the bed. With faltering movements Rost stripped off his clothes and dropped them on the carpet at his feet, and he approached the waiting woman in all the splendour of his nakedness.

'Let me look at you, my love,' she whispered passionately, 'you're as beautiful as a young god!' She drew him to her. A soft, warm, quivering woman's body clung to him, inseparably, and it contained the whole wide world from the beginning of creation to its end, with the laws of both life and death. They stroked each other tenderly, and scratched and bit and crushed each other as if to annihilate themselves in the joining of one body to the other, until their tangled bodies shuddered in that final convulsion which recalls the spasms of the death throes. And again they caressed each other with glowing faces. A pleasant weariness filled their languid limbs, and they smiled at each other and feasted their eyes on their lovely bodies.

Gertrude slid her fingers over his long, muscular body. 'How strange,' she mused after a moment. 'Until two days ago we had never met. Your existence in the world was not known to me, and mine was not known to you, and now we love each other so much. It doesn't seem real to me.' She nestled up to him and pressed her full breasts to him; they quivered as if they possessed a life of their own. 'The only happiness, the very essence of life — a sin? Whoever thought that up was a stupid fool, a madman. A sin! The last thing left to us in this world — a sin? He must have been a eunuch; a miserable, envious eunuch. I accept this sin gladly, and I am prepared to pay for it for the rest of my life!'

A distant clock chimed three times. The night was mild and mute, and streamed soundlessly through the sleeping street behind the windows. The lamp dangling from the ceiling shed a calm pale-orange light on the two bodies on the bed, the wine-red eiderdown piled up at the bottom, covering their feet up to their ankles.

'Tell me, my love, about your life, about your childhood. I love your mother without knowing her because she gave birth to you, my love, and I love your father.'

'My father is a teacher. He has a clear brow and intelligent eyes. He knows a lot about the world and says little. My mother is big, blonde, beautiful. My younger sister looks like her. My mother has not yet gone grey, and she is always full of love; she loves my father as if she had only met him a week ago.' He told her too about the big river that ran through his little town: how in the winter it turned to ice and the boys skated on it, how the snow was piled a metre high and the peasants wore galoshes — men, women, and children.

'Why did you leave home?'

'I wanted to get to know the world and its people.'

They lay together, loving each other and growing tired and falling asleep for a while and waking up again, until dawn began to break and the windows turned blue. Gertrude Shtift sat up.

'I must leave you. How I would love to stay with you, but life has other rules. Rest and restore your strength, my one and only. Until this evening!' She kissed him on the mouth, got out of bed, wrapped herself in her dressing-gown, and stole out of the room. Rost fell instantly into a heavy sleep, where the one-eyed Jan wept and alternately begged and threatened, with his single eye piercing as a sharp knife. He turned from time to time into Gertrude Shtift, completely naked except for a strange hat with a long feather that tickled Rost's chest and lips, and made him laugh uproariously.

He woke up laughing. His watch said half-past twelve. The sun barely filtered though the heavy curtains, and the room was in semi-darkness. The memory of the past night came to him as something unreal, too marvellous to be true. A smile of satisfaction appeared on his face. He jumped out of bed to the heap of clothes on the floor and began to get dressed quickly. After that he opened the curtains: a burst of bright sunlight poured into the room, together with a vivid joie de vivre. Nearby, the high, clear voice of a woman rose into the air singing a merry song, and in the distance the city throbbed and roared. It was good to be alive, to breathe the air on such a lovely day. He felt healthy, young, free, capable of conquering the world. No power on earth could stand in his way. Once again, he felt that everything was attainable, within reach; all he had to do was stretch out his hand.

In the passage he ran into Erna Shtift and wished her a hearty good morning. The young girl mumbled something unintelligible and made to walk past him. 'Are you in the habit of not answering when people greet you?' he called after her in a jocular tone. Erna stopped and turned her head.

'What a pest!'

'If you think I'm a pest, I won't greet you anymore.'

'I don't know you at all. Who do you think you are?'

'Me? I'm Freiherr von Rost zu Kreltain, Fräulein …'

'Idiot!' snapped Erna and escaped into her room. Rost burst into loud laughter. The door of the drawing room opened a crack and Gertrude Shtift's head peeped out. 'What are you laughing at like that?'

'I remembered a joke.'

She winked at him. When he came up close she pressed her lips to his mouth and whispered, 'Tonight, my love,' and closed the door again.

At the appointed hour Rost sat in the café at a table next to
the window. He looked out at the crowds and the carriages
in the busy street, at the wet asphalt gleaming dully from the
rain that had fallen. Now it had apparently stopped, judging
by the closed umbrellas. Rost was curious. He was eager
to know more about this strange man who was about to
appear, his nature and character, how things would turn out
between them. But his curiosity was that of a disinterested
party, of an observer from the side. Naturally he was also
curious with regard to himself, how his life would develop
and what forms it would take. He knew that will was
important, but he knew that everything also depended on
opportunities, which could not always be foreseen and defined in advance.

Peter Dean entered the café. He spied Rost and smiled
at him over the heads of the people sitting at the tables
between them. Then he approached and eased into a seat
opposite Rost. 'All is well with you, my young friend?'

He took out an expensive leather cigar case and opened
it, offering it to Rost, before clipping off the end of a short,

fat cigar with a little penknife and putting it in his mouth. The cigar gave off a very pleasant smell that mingled with the aroma of the steaming coffee.

Rost suddenly felt a wave of warmth towards the man sitting opposite him with his intelligent little eyes, unhurriedly sipping his coffee between one cigar puff and the next. The image of telegraph poles on a dark night flashed before his eyes. Then he gave a brief account of the room he had rented, skipping the part about the intimacy between himself and his landlady, whom he now called to himself Gertrude, without the addition of her surname. Peter Dean listened in silence.

A couple sitting in the bay of the nearby window were arguing in suppressed rage. Rost could only see the flushed face of the woman, attractive in its excitement. She spoke rapidly and vehemently, spitting out words full of venom, tumbling over one another in a furious rush. Their meaning was incomprehensible to him. Her companion, who was sitting with his back to Rost, interrupted her with curt, isolated words.

Dean said: 'What interests you in particular?'

'Everything. I'm curious.'

'Would you like to learn?'

'Learn what?'

'I don't know, science and so on.'

'I'm not particularly inclined that way. And as far as the conventions of society are concerned, I can do without them.'

'Anyone who ignores the laws of society has to be able to make his own laws. My father was not a poor man, but he said to me: "It's up to every man to make his own way, the devil take it!" And then I set out.'

'Where to?'

'To the ends of the earth. First to America, with a matriculation certificate, a passage on a ship, and twenty gold coins.'

'If not for your father, would you have stayed home?'

'No.'

'And after that?'

'Afterwards I set myself a goal: the first million in five years. And I went to work as a dishwasher in a big hotel. At the end of four years I had made my million.'

'But not by washing dishes.'

'No.' And a second later: 'The first million was the most difficult. The rest followed like sheep after the bellwether. At your age I said to myself: people can be made to go in any direction, you only have to know how to get at them.'

'You were mad for money.'

'For freedom, perhaps for power. Money is an important basis. Setting a goal means sacrificing the present for the future.'

'As for me, I wouldn't want to give up a single moment for the sake of some uncertain tomorrow.'

'Of course. Sometimes a person travels for the sake of the journey itself and not in order to reach a certain destination, but for this too you have to buy a ticket.'

'You can also go by foot.'

'A matter of preference. You can't go far and, besides, you get tired.'

Dean drank a little water from one of the glasses on the nickel tray. 'Man is given a limited time on earth, and he spends most of it without thinking, for otherwise he finds himself in an empty void, and on the horizon, death, which is certain to the point of despair.'

Outside, it was raining again. Close to the asphalt the raindrops seemed to spray in the reverse direction, going up instead of down. The coats of the horses drawing the passing carriages were wet and glistening. Dean went on. 'Man is always alone in his sorrow, his boredom, his joy, and this gives rise to the frenzied flight from himself and his solitude to anything and everything, sometimes even to death itself. The overriding element in the make-up of a human being is fear, and all his efforts are directed towards distracting himself from it, hiding away.'

The café was full. The waiters in their white jackets rushed busily about with trays that carried glasses of pure water, drinks, cakes, and newspapers. Music poured in from the adjacent hall, five steps up: light, somewhat yearning, and incompatible with the growing greyness of the rainy day outside. The quarrelling couple at the next table stood up and left.

Rost said: 'You are a man of experience. In your opinion, should a person aspire to some goal?' He himself thought that there was no need for anyone to strive for anything beyond oneself — life, just as it was, was interesting enough. If anyone had asked him what he aspired to with all his heart and soul, an eighteen-year-old like him, he really wouldn't have known what to reply. A thirst for life and a healthy dose of curiosity — these were all he was sure of.

'People are always striving for some goal, consciously or unconsciously,' said Dean, 'according to their strength and their courage. Overcoming obstacles provides a momentary satisfaction, but no more than that. The fulfilment of physical needs also provides a certain satisfaction, on a more primitive, animal level, apart from love, which also belongs to this category.' He continued: 'In my opinion most men of action invest themselves in activity for the sake of the activity itself, in order to save themselves from the boredom and emptiness of doing nothing, and the goal is only incidental. There are other people of a more passive inclination. They enjoy themselves by observing, and abandon themselves to chance. And as for you, how do you intend to live?'

Rost, while being of an ardent temperament that was liable to abandon itself utterly to the object of its desire, always kept some corner of his mind clear, like a little window in a dark room, from which a small ray of light shone on his escapades and experiences at the same time as they were happening. 'I don't make plans in advance. And I don't have any fixed goal to aspire to.'

'And why did you set out into the world?'

'Out of curiosity. I want to come to know life, people, myself.'

'A goal like any other.'

'And I want to live. To penetrate all the hidden corners. I think I belong to the category of active people. This is not a value judgment, simply a question of classification.'

'And what about material means?'

'That isn't a problem. I don't think it's difficult to get hold of them when they're needed. Either by work or by ...'

'What?'

'Personality. I'm confident of myself.'

'All means are equal in your eyes?'

'There are some people to whom the usual rules don't apply. They weren't made for them. You said so yourself.'

'It's not hard to say. Doing is another matter.'

'I feel that I have the strength.'

Dean gave him a quick, questioning glance, and then gazed into the distance, twenty years and more, back to when he was a young man himself. Washing dishes wasn't an easy job, especially for someone whose blood was boiling in his veins, itching to conquer the world. Then came the long journeys to the borders of Canada and Mexico, the nocturnal meetings with all kinds of shady characters who belonged to no society or nation, and the traces of whose origins had been effaced long ago. That was a testing ground where the measure of a man's strength and courage was taken. A modicum of brains was necessary too, for the manoeuvring between the police agents on the one hand and the opium and marijuana smugglers on the other.

At that moment he felt an imaginary pain, like a distant memory of the scars remaining on his body from that time. He remembered the night when he wrestled the Irish sailor, the two of them struggling in silent fury on the quay of the harbour, first one on top and then the other, and he felt the cold stabbing of the knife, stabs that registered in his consciousness only as the chill of the metal, not the pain, which he did not feel then at all. And afterwards, when the last spasms of the other's body subsided under his throttling hands and it grew stiff and motionless, when he detached himself from the body grown strange and sickening in its sudden transformation, feeling tired to death and only now aware of the pain of his bleeding wounds — instead of leaving the dead body and hurrying away to seek shelter and succour for his wounds, as common sense demanded, he gave way to an irresistible compulsion to place himself in danger, and he lit a match to examine the still face of the dead man, whose right eye was slightly open to show the shining white, and the tip of whose tongue was poking out of his mouth. He dragged the body to the edge of the quay with the last of his strength, in spite of the profound sense of nausea the corpse aroused in him, and pushed it into the black, oily water.

From the entire episode, what remained with him for a long time afterwards was the gurgling sound of the water closing over the dead man. He remained for a brief moment on the edge of the quay between the still, anchored ships, weak and bleeding in the face of the giant vessels on which nothing moved and which looked like gigantic black tombstones in a huge graveyard, listening to the muffled ripple of the waves. All at once he felt a despairing, suicidal loneliness. This feeling, which struck him so suddenly, blew like a chill wind straight from down there, from the place where the water had swallowed the sailor's body, and it made him forget his pain and the danger of staying where he was, and gave rise in him to a shadow of remorse. He could not muster the strength to leave, to detach himself from the dead body, which was presumably still close by — a little beneath the surface of the water but still there at his feet, even though he couldn't see it. He felt as though if he left now he would bear this loneliness like a wound that would never heal.

Some strong, hidden force riveted him to this place and to the vanished body and made it impossible for him to move. He stood leaning forward and staring spellbound at the black water without seeing anything, and then a ship's siren blared forth in a loud, mournful wail that sent cold shivers down his spine. He felt a sudden chill on the hot summer night and made off in a hurry, almost at a run, despite his exhaustion after the fight and the loss of blood, and he did not calm down until he emerged from the harbour into the streets of the town.

The same feeling came back to haunt him whenever he remembered the incident at the harbour, although in the course of time it diminished in strength. Not that he felt remorse or pangs of conscience, but he felt himself always tied by invisible bonds to the spot where the deed had been done, and where that chill wind had blown on him, as if his own life had been limited and diminished by the taking of another's, and it was this absence which was the source of his loneliness.

A prostitute bandaged his wounds with strips torn from her nightgown in a poor, barely furnished room. She took care of him with the devotion of a nurse, and the acuteness of his loneliness was lessened a little by her care, as well as by the persistent pain. Afterwards he spent two months in the hospital until he was completely healed. At this stage he put an end to his connections with this class of people: he wanted to do business with a different class, and he had the means to do so.

He joined an oil company and by means of various stratagems succeeded in taking over the majority of the shares, and when the value of the shares rose he sold them. Then he was overcome by revulsion and disappeared. For a year and a half he roamed the world, observed the ways of men in different lands, was implicated in all kinds of adventures, and in the end returned to New York and retired from most of his business affairs. He retained certain stocks and deposited money in banks in America and Europe. He was thirty-two years old then, and he took a wife.

'And if you had money, a lot of money?'

'I would spend it.'

'There are sums that can't be spent, only thrown away.'

'You could give the money to others who need it.'

'Why should I?'

'You don't like them.'

'I know them: they're weak or bad, or both.'

'Perhaps they're mainly unfortunate.'

'That too. But I am not a merciful man. There is only one way to deal with them — master them, or they'll master you. And the end is the same for everyone. Everyone dies alone. Completely alone.'

Rost smiled to himself. 'You don't like them, and yet you are attached to them.'

'Without them, life would presumably be very boring.'

Dean leaned back on the soft blue plush of the upholstery and puffed comfortably on his pungent cigar, half of which had already turned into ash, his eyes alternately on the interior of the café and the rainy street outside the window, with an occasional glance at Rost. He sensed a certain affinity between Rost and himself, a kind of inner kinship, despite the obvious difference in their personalities, and was intrigued by the idea of reliving his own youth in a slightly different way and under different conditions. He wanted to follow the young man's development.

A few days before, when he accosted Rost next to the display window, prompted by some obscure impulse with no particular intention in mind, already then, after their first exchange, he had felt drawn to him. This attraction had grown in the past few days and was now stronger than ever. In this young man sitting opposite him he sensed a definite inner strength: it was clear that he would never bow to the opinions of others or submit his will to theirs.

'Would you like to dine with me this evening?' he asked Rost.

'There's nothing to stop me.'

'I'll just call home and then we'll go.'

He got up and went to the telephone, and a few minutes later they left the café.

It had stopped raining. Only the streets were still wet and gleaming, dotted with little puddles of rainwater. It was twenty to seven. The day had darkened early from the heavy grey clouds massed low over the rooftops. The lamplighters in their dirty overalls, long bamboo poles tipped with smoky flames in their hands, were already running in zigzags to light the gas lamps on either side of the street. They strolled up Kärntner Strasse, turned into the Ringstrasse, passed the opera house, and entered a famous, elegant restaurant in whose spacious hall a number of early customers were already seated, most of them senior army officers in the company of fashionably dressed women. Dean greeted a few of them from afar, and Rost noticed that they returned his greeting deferentially. In other words, in the eyes of his acquaintances he was regarded as a person of consequence. Dean glanced at his companion and saw to his satisfaction that the young man comported himself with the confidence of someone completely at home in his surroundings, although he had certainly never set foot in such a fancy restaurant before. No, he had not been mistaken about him; without a doubt he was one of those people whose quick wits and sharp perceptions enabled them to grasp the unique features of any new environment in the blink of an eye and act accordingly. A characteristic of great actors who can play any part in the world without blurring the clear outlines of their own personalities, and are always able to remain above the role they are in and be its master.

Dean chose a table next to the wall, from which it was possible to survey the whole hall. Imposing waiters in dazzling white jackets served the customers with practised, elegant movements, or stood ready with an air of modesty. The manager, a bald man in a tuxedo, bowed in deference to every new face. Roses and carnations in porcelain bowls decorated the tables covered with spotless white tablecloths. The hall gradually filled with people. A pretty blonde woman of about thirty, with an erect bearing and dressed in high fashion, stepped quickly into the hall and made straight for their table, with a little puppy that looked like a ball of fluff scampering behind her with tiny, tapping steps. In the middle of this ball of fluff were set a moist nose and a pair of intelligent black eyes. It seemed as if a strong gust of wind would blow the fluff away, and nothing would be left of the puppy but for two eyes and a nose suspended in the air close to the ground.

'Here comes my wife,' said Dean. He rose to meet her, and when she came closer he introduced them: 'My young friend, Herr Michael Rost.' Rost bowed and kissed the back of the hand she offered him after pushing her glove down to her fingers. After she sat down she called the puppy: 'Waldy! Come here!' She seized him by the scruff of his neck and set him down on a chair. Her voice was clear and caressing, full of warmth.

'Did you come in the carriage?' asked Dean.

'Yes, Franz is waiting. I thought you might need him.'

'And yourself?'

'I'm going to the opera, to *Lohengrin*.'

'On your own?'

'With Felix.' She gave him a loving look. 'Perhaps you'll join us?'

'I don't feel like it this evening.'

After that she sat there with an airy, haughty look, and with dainty movements extracted the white meat from the red carapace of the lobster Dean had ordered for the first course. From time to time Rost stole a look at her. A smell of violets wafted from her. He mused: a light day in early spring, gold and azure … Suddenly a feeling of pure joy welled up in him for no apparent reason and lit up his face. He was young, and the world was as young and handsome as he was, and outside it was raining, and that too was beautiful and incapable of lowering his spirits to the slightest degree. He patted Waldy, who was sitting on his chair and contemplating the table with a calm, philosophical air.

Rost sipped the chilled champagne. It dissolved in his mouth and became something abstract, spiritual, pure air, and sent a lovely warmth coursing through his limbs. He also felt a kind of happiness for Peter Dean, and a sudden excess of affection for him because of this woman, who obviously loved him very much. And by some unconscious process of association, the previous night in Gertrude's arms flashed before his eyes like a dark stream buffeted by waves of black fire. The passionate lust he had aroused in this older woman added to his self-esteem and made him feel more powerful, as if the strength of her lust made him stronger.

Only now did Rost become aware of the pleasant, unfocused expectation which had been radiating through his body all day in anticipation of the night to come. He could still feel the touch of her body on his; even now he could sense it on his skin, as if he were deliciously enveloped in a gauzy veil of mist. And he went on feeling the warmth of her body dreamily pervading his skin, if only in order to arouse a cherishing affection for his own body, which became precious to him because it was precious to her.

The hall was already quite full. Between the occupied tables the waiters moved silently and swiftly, agile as jugglers. From the far end there floated on waves of bright light the yearning strains of the violins of the gypsy band, full of longing and suppressed passion. The wildness of the Puszta — the plains of eastern Hungary — rose from these tunes, a spirit of unrestrained passions, strong as death, of harsh tyranny, of helpless, childish tenderness, of supplication, of the yearning for freedom. It expressed the desperate pursuit of an elusive happiness, a stubborn and persistent search for that which the more you chased the more it fled from you, and even as you imagined you had it in your hands it suddenly slipped between your fingers and left them empty again.

When they finished drinking their coffee it was already half-past nine. Dean's wife rose to leave and gathered Waldy into her arms. She bestowed a faint smile on Rost as she said goodbye. Her husband accompanied her outside, and after a few minutes he returned.

'The carriage will be back in a moment. 'If you have nothing better to do, you can come with me to the club.' He called the waiter and paid. 'Washing dishes, as you see, does not suit everyone. It is not the only possibility.'

Here and there stars shone moistly between the clouds.

The air was fresh and washed clean. Two rows of lamps stretched along the Ringstrasse. Brilliant lights announced the splendid Bristol Hotel and in the distance the Continental, and on the left the lights drowned in the darkness of the gardens surrounding the fort. A light wind sent a flock of white clouds scurrying across the sky.

Dean said: 'I will deposit in your name a sum of ten thousand kronen in the bank. I am giving you this sum as your allowance for a year, but you are free to use it as you wish — that goes without saying.'

Franz saw his master coming in the distance and brought the carriage from the next street to the front of the restaurant. He sat high on his perch in his livery, his luxuriant moustache twirled up in waxy points, his face impenetrable.

'I don't know if I can show the proper gratitude.'

'Enough of that!' Peter Dean cut him off with a dismissive wave of his hand. 'In most cases it is the giver who owes thanks. The matter will be arranged tomorrow morning.'

The two chestnut horses turned their haughty heads in Dean's direction and pawed their hooves on the paving stones. He patted one of them affectionately on its long neck. The doorman of the restaurant, in his blue livery with its gold buttons, leaped to open the door of the splendid covered carriage, closed it behind them, and felt the weight of the coin in the palm of his hand where Dean had deposited it. Dean arranged to meet Rost the next morning at the credit bank.

They did not have far to go. The carriage drove smoothly to Schwarzenbergplatz and turned into a quiet, affluent street composed mainly of ancient palaces hidden in silent gardens and invisible from the street. On either side all that could be seen were the high iron fences, through whose lattices an ancient, secretive silence, saturated with the mould of generations, stole into the street. From time to time sparks flew from the iron-shod hooves of the horses. Their rhythmic trotting in unison made a monotonous *tick-tack* sound that lulled the occupants of the carriage into an agreeable sleepiness after their good meal, and they sank contentedly into the padded seat without exchanging a word.

Snatches of thoughts and images flitted through Rost's mind. He saw himself again getting off the train at the Nordbahnhof into a cold, gloomy winter morning, without any money but in good spirits nevertheless. For a few minutes he had lingered in the bustling street, full of the creaking of heavy freight carts, the clatter of hurrying trams, the hurly-burly of people, standing and taking it all in before he made for the centre of town. An obscure feeling arose in him: that, thanks to some mysterious power, all this movement was under his control. Then he turned away and went out fearlessly to face the foreign city.

Again he saw his mother in front of him. Now she was presumably getting ready to go to bed. The familiar bedroom rose before his eyes, with the heavy old-fashioned wooden beds. His mother, who was no doubt at this moment thinking of him, her beloved son. Abstract thoughts in an aching heart, without any anchor in reality, since she had no idea of his whereabouts, or the context in which to relate to him. A warm feeling stirred in him towards this mother, whose every movement he saw clearly as if in a vision — how she took off her clothes, loosened her hair and combed and plaited it into a golden braid, opened a book to read in bed before she fell asleep, and how his figure peeped at her between every word, the figure of the son who had abandoned her, until she no longer saw the letters. Such was the fate of mothers — the world robbed them of their sons.

'Do you play cards?' Dean broke into his thoughts.

'Sometimes.'

'We've arrived.'

4

It was about an hour after midnight when they left the club.
A cold starry sky spread over the city. Millions of people
were now sunk in sleep, and the city with its blind, heavy
buildings seemed deserted and abandoned by its masters.
As they stepped out of the door, the crisp night air hit them,
somewhat dispelling the intoxication of the game. Rost felt a
certain sadness rising inside him, a kind of sorrow for something that had been lost. During the course of the evening
he had won more money than he had ever possessed in
his life, and yet he felt a strange emptiness mingled with a
kind of regret, as if he had somehow been impoverished
by his enrichment. Peter Dean spied his carriage in the
distance among the row of grand carriages parked along
the pavement with their elegant harnesses, their coachmen
huddled drowsily on their high perches.

Franz straightened up respectfully as they approached.
Rost suggested that they walk a little, and they proceeded
at a leisurely pace towards the centre of town, descending
the sloping street with the carriage following a little way
behind them.

'You won a handsome sum tonight, I think,' said Dean, breaking the silence. 'Eight or nine thousand. But you don't look happy.'

'I don't know. The world seems a little emptier.'

The Ringstrasse lay before them abandoned and exposed, broader than by day. The rows of leafy trees lining it on either side were still. Night watchmen rattling huge bunches of keys; solitary passers-by; prostitutes swinging their handbags demandingly from side to side, pacing to and fro on their piece of the pavement, alone or in pairs, throwing out the same business-like *'Kom, Schatzerl'** to every man that passed. Homeless people parked here and there on shady benches; illuminated stalls selling piping-hot sausages on the street corners; gigantic policemen planted in the middle of the pavement; an occasional carriage going by, the echo of its galloping horses' hooves coming back from the dead buildings, clear and full.

'Should we drop in somewhere for a drink?'

Dean had no objections to this proposal. They turned into Kärntner Strasse and from there into a side alley. Close to the alley's entrance, electric lights blinked alternately in red and blue, advertising the most famous nightclub cabaret of the day. The smell of perfume mingled with that of tobacco, garish lights, beautiful women in magnificent evening gowns and glittering jewellery, and men in tuxedos or army officers' uniforms, with severely bristling moustaches and monocles. With every opening of the door, snatches of sentimental music fluttered through the air like a swarm of invisible butterflies, and two red-coated doormen executed mute

---

*   German: 'Come, sweetheart'.

bows, ceremonious and at the same time rather automatic.

A number of wide steps covered in soft wine-red carpet led down to a round, spacious lobby lit by a blue light. On either side loomed marble statues and giant pots holding dwarf palms, which were multiplied in the mirrors covering the walls up to the gilded ceiling. From there three openings led into a spacious hall divided into alcoves, curtained off by screens taller than the height of a man and surrounded by a balcony. There was a loud hubbub. Gleaming bald pates and curious women's hats resembling exotic birds were scattered all over the hall. Dancers wriggled their backsides and naked bellies between the tables of the guests. From the heights of the stage poured an avalanche of ribald tunes. Singers sang '*Puppchen, du bist mein Augenstern*'[†] and similar ditties, accompanied by rude gestures. Waiters poured champagne with a flourish; elderly men, with fat cigars stuck in their well-fed faces, pawed ambiguous young women who could see nothing but their money; and a stupefying smell of tobacco, perfume, alcohol, and sweat congealed in the air. It was hot in spite of the fans, which never stopped turning. The atmosphere was one of artificial revelry, forced and exaggerated, which did not break forth spontaneously from the soul, and whose phoniness was immediately apparent, as in most places like this one.

Rost sipped the champagne and nibbled salted almonds. The previous feeling of emptiness did not leave him. He looked at the musicians opposite him, their faces pale and

---

† German: 'Darling, you are the apple of my eye' — a refrain from a popular operetta of the year 1912 by the German composer Jean Gilbert (1879–1942)

jaundiced in the garish light after sleepless nights, and thought to himself: *They certainly aren't enjoying themselves.*

'Is this all?' he asked Dean, making a comprehensive gesture with his hand. 'Is this all there is?'

His companion looked at him for a moment in silence, and finally said: 'A little oblivion purchased by money. Anyone who brings joy with him will find it here too.'

Sitting at the table next to them was a merry company of two men and three young women. One of the women, a slender brunette with mocking eyes, sent frequent glances in Rost's direction, a fact which did not escape his notice. In the end she stood up, excused herself to her companions, saying that she would be back in a minute, and sailed off in the direction of the lobby. Rost waited a few minutes and then rose from his seat and followed her. With her back to the doorway, she was powdering her face in front of a mirror in which the whole of the interior was reflected. There were a few other men and women standing about in the lobby. Rost made his way between them and picked up her handkerchief, which had slipped from her hand at that very moment and fallen to the floor.

'If you please, madam.'

With the tips of her delicate fingers she took the handkerchief and put it in her handbag. With an alluring smile she thanked him.

'Perhaps we could meet tomorrow?' ventured Rost.

'The two of us? What for?'

'Just for a chat. For a chat about the political situation in Europe and in general.'

'And you think you can shed some light on the subject.' The young woman laughed.

'I hope so. Why don't we see, at five o'clock in Café Graben?'

'Fine.'

Rost returned to his table. 'Do you happen to know the people sitting next to us?' he enquired. Dean didn't know them. He only knew that the brunette was a dancer, Vita Kersten. Rost called the waiter and paid. As he rose to his feet he exchanged a meaningful look with the brunette. Dean accompanied him home in his carriage.

When he turned on the light in his room, Gertrude raised her head from the bed and supported herself on her elbow. Her blue silk pyjama top was unbuttoned. One full breast was exposed and also a little of her white belly down to the darkness at the groin, where the blanket and pyjama pants had slipped below her knees. Half-reclining, she looked straight ahead, a dark, burning look, her eyes glittering feverishly. Rost went up to her without taking off his clothes and kissed her on her mouth, on her eyes, on her nipples, on her belly. Her smooth body was suffused with the warmth of sleep. His kisses and caresses gradually dispelled the dregs of the sadness that had settled inside her and, with the continued disappointment of her expectations, had grown into the resignation of despair. Hers was the extreme loneliness of a woman left alone, with the desire of her body stretched to breaking point in the anticipation of her lover — in vain.

For two-and-a-half hours she had been lying here. The faintest stirring in the sleeping street was caught by her tense, sharply honed senses. She was on the alert for any rustle, any footfall in the street or on the stairs, the sudden howl of a cat or roar of a tram in case it signalled his arrival.

Eventually she sank into an irritable sleep, permeable and riddled with holes as a sieve, infiltrated by every sound and deprived of any beneficial effects. When he turned on the light, she had woken up immediately, feeling wide awake and as if she only closed her eyes a moment before, just as the room was flooded with a pale-orange light.

'I waited for you. The night is short. Life is short,' she said slowly, in a voice that was passionate and a little muffled, as if wrapped in cotton wool. Rost got up and began to undress. When he lay down beside her, her body consumed him like fire — he felt as if he would die in her embraces. In her lust there was now pain and despair, a dread of the imminent parting, an effort to suspend this moment in time, to make it last forever.

'You're sad today.'

'I'm happy. Perhaps a little sad too, only a little. I felt suddenly afraid. The whole day was empty. All the time my body felt the touch of your flesh, and you weren't here. And it cried out to you at the top of its voice without being heard. And then the foolish fear came to me that I would never see you again, and the fear grew greater, and I felt the loneliness of death. Perhaps it isn't good to love you so much.'

'Perhaps it isn't. A person should leave some space inside himself, a refuge he can escape to in time of need.'

'When a woman like me loves, it's with all her heart and soul, without holding anything back.'

Rost reached out his arm and drew the little smoking stand to the bed. He lit a cigarette and stuck it between her full lips, red with lust.

Gertrude took one puff and passed it back to him. She didn't know how to smoke. The night lingered with them and drifted on, still and motionless. The silence was audible. Threads and tongues of blue-grey smoke clung to the ceiling of the orange room like an airy, transparent scarf. For a minute they remained still, then they began to flee in a panic-stricken rush towards the open window, as if drawn by an invisible hand. The silence was interrupted by the muffled hoot of a locomotive, cut short and not repeated: the Sudbahnhof, Rost surmised, and crushed the end of his cigarette in the ashtray. He had every reason to be content. He had plenty of money, he had a lover with ardent flesh and snaky black hair, he had an affectionate friend. And apart from that he had an appointment to meet Vita Kersten, who had intelligent, mocking eyes, a passionate, capricious mouth, and an astoundingly shapely figure. He would see her tomorrow. It was good to be eighteen, and good to love women, to covet them even when they were attainable.

Rost stroked the calves of the naked woman lying at his side. Despite its mature abundance, her body looked like that of a virgin. Only the thin line of hair stretching down from her navel, as if drawn by a pencil over the slight curve of her belly, hinted at pregnancy and birth.

Rost sat up. He looked curiously at her body. Every part of it was brimming with effervescent life, every part of it had a soul of its own, and the play of light and shade threw each part into relief in the framework of the open blue pyjama top and the wine-red blanket at her feet. Rost added an imaginary black cat to the picture, to emphasise the white glow of her body, because it reminded him of a painting by Manet, of which he had once seen a reproduction. He went on surveying her thus for a while, and the survey already held the seeds of conquest.

Gertrude smiled at him, a smile of gratification and submission. She felt his gaze like the caress of his warm hands. The vestiges of her sadness had already evaporated completely. She was happy to be surveyed by his eyes. Happy with a quiet, tender joy, treasuring her happiness inside her, and revealing herself utterly to his gaze. She did not want to interrupt by speech or movement this unique moment of full, calm joy. It was a situation she was experiencing for the first time, and she could not recall any other like it. She thought of her husband, who would go to sleep immediately, leaving her alone, boiling, frantic with excitement, her blood racing and her heart beating fit to burst. Then she would be left in an empty abyss, a desolate wilderness, all alone, her blood raging as if demented, with no one to rescue her. A woman is always left empty-handed. In the end everything slips through her fingers and she needs a concrete, living presence. She more than the man, because she is always alone. Alone till death. And he, the husband, snores at her side, at first hesitantly and then at full blast, freely, in the contentment of physical satiety. At these moments the seeds of loathing for her husband were sown in her, loathing mixed with contempt, which grew stronger with the repetition of such scenes. She could have murdered him; she could have screamed at the top of her voice, called for help in the distress of her body, or got up and gone outside, into the night streets, to solicit anyone passing by.

Most women, Gertrude knew, were like her, existing in a state of constant thirst, forever unsatisfied. Some rebelled and some despaired, imprisoning themselves in a situation of enforced renunciation. She too would fall asleep in the end, and wake up in the morning with a headache after a night of nervous, unhealthy sleep, and the dregs of her resentment against her husband settled into her soul and lay there like a heavy mass, colouring her day and her mood. Under a camouflage of external calm she was always seething inside. She flared up easily, lost her temper, and her suppressed anger would break out for no perceptible reason, in relation to trivial things of no consequence in themselves. Such outbursts made her seem ridiculous even in her own eyes, but she could not stop herself. They erupted of their own accord, like lava from a volcano. When her brother-in-law went away, she persuaded her husband to agree to rent out the room — even though there was no material reason for it — in the hope of acquiring a respectable lodger. She had no intention of renting it to just anyone who came along. She was in no hurry and she rejected a number of applicants on various pretexts, but she took to Rost from the instant she set eyes on him.

Rost lay down on his side again, facing her. 'You're deep in thought today.'

'Are you worried?'

'No, why?'

'I'm happy. Utterly happy. My day has a new complexion now. I'm full of joyful expectation. Do you have days when it seems that the sun is shining for you alone? In your honour and for your enjoyment?' She suddenly fell silent and seemed to be listening. After a moment she whispered: 'Didn't you hear anything?'

'Where?'

'I thought I heard footsteps in the passage.'

Both of them lay without moving, their ears on the passage, but they didn't hear a sound.

'Perhaps it was Mitzi the maid. And perhaps I only imagined it.'

Nevertheless, Rost got up and went to look. After switching off the light in his room he carefully opened the door, stepped into the passage, and turned on the light. At that very second it seemed to him that a long, white, spectral figure had disappeared into one of the doors at the end of the passage. He suppressed a cry of surprise and made as if he were going to the toilet. So, he had to be prepared for complications: the child was rather temperamental. He returned to his room and lay down next to Gertrude.

'I didn't see anything,' he said in reply to her questioning look. After a brief silence: 'How old is Erna?'

'Fifteen and a half.'

'She's very well developed for her age.'

'In our family the girls mature early. I got married when I was only seventeen.' She pressed up strongly against him, as if to wipe out the years separating them and abandon herself to him in all the purity and fire of her youth, dazzled by the first, innocent passion of a girl who had just become a woman. The night was coming to an end. A hint of bluish-green light dawned in the still, fresh air outside. It was time to part. The night could not last forever. The creaking of cart wheels was already echoing in the streets nearby, and Gertrude got out of bed and put on her pyjamas. Quietly she opened the door, listened for any sound in the passage, and then stole away. Rost switched off the light and fell asleep immediately.

5

In the afternoon Rost visited a few of the shops on the main streets in the city centre in order to complete his wardrobe. He ordered his purchases to be delivered to his address. Then he went to wait in Café Graben, a quarter of an hour before his rendezvous with Vita Kersten. He sat at a table not far from the window and was able to feast his eyes on the glorious day outside and the crowds of people passing by, of whom only the upper halves of the bodies could be seen. He ate cakes and cheese savouries, smoked fragrant cigarettes, and felt in a good mood. The appointed hour went by. She was already twenty minutes late, but he didn't mind. If she was playing a practical joke on him — too bad. He was in no mood today to die of sorrow for the sake of such trifles. On the contrary, he felt a particular zeal for life today, and no rendezvous that failed to take place was capable of spoiling his good mood. In any case, his heart told him that she would come.

And come she did. He was looking at a waiter with a round head as bald as a eunuch's, with ten wisps of colourless hair combed horizontally from ear to ear over his shining pate, and a permanent friendly smile on his round, clean face, when she came in. Wearing a white coat and a broad-brimmed white hat and smiling a genial smile, she greeted him simply, like an old friend. When she sat down opposite him Rost said admiringly: 'Allow me to compliment you at once and say that white suits you very well. We can continue on this basis.'

'The more the merrier,' said Vita Kersten, laughing. She sipped her hot chocolate with charming little sips, holding the cup with the tips of her slender, dainty white fingers. Her movements were rather affected, perhaps even a little theatrical, as if she were performing some rite to a mysterious divinity. She repaired her make-up and lit a cigarette.

'And where did you buy those black eyes of yours?' he joked.

'I don't remember; in Mariahilfer Strasse, or in Spain.'

'In any case, you have excellent taste.'

'Haven't I?' The young woman laughed again. And after a minute: 'But you too aren't Viennese born and bred.'

'To my regret I was not so fortunate. And I'm not even a real Russian.'

He beckoned a flower seller passing from table to table and bought a bunch of violets. Vita breathed in their delicate scent and put them in the glass of water on the nickel tray. A faint smell of coffee and chocolate pervaded the hall, mingled with the aroma of fine tobacco and the fresh print of the afternoon papers, which had just been delivered. Rost leaned back in his chair and contemplated his companion, who was the recipient of a friendly smile and greeting from an officer who had just entered the café. The happy thought crossed his mind that he now had eighteen thousand kronen in the bank, a sum that, even if it was not increased by unexpected profits, would enable him to live for a time without worries and without denying himself any pleasures. The officer who had greeted her was no doubt a distant acquaintance. A small part of her existence, which was unknown to him; a full and variegated existence composed of a great many trivial and perhaps also important things, and populated by all kinds of people. He knew nothing of all this. As far as he was concerned she had only come into the world the evening before, just as she was, fully formed and perfect. The reality of her existence up to now could be denied at his will. For him she had begun yesterday, not before.

Rost suggested going for a drive in a carriage. Soon the two horses were cantering down the wide tree-lined avenue towards a distant horizon already painted the faint, rosy pink of sunset, gradually shrinking to a narrow crack shaded by the branches of the trees. On either side of the avenue, strips of loose soil unfurled like long ribbons: these were the bridle paths, where the sound of the galloping hooves was muffled as if by a soft carpet. Men and women riders stormed past them in both directions.

They sat facing the evening in the gently swaying carriage; before them, the broad back of the driver, immobile as if cast in iron. A light breeze brushed their faces. The cafés were full of people. Shades of white, black, red, blue, yellow, and pink glimmered between trees in full bloom. Green meadows at the roadsides turned grey as night approached. Snatches of merry music burst into the carriage trundling soundlessly on its tyres, pursued them for a while, and disappeared, only to break out from among the trees again. A carriage brimming with youthful laughter came towards them and passed them by, spraying them in its wake with a dust of bright, budding life. In one of the meadows young boys shot a big football into the air. Nannies with babies; lovers slipping arm in arm into the adjacent woods; a railway bridge arching from one side of the avenue to the other with the many carriages passing beneath it; and the air a little moist, cool, and fragrant. A train puffed across the bridge and disappeared into the dense foliage of the trees. Its heavy breath receded into the distance, becoming fainter and fainter until it turned into something abstract and immaterial.

'I'd like to be a poet,' said Rost, 'and preserve an evening like this in words to keep and treasure.'

'No banalities, if you please.'

'I feel a little sentimental now, forgive me.' And after a minute: 'Do you like trains? I'm mad about them. They always take you somewhere else. Always somewhere else. Staying in the same place means death.'

A last orange light rested on the treetops and flickered there faintly before it died. The sun had definitely gone down. A gust of wind emerged from the approaching darkness, about to lick their faces with its chilly tongue. Vita tapped the coachman's shoulder and told him to go back. She declined Rost's invitation to dine with him: she had a previous engagement; another time, perhaps. Next to the opera house he said goodbye to her. The evening had already settled on the rooftops. For a while he strolled along the street, then he mounted a tram going in the direction of the canal.

At Stock's, people were eating dinner. The air smelled of roast meat, onions, and sauerkraut. Misha the anarchist was busy polishing off a stuffed chicken neck, a task he performed with dedication and skill. The heroic tenor at his side gnawed on a drumstick, giving vent from time to time to a hoarse grunt of satisfaction. Reb Chaim Stock circulated with a measured tread, his hands behind his back and his pince-nez on his nose.

'Sit with us, sir,' invited the tenor.

Misha raised his eyes and stopped chewing for a moment. 'Be careful of Jan, kid. He's itching to tickle your throat with the tip of his knife.'

'Where is he?' asked Rost.

With a jerk of his head Misha tossed back his hair. 'Taking care of his eye,' he said, and looked down at his plate again.

'And Yasha?'

'He hasn't been here yet today,' said the tenor. 'Maybe he'll turn up later.'

'He'd better look out for his other eye, Herr Jan,' said Rost. 'Will you have a drink with me? It won't do us any harm.'

He ordered roast chicken.

Max Karp was leaning over the bar and whispering to Malvina. One of his feet was poised on his toes, revealing a large hole in the sole of his patent-leather shoe. From time to time he glanced in their direction. Then he approached them and asked Rost if he could spare him a moment: he had something very important to tell him alone. Rost stood up and retired to a corner of the room with him.

'It seems you're a rich man now,' Karp said with an obsequious smile.

'Yes, it seems I'm rich now.'

'I have a favour to ask you, a trifle in your eyes.'

'Well?'

'Would you like to lend me twenty kronen?'

'No.'

'You don't want to lend money to a man like me?'

'I don't want to lend money to a man like you.'

'You're so worried about such a trifling sum?'

'I'm not worried.'

'We're going to bring out a literary journal for young people.'

'Congratulations.'

'You can be part of it.'

'How?'

'You can publish things.'

'I have nothing to publish.'

'You don't write?'

'I don't write.'

'How come? But it's probably for the best. It's obvious to me that you have no talent.'

'I have no talent.'

'But I could help you, instruct you; I could write for you, and you could sign your name.'

'No thanks.'

'And the twenty kronen?'

'Not a chance.'

'I could get it here for the asking.' He turned his head in the direction of the bar. 'All I have to do is ask. But I don't like to.'

'That's a pity.'

'Why is it a pity?'

'Because you'll remain without twenty kronen.'

'You really don't have any talent. You're a scribbler, a hack!

You'll never write a single word worth writing — you'll be sorry!'

'I like being sorry.'

'Maybe you'll give it to me anyway?'

'No, I won't.'

'I'll give it back in eight days' time, believe me; you'll have it in your pocket.'

'You're wasting your talent for nothing.'

'I demean myself by talking to this person, and he doesn't know how to appreciate it!'

'No, I don't know how to appreciate it.' Rost returned to his table and finished his dessert.

Then, with his finger, he beckoned Max Karp at the bar, and when the latter approached the table Rost asked: 'Will you have a drink with us? Alfred! A bottle of slivovitz.'

Rost poured. 'To the literary journal for young scribblers — raise a glass with me, Herr Karp!'

The latter smiled an embarrassed smile and raised his glass.

'How much is required to bring out a journal of that kind?'

'Hmm … two hundred kronen to begin with.'

'Not much for such an important enterprise, not much at all. And you want me to participate to the tune of twenty kronen, right?'

'The more the better, of course, if possible.'

'The more the better, of course, eh? Did you all hear that? And will there be a section for music too?'

'For music?'

'Certainly — for example, our famous tenor here could contribute an aria or two.'

Max Karp parted his lips in a sycophantic snigger. 'Hee-hee.'

'Shut your trap! You young pup!' the tenor cried hoarsely.

'Keep your hair on, you old dog. And here, Herr Karp, is one krone for you!'

'One krone?'

'For your journal I won't give anything, not a penny. Only if you set aside a section for the singing of our tenor, otherwise not a penny. But here's a krone for you, for your personal needs, because you're not a scribbler but a great talent. One krone!'

'How about, hmm … two kronen? A florin at least? In eight days' time …'

'No, one krone and that's it.'

'Good, you've caught me in an hour of need.'

'You hear, I've caught him in an hour of need! Here you are, one round, genuine krone, not counterfeit!'

'So you're still among the living, Rostel! Stirring up trouble here again?' roared Yasha the Odessan, who had just come in. 'You taught Jan a good lesson! Bravo!' He brought up a chair and sat down. Rost ordered another bottle and a glass for Yasha.

'He'll have me to deal with if he dares to touch you! I told him I'd crush him to a pulp.'

'He wanted me to give back the thirty kronen he lost to me; he found the right person!'

Max Karp stood up, about to leave.

'Sit back down!' ordered Rost. 'Drink with us. Isn't our company good enough for you?'

'No, no, not at all, on the contrary, it's only …'

'Sit down! Do you know each other? A great talent about to bring out a literary journal, my friend Yasha.'

'But we already met long ago.'

'All the better!'

Loud, drunken voices and the boisterous strains of a harmonica rose from a neighbouring bar. A dog gave voice to brief, hoarse barks that sounded like coughing, interrupted by the despairing wail of a baby. Nevertheless, none of this could mar Rost's blissful mood, because it was springtime and he was in the full bloom of youth, and the little evil in his heart, which occasionally found expression in his actions — even that could still be seen as no more than youthful indiscretion.

Max Karp sat down reluctantly with an expression as sour as if he had swallowed a lemon. His round protuberant eyes were dim behind his spectacles, and his fleshy lower lip sagged like that of a tired horse, revealing big, yellow, irregular teeth. His face looked detached from its bones: weak, slack, and helpless. Rost was suddenly seized by a feeling of physical revulsion for the man.

'But if you're in a hurry, we won't detain you.'

'No, on the contrary, I can remain a little while longer in your company. It would be my pleasure.'

'And the great, terrible assassination, when will it take place?' Rost turned to Misha the anarchist, who was leaning back with his long legs stretched out in front of him.

'You'll read about it in the papers after it happens.'

'I'm on tenterhooks, as long as the target isn't me.'

'You needn't worry. People like you aren't even capable of doing any harm.'

'I'll take that as a compliment and a mark of affection,' Rost said with a laugh. 'Listen, Misha, perhaps you should get married instead. It's less dangerous than assassinating someone. I think dealing with a baby would suit you better than dealing with a bomb.'

Yasha laughed loudly.

'You'd do better to mind your own business and stop trying to be so clever.'

Nobody knew the details of Misha the anarchist's life. About a year ago, he had turned up at Stock's, tall and sinewy, and ever since then he had been a frequent visitor. For the most part he kept quiet, listening to the conversation without engaging in it. He seemed to be deliberately withholding his real opinion, for the most part dismissing his interlocutor with some banal remark that put an end to the argument, a remark that perhaps held a hint of buffoonery, of ridicule, even when it was pronounced gravely, with a kind of affected pathos. It was known only that he worked in a factory that produced electric globes; he made no friends, and nobody knew where he lived. He seemed ageless. He could have been twenty-five or thirty-five. He appeared highly educated, even though he didn't show it off. He would sit in their company for hours at a time in silence, smoking, observing, without offending anyone, although it was evident that he was not lacking in courage. There was an obdurate look in his eyes, a look of suppressed fanaticism. His presence aroused in his acquaintances a vague feeling of fear, or rather of unease, without any specific, obvious reason.

Sometimes he would cough, a brief, hollow cough that gave rise to the suspicion that his lungs were unsound. Sometimes he sang to himself in a whisper, in a foreign language that sounded like Mongolian, a very melancholy tune full of longing, conjuring up a strange, unfamiliar landscape, glorious in its wildness, which may have been real and may have been imaginary, in which straight-backed young girls went to draw water from a well, surrounded by green mountain ridges; a landscape that filled a person with sadness and joy and yearning in the splendour of its beauty and its solitude — even a feeling of transcendence.

This Misha interested Rost to a certain extent, and he was only teasing him now in the hope of making him lose his temper and say something revealing, of provoking him into betraying a hint of his true nature. But Misha did not fall into his trap, and Rost was disappointed once again.

'Don't take it the wrong way, Mishka; you know I was only joking.'

'I spit on it all!'

'Restrain yourself, don't spit. We'll both spit together!'

The little street was steeped in the mild evening air. Small children were still playing one last game before going to sleep. Outside the entrances to the buildings, women were chatting, some of them having taken their dogs out for a walk, some sitting on chairs they had brought out from their apartments and gossiping about their neighbours with the doormen, who were puffing on long-stemmed pipes. A woman's voice called: 'Surel, hurry up! Don't forget the keys!' And Surel answered from the open window: 'Shut your trap, you cow!' Someone laughed loudly. The blacksmith Glekner was punishing his son as he did every evening at this hour, and the sound of the boy's yells broke out of the basement windows and echoed down the street.

Misha said, 'I once had a friend with a compassionate

heart. He took a girl out of a brothel and married her. He thought these girls were more deserving of pity than others. She stayed with him for over a year, gave birth to a son, and then ran away. Later on she was seen in another brothel. He took care of the baby for a while on his own, without earning any money. In the end he put him in an orphanage, and the child died before he was one year old.'

'Your story is not very interesting,' mocked Rost.

'If you want something interesting, read detective stories. In real life things are less interesting and sadder.'

'And what happened to your friend in the end?'

'In the end? Siberia. Hard labour.'

'O-ho! And all because of that whore who ran away from him?'

'Perhaps because of that too,' Misha replied simply. 'He was desperate. He had lost his faith in humanity.'

'So he loved her?'

'He didn't love her. Or perhaps he did. Perhaps he loved her without knowing it.'

Rost remembered the young men in his town who preached revolution in clandestine meetings of tailors' and carpenters' apprentices and the like: 'Comrades, all of you exploited workers! Rise up as one man! Break your chains!' And so on and so forth until they were caught in the net and sent to Siberia and turned into martyrs of the revolution. Their parents made money in timber, in grain, in speculating and profiteering, opened all kinds of little shops huddled together, and lived in dread of pogroms. On Sundays and feast days the priests incited their congregations against the Jews, and terrifying rumours spread: 'They're getting ready …' The youths went round the villages setting the peasants against the oppressing landowners and the Czar, and the flames fanned by the sons in the end wrought havoc with their parents.

The restaurant was emptying. Only a few customers were left here and there, sitting at the tables and finishing their dinners. Malvina emerged from behind the bar and came to stand next to Max Karp. 'Herr Karp, perhaps you have a moment to spare? The gentlemen will pardon me.' She pronounced the word 'Karp' with a special pout of her thin lips, which was meant to be coquettish. He stood up and followed her to the bar. Immediately afterwards it was evident from their movements that a lively, low-voiced argument had sprung up between them. Presumably she was scolding him for his long absence, for preferring the company of others to her own. And she had a dull, boring foretaste of what their forthcoming marriage would be like after ten years, when they were familiar ad nauseam with each other, down to the slightest grimace, every little nuance in their voices, every shift in their moods; and there would be nothing between them but the bonds of mutual loathing and undying hostility, which would keep them tied to each other forever. He would be a petty clerk or a teacher, or a small-time businessman with a paunch and a bald head and felt slippers under the bed and flat feet, the hopes of his youth buried at the back of a desk drawer in a yellowing moth-eaten old notebook: his unpublished literary remains. And he would blame his failure and his nothingness on his wife and children, because of whom he never became what he was destined to be. And the possibility of seeing himself as the victim of family life would no doubt afford him a degree of consolation and satisfaction, and he would even enjoy his self-pity, and often be heard to say with a sigh: 'Ah, but for the circumstances, the wife, the children …'

Outside, the commotion gradually died down. The silence of night came creeping in, forgotten and forlorn. Only from the nearby bar did sounds of raucous celebration still rise from time to time. And between the drunken cries, stifled whispers drifted in, presumably from lovers standing in the doorway close to the window.

Rost called the waiter and paid. He parted from the others and left with Misha. They walked silently side by side to the bottom of the little street, which ended at the canal.

'With your permission, I'll accompany you for a while,' said Rost.

'As you wish,' Misha replied, without interrupting his stride. They turned into the gardens lining the canal banks, where a few couples, their bodies entwined in a daze of love, sat on the benches opposite the flowerbeds, which gave off a cool, pleasant breath of night. The bare-headed Misha took big strides with his long legs, making it difficult for Rost to keep up.

'Listen, Mishka, if you need a bit of money, fifty or a hundred kronen, I'd be only too glad.'

'There's no need.'

After a while he changed his mind: 'All right, fifty will suffice.'

They sat down on an empty bench. Below them the city train trundled noisily past on its tracks next to the canal. For a moment the smell of coal lingered in the air. Stars twinkled between the tree branches.

Without a word of thanks Misha stuffed the fifty-kronen

note nonchalantly into his pocket. He lit a cigarette. He behaved as if he were sitting there by himself, and for a long
time took no notice of Rost. Suddenly he spat in a long arch
between his teeth: 'The end is close, do you understand?
A certain, absolute end, like the station seen through the
window of a train unable to diverge from its course. You're
heading directly for it, as if on railway tracks. And you are
always aware of its closeness, whether dreaming or waking,
in action or idleness, and you can't stop being aware of it.
Everything will remain as it was, and only you, only you will
be missing … And the world will come together again in the
blink of an eye, like water you can't make a hole in, and
the empty place will not even be felt. And nobody will give
a damn.'

After a brief silence, he went on: 'The bubonic plague
would be better! To go from town to town and poison the
wells; for them all to be wiped off the face of the earth
together with you! That would be the only satisfaction.'

'How you hate them!'

'I hate them so much it drives me mad! If only I was the
chief inquisitor.'

'I don't know if they're worth such hatred; a little contempt would be enough.'

'You don't know? A little contempt? Peace and quiet,
without disturbing the status quo? God forbid! It's no job
for people as bloodless as you, but I do know. The pulse
rate — a hundred and twenty a minute, understand? The
blood — exactly where to cut! There's no room here for a
little lukewarm contempt.'

He gave a few barking coughs, as hollow as if they came
from an empty barrel. In the row of houses opposite, on

the other side of the road, most of the lights had already gone out in the windows, which looked like square black holes in pale walls. Behind them lay rooms packed tight with sleep. The roar of the city was receding into the distance. From somewhere or other came the hoot of a tram. The red bricks of the nearby barracks were wrapped in a dense, dusky silence. Outside his narrow booth, the figure of a sentry with his gun materialised, a dark, frozen silhouette. His Imperial Majesty was no doubt already dozing on his bed with his grey beard spread around him.

'To poison the lot of them!' Misha repeated in a hollow voice. He kicked the gravel a couple of times and stared into the void. 'An old mother and her daughter raped in front of each other's eyes — ha, what do you say to that? And afterwards, the daughter lies on the ground with her legs apart, her beauty in ruins, in a pool of blood and drifting feathers from the torn pillows, and her mother sits silently next to her without moving. This mother has no more to say. But her eyes — the look in her eyes can drive you mad! You think a little contempt is enough for this too?'

'Of course not, but I think action should be taken at the time, against the people responsible.'

'And how do you know it wasn't? A few villages round about were set on fire. A few of the leaders were killed. But from then on your attitude towards the world is fixed. Those images are etched on your soul forever.'

A policeman walked past and gave them a hard look. There was a silence. Rost felt a pang of pity for the tall man sitting next to him, who always saw these atrocious pictures before his eyes and who always saw his approaching end before him. Neither of them said anything. A woman in a broad-brimmed hat came and sat down beside them. Her features were indistinguishable in the semi-darkness.

'Why don't we go somewhere to have a drink?'

In his hometown the lads of the neighbourhood were also familiar with the sight of women like these, who would sometimes stroll down their streets on a tranquil afternoon, in twos and threes, cracking peanuts and nibbling sweets, on their guard, like foreigners, as if they didn't belong to this town or this afternoon, speaking hesitantly or the opposite, raising their voices and laughing in a reckless, exaggerated manner. Their clothing, although not brazenly loud, always attracted attention by something excessive: brightly coloured ribbons or sequined scarves, testifying to an empty, vacuous life, a life without duties or obligations.

'I'm going home,' said Misha.

'And leaving me here alone?' asked the woman in a slightly smoky voice.

'You should go home too.'

'And who told you I have a home to go to?'

'If you want a krone you can have one, as long as you don't tell the usual sob stories. We've heard them before.'

'Why so high and mighty, stork legs? For a price like that you won't get anything.'

'I'm not asking for anything. Here, take it!'

'Give me four, all night for four.'

'Take it, or you won't get anything!'

She took the coin from Misha. 'Will you look at that: such generosity! And you, my little one,' she turned to Rost, 'aren't you up for it either?'

'I'm not up for it either.'

'A fine pair you are, I must say! In that case, let's go and have a beer together. My treat. No one can call black Hedwig stingy!'

'That's enough!' said Misha and rose to his feet.

The woman threw after them: 'Some men you are! More like snails than men.'

After a few steps Misha said goodbye and walked off with his long strides. Rost got on a carriage and rode home.

6

At about five in the afternoon Rost went for a stroll in the Volksgarten, which was bathed in sunshine and shades of bright green. The army band was playing spirited marches, which no doubt gave rise in the hearts of the maidservants to thoughts of their beloved Hussars. Afterwards they played a waltz by Strauss. Strolling there were smart military men and elegant women, as well as ordinary citizens and idlers. The glorious flowerbeds were as flat as precious, intricately woven carpets. The subtle scent of an undefined happiness, distant but nevertheless close enough to touch, wafted through the air. Rost lounged at his ease in a deckchair, and saw his future life stretching out before him, bright and open as a long, blooming summer, and he, Michael Rost, always full and hungry at once, was greedy for it all. He wanted to plumb the depths of life in all its shades, in its good and in its evil, to exhaust all the possibilities inherent in himself. Was he responsible for the needs of his nature? They had been ingrained in him from the day he was born, and he was under no obligation to make any corrections in them. A man was the sum of his parts, an indivisible whole, and he could not be changed to the slightest degree.

Rost recognised Erna Shtift walking with another girl in the distance. They turned into the path where he was sitting. When they passed him he looked straight at Erna without greeting her. To his satisfaction he saw a blush on the cheek facing him. A moment or two later she returned on her own and came straight up to him. 'You're rude!' she exclaimed, red with anger.

Rost stood up and smiled. 'Me? Why?'

'Rude and badly brought up!'

'Why don't you sit down for a minute? It's a glorious day.'

'Perhaps you think that you interest me?'

'No, I don't think so.'

'As far as I'm concerned, you're air.'

Already a woman in every respect, reflected Rost.

'I'm happy to be air for you. Why don't you sit down anyway? You can say whatever you want to sitting down; you'll be more comfortable.'

For a moment she appeared to hesitate, and then she sank into his chair.

Rost pulled up another chair.

'Why do you treat me like this?'

'How do I treat you?'

'You think I'm a silly little girl.'

'Of course not,' replied Rost gravely.

Erna said disconsolately: 'I know I'm only a silly little girl, but it's nobody's business! Yours least of all.' Rost said nothing. 'And when you see an acquaintance walking past, you should greet her!'

'Of course I should.'

'I don't mean myself. I'm not an acquaintance of yours.'

'Has your friend left already? A pretty girl.'

'None of your business. And she isn't in the least pretty, with that snub nose of hers.'

At that moment a flower seller walked past. Rost bought a bunch of mayflowers and offered them to her.

'Keep your flowers for … for yourself! I don't need your flowers.'

'Why are you really so angry with me? I haven't done you any harm.'

'Because, because I can't stand you! And altogether, you make me sick!'

'Is that all?'

'You're a horrible person! A monster!'

'Pardon me, but you really are a very pretty girl.'

Erna sat in silence, her eyes downcast. The orange sun climbed to the top of the buildings that overlooked the trees and the iron grille of the fence. Close by, an excited little girl ran after a big hoop, with a huge blue bow in her straw-coloured hair. A young nursemaid raised her head from her book and called, 'Zuzi! Don't go far!' The band went on playing, and Erna was silent. Rost had an impulse to take this Erna, with all her sixteen helpless years, to race for hour after hour in a train, to arrive at some strange village in the mild spring evening with a cow mooing contentedly, to retire to a long, low room in the only inn, with its simple, heavy, sturdy, old furniture, which preserved the smell of two gene-rations ago, while on the other hand the sheets gave off the fresh scent of soap and the hands of a strong, clumsy peasant woman. And afterwards, to lean on the windowsill and stare bemusedly at the still, bare village, where only a stray dog roamed the streets; to feel her sixteen years burning and trembling next to him, to feel them until he couldn't breathe and his legs gave way beneath him; and then to get onto the racing train again, and to go on travelling, further and further, in order to find the happiness that existed inside … *You're getting almost sentimental*, Rost mocked himself.

Erna suddenly jumped up, as if she were in a great hurry. Rost rose to his feet too. 'If you allow me, I'll see you home. It would be my pleasure,' he said. She made no reply, and Rost set off next to her. Her previous agitation appeared to have died down, and she now seemed sad, even shy.

Outside a fancy café in the Ringstrasse, he urged her to go in with him for half an hour. She agreed without a word. They sat on the terrace. Patches of pale green and orange were reflected in the crisp, cool air. The sky was stained a rosy pink, and fluffy clouds were suspended in it as if by the light touch of a paintbrush. The sun had already sunk to just above the rooftops; screeching trams rushed to and fro, packed with people. Light carriages glided past; passers-by hurried to unknown destinations, while others strolled at their leisure. His heart began to tremble in anticipation of something undefined.

'Is your mother at home now?'

'She's gone out.' And then: 'What's it got to do with you?'

'I only asked.'

As if in all innocence she said, 'My father will be back in three days' time. He wrote.'

At that moment Rost, to his surprise, saw Gertrude Shtift. He stood up and called her.

'You're here?' She addressed Erna in a somewhat indignant tone.

'It's my fault,' said Rost. 'I met her in the park and dragged her here. I'm ready for any punishment you think fit,' he concluded with a laugh.

'It's no great crime,' said Gertrude, but her face betrayed her annoyance. She made a few remarks in a rather reserved tone and had no desire to remain in the café. They had to get back in time for supper.

There was a kind of tension in the air. Erna too seemed annoyed, and he could feel the hidden sting in the few words that escaped her lips. He paid and set out to accompany them home.

They did not have far to go. Rost spoke about the weather and then fell silent. When they reached the house, he retired immediately to his room. It was about half-past six. He put on a dressing-gown and sat next to the open window. For a while he leafed without interest through a new novel that had earned a reputation in a short time. He didn't like it at all. The style was bombastic, unnatural, fussy, flaunting its cleverness under the nose of the reader as if to say: *Look at me! I know this and this and this too! Don't forget whom you're dealing with here!* The reality in this novel was counterfeit, false, and without any natural, direct relation to things. The writer possessed intellect alone, without passion or art.

Rost put the book down, dismissing it with contempt, and stood up to look out of the window. A few citizens hurried home from the city centre and vanished into the entrances of the buildings. The day was drawing to its close, already pale with exhaustion. The smiling face of a girl appeared in an open window. Perhaps she was smiling at him, at Rost.

No, Gertrude was apparently not pleased. He had never seen her like this before. And all because he had taken Erna to the café? That, at any rate, was not reason enough. After all, she was already quite grown up. Perhaps even more so than her mother imagined. Never mind, he had the time and patience to wait for the air to clear.

He sat down to write a letter to his mother, and about half an hour later he got dressed and went out. In the passage he bumped into Gertrude. She whispered that he should wait for her in three-quarters of an hour in the gardens on Karlsplatz.

He had supper in a nearby diner and then set out for the gardens. Gertrude was already waiting for him outside the entrance. She linked arms with him and drew him after her, in the direction of the Ringstrasse. Evening had already settled on the city. The busy road was brightly lit. The sound of music rose from the cafés. The revolving doors never stopped turning. Rost suggested sitting in a café. When they were seated Gertrude said: 'Erna doesn't want to hear your name. She hates you. I ask myself why.'

Rost stopped sipping his coffee. 'At that age they're capricious.'

'What do you want of her?'

'Nothing.'

'There's no need to show her the way to the café. It's too soon for her.'

'Somebody will show her the way in any case. She isn't a baby anymore.'

'But not you. I won't have it, you hear?'

'Why not me of all people?'

'I won't have it,' repeated Gertrude. 'I won't allow it!'

'You'll have to lock her in her room, and I doubt if that will help.' After a second he added: 'I don't understand, why all this fuss? Nobody did anything to her.'

'She's a high-school student! She should occupy herself with her studies!'

'All for the sake of education?' joked Rost. 'By the way, I suspect she knows all about our relationship. She's not so innocent.'

'Where do you get that from?'

'I have a feeling.'

'There's nothing to it. I'm not afraid of anyone!'

'She suddenly announced out of the blue that your husband was coming home in three days' time. It was obvious that there was something behind it.'

'I don't care! I love you. Nothing else matters.' She stroked the back of his hand lying on the table. 'Nobody can come between us.'

'And when your husband returns?

It made him feel strange to speak of her husband, who as far as he was concerned was an abstract idea. It was hard for him to imagine this Gertrude, who had become one flesh with him, and whom he felt he had always known just as she was now, with her smooth, warm, different, penetrated flesh, with its strong, stunning smell merging into his. To imagine her uniting with some other man called her husband in exactly the same way, with the same dedication, the same transcendence and utter loss of self — it was a strange image, not without a hint of absurdity.

'When he returns, he'll be here.'

'And you'll go to bed with him as his lawfully wedded wife?'

'Are you jealous of him? It seems to me that I'm cheating on him, not on you.'

'I'm not jealous. But the idea of a relationship with limits doesn't appeal to me.'

'You may be sure that I never gave him what I give you. Never. Perhaps you're still too young to understand this, but I'm telling the truth. I was with him, I had a child with him, and, nevertheless, you're the first one, as if I never knew a man before you.'

'And you didn't love him? So why did you marry him?'

'I thought I loved him. A young girl doesn't know how to distinguish between one feeling and another. I found him sympathetic, and he loved me very much; he still loves me today. A girl of that age yearns for caresses, kisses, tenderness. And she's also curious. So I imagined that I loved him, but I soon realised that it wasn't true love. It was only a poor substitute. In fact, I have never loved him at all. I can't say that I hate him or hold him in contempt, not that; but going to bed with him is only a poor imitation without real arousal, an old habit.'

She was telling the truth, but it was quite possible that she was lying without being conscious of it. Since her former feelings for her husband had changed over the course of time, she was no longer able to conjure them up and feel them as they once were. And because she was now unable to describe them to herself, she was inclined to deny their reality in the past too — like someone reading a letter that he wrote a number of years previously, and that now seems to him to have been written by a stranger, not himself.

Rost watched her as she sipped her coffee, which had grown cold in the meantime. She sensed him watching her and looked up at him with a joyful smile.

'Why don't we have a cognac together?'

When the waiter brought the cognac, she took a sip from the round-bellied goblet with its long slender stem, and offered it to him. 'You know, sometimes I feel as though you're my son, born between my thighs, and it drives me wild with joy.' Soon afterwards she said: 'Let's go home now, shall we?'

They left the café. For a while they strolled through the sleepy alleys, Gertrude hanging on his arm with all the weight of her eager body, and the murmur of the city receded behind them, faint and vague and insubstantial. Gertrude's excitement infected Rost. A tremor ran down his legs. He stood still and kissed her on the mouth in the middle of the street, and as he felt her soft lips and the tip of her tongue pushing between his teeth to his dry palate, he was overcome by a slight dizziness. After that they hastened their steps.

7

Straight after supper Erna's mother announced that she was going out for a little walk. For a while Erna went on sitting where she was in the dining room without moving. Mitzi cleared the table and tidied up, and Erna looked at her without seeing her. She guessed where her mother had gone; she was almost certain. To a rendezvous with him, without a doubt. They would meet at a pre-arranged place and he would kiss her and kiss her again — oh, how loathsome he was!

The electric light cast a still, pale-orange glow over the room. The heavy curtain on the window moved a little when Mitzi opened the opposite door. Mitzi had colourless hair and broad hips, and her buttocks shook like a piece of heavy machinery when she walked. The floorboards creaked under her tread.

'Listen, Mitzi, do you have a lover?'

'Fritzel, *gnädige* Fräulein, Fritzel the welder.'

Erna paused. 'And does he kiss you a lot?'

'Like lovers do.'

'Like husband and wife?'

'Fritzel will marry me later.'

'Listen, Mitzi, you have to tell me everything. Everything, you understand.'

'You're still too young, Fräulein.'

'I'm not too young. I already have a lover too, I promise you,' lied Erna. 'He's already kissed me too.'

Mitzi leaned her red elbows on the table. Her full breasts escaped from her polka-dotted blouse and strained it to bursting.

'And do you lie naked? Completely naked?'

'Sometimes naked too. But the Fräulein is very curious.' Mitzi laughed.

'And is it nice to lie like that?' Erna questioned her again, blushing all over.

'Very nice. At first it hurts, but afterwards it doesn't hurt anymore.'

'And does he stroke you like this? Everywhere?' Erna reached over the table and touched Mitzi's breast. She recoiled with a laugh.

'Tell me please, Mitzi, look at me hard, am I pretty?'

'The Fräulein is very pretty.'

'Come here,' said Erna, sitting up straight, 'look from all sides.'

'The Fräulein is very pretty, nobody can deny,' Mitzi delivered her verdict, 'I wish I was as pretty as she is.'

'But here, feel.' Erna took the maid's hand and placed it on her breast. 'There's hardly anything there.'

'They'll grow bigger.'

'Do you think I'm attractive? Tell me the truth.'

'I promise you. All the men will be crazy about you.'

'You see, Mitzi, I always think that I'm ugly.'

'The Fräulein ugly? Don't make me laugh! The Fräulein

is a real beauty.'

'But which of us is more beautiful, my mother or me?'

'There's no comparison. The mistress is beautiful for an older woman. It's completely different. And the Fräulein is beautiful as a young girl.'

'You're a nice girl, Mitzi. Wait a minute. Come to my room later, I still have a lot of questions to ask you.'

'Yes, I'd better go now. I still have to wash the dishes.'

Erna retired to her room, which was long and not very large and furnished in white. She started stripping off her clothes in feverish haste. When she reached her petticoat, she hesitated before taking it off too. She shivered slightly, even though it wasn't cold. She removed the little mirror from the wall over the washbasin, and began examining her body bit by bit, with great interest. She had already had the opportunity to see her body, or part of it, many times before, but she had never studied it so intently. She had always taken it for granted as something that did not require any special attention. Everyone had a body, obviously. But it wasn't obvious today. Looking at her body gave her a strange feeling, pleasant and disturbing at once. She contemplated it as if she were contemplating a body that didn't belong to her, and she showed it to herself as if she were showing it to a stranger. Yes, she had a secret feeling that a stranger was looking at her nakedness, she felt a stranger's eyes caressing her skin, and she was filled with shame, but this did not prevent her from studying the reflection of her little breasts, round as apples, in the mirror, and then putting it down and cupping them in her hands as if to weigh them, and then picking up the mirror again, while cold shivers ran down her spine.

After that she sat on the edge of her bed and looked at the reflection of her smooth belly, with its straight line of black hair. She stroked this warm belly tenderly and felt her hand as the hand of a stranger. She tried to probe the modest place that was the source of life. She turned the mirror every which way and tilted her body, and she was ashamed, but she didn't stop. Were all women the same? Exactly the same? If so, then perhaps they were all ugly in this particular place, or perhaps they weren't all the same. And her thighs, they were far from pretty, she had to admit. Her mother's were more beautiful, round and smooth; she had already seen her in the bath.

She hung the mirror back on the wall, and then opened the door a crack and called Mitzi.

The maid shouted from the kitchen: 'In a minute! I'll be done in a minute!'

The whole house was silent. Only the muffled clatter of dishes rose from the kitchen. Erna lingered at the door for a while and looked absent-mindedly through the crack at the dim, silent passage. A faint ray of light shone obliquely from under the kitchen door at the other end of the passage. Erna felt the hot breath coming out of her mouth. Her mother wasn't back. She felt full of nervous tension, waiting for something, she didn't know what. Her mother wasn't back and it must be late. She went back into the room without closing the door. The little alarm clock on her table full of books and writing materials said it was a quarter past ten. She sat on the bed with her feet on the floor. Outside, someone was standing and singing in an old man's drunken voice. Afterwards he delivered a speech denouncing the authorities right under the window. He declaimed a few vague, unconnected sentences and suddenly concluded with a vulgar epithet that left no room for argument. A few houses further along, he started singing again.

Mitzi entered the room without her white apron. She hesitated at the door: 'Oh, is the Fräulein already going to bed?'

Erna stood up. 'Come here, Mitzi, come closer. Do you think I'm pretty? Tell me the truth.'

'Very pretty. What sweet little breasts! Just asking to be kissed.'

'And are all women the same? Exactly like this?'

'Of course they are! Doesn't the Fräulein know that? Only some are prettier and some are uglier.'

'Just like me?'

'Just like you.'

'And you yourself?'

'Me too.'

'I want to see.'

'What is the Fräulein saying?' Mitzi giggled. 'How can I, just like that ...'

'Why not? You're a nice girl, what do you care? I want to see.'

'It's very funny without a man.'

'Kiss me here, Mitzi.' Erna pointed to her breast.

Mitzi stood still and looked at her with a stupid smile plastered over her face. She didn't move.

'Kiss me here,' Erna repeated. Then the maid bowed her head and kissed her. Erna pressed her head strongly to her breast and let out a moan. 'Well, Mitzi?'

'If the Fräulein insists!' She giggled and began rather reluctantly to unbutton her blouse.

'Your petticoat too,' demanded Erna. Then she examined

her from all sides. Mitzi was not tall, rather ungainly, with big, clumsy limbs. 'You're broad here.' Erna pointed to her hips. 'Not like me.'

Mitzi felt out of place, like someone suddenly and disagreeably left with nothing to do, superfluous, with no possibility of distraction. Her clumsy arms hanging at her sides, she stood in the middle of the room, fleshy and crude, a small, embarrassed smile on her face. She was alarmingly naked. Her nakedness filled the room. One hand started absentmindedly scratching her round belly. Being naked for no particular reason utterly robbed her of her worth, deprived her of her vocation. Clothed, she was good for various roles, even the role of love; naked, she was worthless.

Erna came closer and put her arms round the maid's waist, and drew her to the nearby bed. The two of them sat there without saying a word. The silence was emphasised by the assertive ticking of the alarm clock. The two women breathed heavily and unevenly. Then Erna raised herself to sit on Mitzi's lap. She pressed herself violently against her breasts; she was on fire. Mitzi began to stroke her belly, her thighs, with hands rough and calloused from hard work.

'Is this how he does it to you?' whispered Erna and pressed herself closer.

Suddenly Mitzi stood up. 'The mistress could come home at any minute. I have to get out of here.'

As if through a veil Erna saw her picking up her clothes and leaving the room. For a while she went on sitting on the bed without moving. Mitzi had forgotten a stocking on the chair. She got up and fondled it as if it were a living thing. Her heart beat wildly. Her burning body seemed to burst at its boundaries, reaching for something. Her mother had not come back, and neither had he. But her father would come back. In three days' time. She hadn't done her homework. Her teacher, Herr Stark, would purse his lips until the hairs of his thin moustache stood on end.

In the park he had asked about Friedel. But she wasn't in the least pretty, Friedel Kobler. And yet she flirted with Willy Martin from the seventh form. Maybe he even kissed her. She herself didn't fancy him in the least, with his pimply face and his hoarse, broken voice and his ratty little eyes. A callow youth of no interest at all. But him? He was loathsome without a doubt, and conceited. But ugly he wasn't. And she, Erna herself, was only a silly little girl, and as such he probably despised her. Today she had behaved like … a baby in the first grade. He was probably laughing at her. She would never speak to him again. What was he to her? She detested him from the bottom of her heart.

What if he were to see her just as she was now? She was suddenly flooded by a wave of shame. She made an empty, unconscious gesture with her hand, as if to cover herself. Then she stood up and went to the mirror. She raked her fingers through her hair and started to comb it carefully as if in anticipation of meeting someone she wanted to impress. Her curls reached halfway down her back and made faint crackling noises when they came into contact with the comb, like dry straw catching fire. Outside, a cart trundled past and dissolved into the night. The tear in the silence closed up again. Only the ticking of the clock riddled it ceaselessly, puncturing it with tiny holes.

Erna gathered her hair in her hands and brought it to her face. A black shadow on the whiteness of her neck and chest. She took a handful of hair, raised it to her mouth and nose, and breathed in a vague, distant smell of soap. For some reason she felt an inexplicable need to cry. To sit and weep soundlessly in the silence of the night, not out of sorrow or anguish but for no particular reason, perhaps because of the vibrant inner life stifled within her, trembling in anticipation of meeting some unknown and unbearably mysterious stranger; and because it would not allow itself to be given a name or a form, she, Erna, could not do so, and remained completely helpless before it.

She imagined hearing footsteps in the passage and leaped into bed. She switched off the light and lay still, intent on hearing the slightest sound coming from the passage. The key turned in the lock, and the two of them entered the house. She heard the door to her parents' bedroom, next to hers, opening, as well as the door to another room, at the other end of the passage. With bated breath she listened to the muffled sounds coming from the room next door. As clearly as if she could see them, she followed her mother's movements; saw her taking off her skirt, her blouse, her girdle. Erna felt hot, but she was afraid to move a muscle.

Then the door opened and her mother came out, wearing slippers. After a few moments she returned. The noise of water splashing rose from the end of the passage. Not a sound came from the room next door. A dense silence reigned. So, she had gone to bed. What was going on there? Erna couldn't understand. It seemed to her that an eternity had gone by since her mother had entered her room for the second time. Nothing stirred there. Nothing at all.

Erna was beginning to give up when she seemed to hear the door being stealthily opened. A soft creak confirmed it. With sharpened senses she heard barely audible steps absorbed by the carpet in the passage. For a long time she went on lying there without moving, listening to the silence. Outside, at a little distance, someone whistled a merry tune. Erna got up quietly and put on a nightgown. She didn't turn on the light. She crept into the passage and walked very slowly down it, setting her bare feet down as carefully as if stepping on an ice-rink. At the other end she stood still for a moment, breathing heavily, as though she had just completed a long, arduous journey. Then she took another step and put her ear to the door. She heard the sound of whispering, interrupted from time to time by brief laughter. Sometimes there was a silence. And then the whispering rose again. A strange, heavy, stunning breeze blew from inside the room.

Erna stood outside the door without moving. Her beating heart was fit to burst, and cold shivers continued to run down her body. She was all alone in the whole world, miserable and forsaken in the silence and stillness of the night, in which strange and incomprehensible things were happening nevertheless. She felt very small and helpless. Once or twice she felt a strong desire to break into the room and disturb them, spoil the happiness that left her out. On the other side of the door, something was happening that she did not understand but that put an end to solitude. Over there, there were two of them to face the night together: there they laughed, knew what to do with themselves, with their bodies, reached the limits of their being. And here the night was wide open and empty and terrifying, and a vulnerable body burned and struggled and trembled without any aim or limit in mind. All this Erna felt obscurely, without giving an account of it to herself. Suddenly she was overcome by a rush of hostility towards her mother. Suddenly her mother seemed alien to her, foreign, not the mother she knew but an enemy. It wasn't only her father she had betrayed but also Erna, and at the same time her mother now aroused her curiosity in a completely new way. It appeared that Erna had never known her at all. The idea that her mother had never really loved her thrust itself into her consciousness. Not her, and not her father.

Inside the room they were laughing again. Erna turned away and groped her way back to her room. She switched on the light and lay in bed without covering herself. She felt hot. For a while she lay still, staring at a black spot on the cornice, perhaps a sleeping fly. Then she slipped off her nightgown and began desperately stroking her body, her breasts, her belly, her thighs, as if with the hands of a stranger. Her mounting excitement, which grew increasingly frantic as her fingers stroked a certain place in her body, now approached an unfamiliar extreme, a kind of release. She repeated these movements a few times until her whole body shuddered and convulsed. The shudders gradually died down, and her limbs relaxed. She switched off the light and fell asleep immediately.

8

Friedel Kobler was not an intimate friend of Erna's. Her true bosom friend was Gretel Milner, who had spent the past three months in a sanatorium for lung patients. Erna had always treated Friedel with a certain contempt. But the latter nevertheless latched on to her and sought out her company, and in Greti Milner's absence, Friedel took advantage of the situation to come closer to her. Erna did not protest. Friedel sat next to her in class. Her schoolbag was always full of chocolate and candies, and her mouth never stopped chewing. She already looked just like her fat fifty-year-old mother, Frau Emmy Kobler, apart from the wrinkles round her calf's eyes, which she tried in vain to hide underneath a thick layer of make-up.

After class, Erna invited Friedel to come round to her house after lunch. Friedel lived not far from her. The two girls took the same way home until Karlsplatz. On fine days they would linger in the gardens; at this midday hour all the infants had left. Only a few workers sat here and there on the benches eating the lunches their wives brought them in knapsacks. Most of them were builders or pavers working in the vicinity. Today, Erna avoided entering the sunny gardens, parted from her friend, and hurried home. At lunch she spoke little. She sat opposite her mother, and from time to time she stole a glance at her. Her mother's face had a quiet, contented expression. Her full mouth was ripe and satisfied. There was a smell of roast beef and lettuce in the spacious dining room, and a feeling of drowsiness in the air. An oblique, amorphous window of sunlight lay on the gleaming floor and the edge of the soft carpet.

'The lettuce is fresh. Take a little more.'

'I've had plenty,' replied Erna.

'Tomorrow we'll go to buy you a new hat.'

Mitzi served a dish of noodles with raisins and cream.

'I invited Friedel Kobler round. We'll go for a walk.'

'Where to?'

'I don't know. To the park.'

'You'd better put on your blue dress. The one you're wearing isn't quite clean.'

As soon as the meal was over, Erna retired to her room. She tried to do her homework, to read a book, but she was unable to concentrate. The words seemed foreign, unrelated to her, incomprehensible. She went to bathe and do her hair. Dressed in a pale-green petticoat, her arms bare, she combed her hair in front of the mirror without looking at it, with slow, negligent, absent-minded movements. Suddenly she started to hurry, as if compelled by some inner force. She parted her hair hastily, pinned it in place, and sat down at her desk. She took a clean sheet of paper out of her schoolbag and began to write carefully in big, round letters:

I don't know you. I don't want to know you. You broke into my room by force and now you're sitting here, at the bottom of my bed, and smiling. Why do you smile like that all the time without any shame? I can't stand the sight of you. I don't love you. I'll never love you. I'll wipe that impudent smile off your face. I'll kill you. I'll bite. I'll put you in my desk drawer and take you out whenever I like and you'll be mine. Mine mine mine! Not yours. Not hers. Then maybe I'll love you one little time and throw you away. Because I won't need you at all. And for the time being get out of here. Please. Leave the room. You may give me one little kiss, here. And now go. If you think I'm pretty, tell me before you go. From the tips of my toes to the top of my head, all of it is Erna Shtift. Me. If you were nice I would carry you with me all the time, but I won't do it. You've got yellow hair and you laugh at night. I'll never love you the least little bit. I love you. If I wanted to, I would come and lay my head on your shoulder and stay like that for a week without eating. We could sail like that on a ship to a world where you would be my lover. I could tell you from morning to night that I'd love you forever. At night, when I was asleep; and in the daytime, when I was eating or playing the piano. I would always be able to draw your face. To fill four thousand notebooks with the letters of your name. Four or five letters. And to smile at everyone out of love for you. But I don't know your face, I don't know your name. And maybe I don't love you. I could cry because I love you and because perhaps I don't love you. If I really loved you, I would even love my history teacher, who looks at me with one eye while the other one looks in a different direction, and smiles a nasty, crooked smile with half his mouth. For your sake I could do my homework properly or even not do it at all. But I don't see you, and if

I did see you, I wouldn't even know if it was you. Perhaps there won't be a sign to show that it's you, and I'll be shy. If you make fun of me I'll be sad. I'll hate you and I'll cry. If I find you there today, I'll know that you're thinking of me. In the whole of the city there's nobody but you — nobody.

Erna

She tore the page to shreds and heaped them into little piles in front of her on the desktop. She went on sitting without moving, a forgotten smile fixed on her face. Then she stood up and collected the scraps of paper to go to the kitchen and throw them into the trash.

In the passage she saw her mother, dressed to go out.

'Oof!' grunted Friedel as she sank into the armchair. 'It's hot today!' Erna hid the scraps of the letter in her hand and tried in vain to crush them into a ball. She hadn't noticed Friedel coming into the house. The latter remarked: 'I met your mother on the stairs.'

'What, she went out?' Erna glanced at her friend, who was flushed and breathing heavily.

Suddenly Friedel stood up and approached Erna, and kissed her on the lips. 'You're beautiful, my dear, you know?' Erna felt grateful. Friedel went on standing next to her and looking at her admiringly.

'You're not meeting Willy today?'

'Yes, he's coming to supper with his sister Suzie and Karl Greener, the art student. Why don't you come too?'

'I can't. I'd have to tell my mother first, and she probably won't be back before suppertime.' Erna stood up. Through the crack in the open door, she called Mitzi to make them coffee. Then she started to fix her hair and get dressed. Friedel, sunk in the armchair again with her legs crossed, watched her friend calmly. 'He's interested in you, Karl Greener.'

'That ugly monkey?'

'Don't exaggerate, Erna, he isn't ugly at all. He's a nice boy, and people say he's a great talent. He's going to paint my mother's portrait.'

The two girls went into the dining room, where Mitzi had set out piping-hot coffee, rolls, butter, and jam. Friedel ate voraciously, as if she hadn't eaten anything for a week. 'He said that you were a very pretty girl,' said Friedel, taking up the conversation again with her mouth full. Then she added: 'Maybe you'll come to us for supper anyway? You could sleep over too; tomorrow's a holiday.'

'I don't know. Possibly, if my mother agrees. We'll see later.'

They went out. Erna led them straight to the park, through sunny, spring-drenched streets that seemed cleaner and more beautiful than usual. She paid no attention to Friedel's non-stop chatter. There was only one idea in her head: *if he's there, it's a sign* — and he was there.

She didn't see him at first. On the path where he had been sitting yesterday, she scanned with a beating heart the people strolling and sitting in the deckchairs, and he was not among them. The disappointment struck her with such force that her knees gave way beneath her. She almost stopped breathing. For a moment she stood still to get her breath back. The crowded park suddenly became empty and desolate. There was nobody there. At the end of the path she turned and retraced her steps in the secret hope that she hadn't looked properly the first time. There were so many people today! And indeed, when they reached the turn in the path, he appeared among the crowd. Erna blushed all over.

Smiling self-confidently, he made straight for them. 'What an unexpected pleasure,' he said, holding out his hand to Erna. Then he introduced himself politely to Friedel. Erna kept quiet for a moment, too excited to utter a word. She felt that she was red in the face, and she was filled with rage against herself, which made her even redder. In her annoyance she exclaimed accusingly: 'You're here again! Apparently you have no other work to do — what a loafer!'

'You're here too, I see. But let's move out of the way; we're blocking the path.' After a few steps he suggested that they sit down on the chairs that had just been vacated nearby. The conversation proved heavy-going, inhibited by Erna's stubborn silence. They talked about the weather, about famous stage actors. Friedel interrogated Rost about his origins.

'They say that the Russians are complete barbarians.'

'Yes, they're cannibals,' joked Rost. 'The Czar, for example, eats nothing but human roast. Every village in holy Russia has to supply a tender young man for the royal table, one by one, every day.'

'Only boys?' enquired Friedel in all innocence.

'Virgins too. A young lad one day, a virgin the next. On feast days and holidays two a day, a boy and a virgin together.'

Erna suddenly burst out laughing. 'What kind of fibs are you telling us here!' They all laughed. Erna was seized by an urge to talk non-stop. She talked about school, described her teachers and fellow students in outlines that picked out their most ridiculous features, to the delight of her audience.

There was something sharp and pointed in her descriptions that cast their objects in the grotesque light of a caricature. Something fixed and definite, so vivid that if you happened to meet them later, you could only see them in the shape she had given them.

'It seems to me that you have some artistic talent,' said Rost. 'Do you want to be an artist?'

'I don't know. I've never thought about it.'

'In any event, I don't sense in you the right material for building a respectable bourgeois family. Being fruitful and multiplying in a swamp of boredom. And all out of dull, joyless habit.'

At that moment Vita Kersten walked past, hanging on the arm of a grey-haired man with a youthful face. She responded to Rost's greeting with a meaningful smile, as if she shared a secret with him.

'That's the dancer Vita Kersten!' exclaimed Friedel. 'Do you know her personally?'

'What a question! We met some time ago.'

Erna watched her closely as she walked away, taking the measure of her upright carriage, her mincing walk, the coquettish, ingratiating way she clung to her companion. Without any clear reason, a feeling of hostility towards this woman rose in her.

'You think you're so clever,' she said.

'Not the biggest fool in the world, at any rate.'

'You can keep your cleverness to yourself! It doesn't interest me.'

'I had no intention of offending you.'

'They say she's an interesting woman, that Vita Kersten.' Friedel Kobler knew everything people said about everyone.

'Go and get us some chocolate, Herr Rost. My friend Friedel is crazy about chocolate.'

'With the greatest pleasure.'

When Rost was out of hearing, Friedel remarked, 'An agreeable man.'

'Extremely disagreeable!'

'Don't exaggerate, Erna. To you everything is disagreeable.'

Rost returned with two bars of chocolate. Friedel peeled off the wrapping and fell eagerly on the chocolate. At that moment nothing else interested her. Erna held the bar of chocolate in her hand, making no attempt to unwrap it, as if it were not meant to be eaten at all. She looked straight ahead, above the heads of the people sitting opposite, to the round flowerbed behind them, most of which was already in the shade. The daylight was quickly fading. Waves of music reached them, interrupted by the noise of the trams beyond the fence and the clamour of the city. Rost smoked in silence beside her. From time to time a whiff of pungent smoke drifted into her nostrils. She breathed it in like perfume. If she were older, he wouldn't despise her and make fun of her. In spite of everything she didn't want him to despise her — no, she didn't! Friedel was a fool, a fool, a fool! Why had she dragged her along? Was it because she didn't have the courage to be alone with him? Nonsense! She wasn't afraid of him.

Friedel stood up. She had to go home to receive her guests. And Erna should please try to come for supper or afterwards. Her mother wouldn't object, and it would be great fun!

After Friedel left, Erna remained withdrawn into herself for a while. The outside world seemed to sail away and dissolve into nothing, leaving her alone in an empty void, with a sweet sadness drifting around her and the twilight silently descending on her, touching and not touching her, and a man, perhaps him, by her side. Not by her side, but inside her, and she was filled with a sudden gaiety, and she began to skip and prance mischievously into the grey depths of the evening, her feet bare and her hair wild, with him behind her, laughing, catching and not catching her, running after her as she evaded him, all flushed and dewy with desire.

Erna raised her eyes. Yes, everything was as it had been. And he, he sat unchanged in his chair, smiling affectionately at her, emanating a kind of warmth and protectiveness. All at once she felt very close to him.

'Tell me, is life very sad?'

Rost did not reply immediately. He looked at her, into her eyes, which were close and at the same time very far away and unfathomable. 'It is and it isn't. Depending on the person. And depending on his mood.'

'When a person is very happy, he becomes sad, just a little sad.' And then she added: 'It must be nice to be free, to be able to do whatever your heart desires. When I'm grown up ...'

'When you're grown up?'

'The world is so big, and there is so much to see! And I would also like to be very beautiful.'

'You are very beautiful.'

'Really?'

'What a question! You don't think you're ugly, do you?'

'Yes, sometimes I do, and then I get sad and think I would be better off shut up in a convent.'

Rost laughed loudly. 'You in a convent!'

Erna laughed too. 'Not really. I've never really thought

about a convent. The idea just came into my head. As a matter of fact, I don't like the nuns at all.'

Erna had to go home. In the Ringstrasse, Rost stopped a carriage. He let her off at Karlsplatz and went back to town. Erna stood still and watched the carriage recede into the distance.

9

The Koblers lived in a large apartment whose many rooms were all luxuriously furnished. They were rich. Herr Kobler, fifty years old with an imperial beard strewn with grey, a Moravian Jew born in Vienna, bought and sold shares on the stock exchange, trading in abstract bushels of wheat that nobody had ever seen and that existed only on paper. He had a company called Kobler Brothers, Export and Import (the firm was named Kobler Brothers for the purposes of re-inforcement alone, since he himself was the only brother — the others had never been born). Somewhere or other he had a large country estate that he never visited, and a handsome villa in Ischl, where they spent the summer months almost every year, unless they went to the seaside or abroad. He was preparing to receive the title of court councillor and sometimes, for his private enjoyment, he would try on the anticipated title in advance: 'Herr Hofrat Heinrich Kobler, eh, Emmy?'

His wife, Emmy, was a Christian from a poor family, and had married Kobler because 'the Jews have money'. She considered herself superior to him on account of her

Christian origins, but the truth of the matter was that she was not an ill-natured woman. Her sole ambition now was to hang on to her long-lost youth, to cling to it with all her might, and her movements and exaggerated girlish laughter made an unnatural and grotesque impression. She did not allow herself to show any sign of weariness, and when it sometimes happened that someone in her company complained of being tired, she would immediately exclaim, 'I'm never tired — I haven't reached that stage yet, thank God!' while all those present thought to themselves: *The old hag!*

But her husband would see her when she woke up in the morning, crumpled and wrinkled, without the armour of her cosmetics and outfits in the latest fashion, and he kept a little blonde mistress who cost him a few hundred kronen a month and with whom he spent the afternoon three times a week. He was in the habit of remarking, 'My wife, Emmy, who comes from an aristocratic family ...' until in the course of time he came to believe it himself. As far as possible he avoided the company of Jews and sought that of non-Jews, especially those with titles. He would emphasise their titles when addressing them, conveying an impression of humble gratitude and pride at the privilege of rubbing shoulders with them and being counted as one of them. He donated generously to Christian charities, especially those that could buy him fame. But his close friends and those who took his money would refer to him behind his back as 'that Jew bastard'.

Apart from Friedel, they had a twelve-year-old son, Johann Wolfgang — after Goethe, because Heinrich Kobler loved classic poetry and Goethe in particular, and giving this name to his son expressed his admiration for the poetic genius on the one hand, and constituted a sly nudge to fate on the other. But Johann Wolfgang Kobler paid no attention whatsoever to his father's secret intentions and was a boringly average boy. He did not distinguish himself in anything, apart from, perhaps, the snub nose and colourless hair he inherited from his mother, which in themselves were regarded as a great advantage by his father, whose family was afflicted with black hair and typically Semitic noses. Johann Wolfgang struggled from one grade to the next only by dint of exhaustive labour, with his body, as it were, preceding his head. Johann Wolfgang Kobler was like a swimmer advancing with great effort, only to be pushed back to his starting point by a new wave, again and again. His friends at school called him by the nickname Wolf, to his father's secret sorrow. And one more little detail that added to the father's sorrow: his son chose, as if to spite him, to befriend precisely the Jewish boys, and there was no way to stop him. Although Heinrich hinted obliquely at his displeasure with these friendships whenever the opportunity rose, he could not speak plainly and explain his reasons in so many words.

Erna arrived at the Koblers' after supper. The parents had gone out, as they usually did on every evening of the week except for Thursdays, when they received guests at home. Friedel and the others welcomed her with glad cries. They were sitting in the drawing room, and Karl Greener was playing the piano. Without stopping, he turned his head and waved his hand. He was playing a piece by Schubert. When he finished he swivelled round on the piano stool, with his face to the room. He reached for an apple from the bowl of fruit on a nearby shelf, and began to eat it ostentatiously.

He looked at Erna, who was sitting close by with a rather impudent air, and she made to turn her head away, but changed her mind halfway and stared back at him with a mocking look. She didn't like him.

'So you like eating apples.'

'Yes, I like eating apples.'

'A praiseworthy characteristic.'

'What do you mean?'

'Apart from which, you have a great future too — Friedel herself told me so.'

'I have a great future too.'

'I don't like great futures.' She pulled a face. 'I prefer people with a present.'

Karl Greener suddenly leaned forward and thrust his face into hers. 'Yes, yes. I want to paint you with exactly that expression.'

'Paint me? You? Not on your life.'

'Why not?'

'Because I don't want to.'

'Well, we'll see about that.' He crossed his legs with an arrogant expression and lit a cigarette.

On the sofa Friedel laughed and chatted vivaciously with Willy Martin and his sister Suzie. Next to them sat a silent, bashful boy who had been introduced to Erna when she arrived as Fritz Anker. He looked as if he were trying as hard as he could to efface himself. Occasionally he smiled a shy, detached smile that was unrelated to the conversation. He was extremely short-sighted and wore glasses with very thick lenses. From time to time he sat up straight, simply out of embarrassment, and immediately sank back into the low sofa. His movements were heavy, embarrassed, rather clumsy, and resembled those of a tired old man. His very being seemed somehow dim. Everything about him was tenuous, vague, uncertain, and even his age was hard to tell. He must have been about eighteen, but he could have been thirty. He had no sign of a moustache or beard — nothing grew on his face. And nevertheless it was old, the colour of parchment. He moved away to make space for Erna, who came to sit beside him.

'Are you bored?' she asked him.

'Bored? No, as a matter of fact, I'm not bored.' He smiled, showing large, yellow, uneven teeth. Then he added: 'But I can tell that Fräulein Erna ... how shall I put it ... is not altogether here; that her thoughts are somewhere else.'

'That my thoughts are somewhere else?'

'I can tell.'

'I think you're mistaken.'

'That's possible too; I am often mistaken.'

'In that case you should hold your tongue.'

'Quite right. I usually hold my tongue for fear of saying something stupid, and in the end I say it, and it sounds even stupider than I thought it would.'

'And do you think that other people always speak words of wisdom?'

'More than I do, at any rate.'

'Not at all. They're simply less modest.'

Her eyes were suddenly drawn to his hands, which were exquisitely delicate and beautiful, slender with very long fingers. Perhaps somewhat feminine. The hands seemed to sense her eyes on them, and the fingers started drumming nervously on their owner's thighs. One glance at these hands was enough to ensure that they would never be forgotten, and the same was true of his entire person, with all its ugliness.

'Your hands … it seems to me that hands like these could never do any harm.'

'I … I'm very ugly.'

'Yes.' She gave him a quick glance as if to confirm the truth of her observation. 'I mean, perhaps you're not so ugly. You're just different.'

Willy Martin took out a packet of cigarettes and the girls practised smoking, laughing and pulling faces. Friedel persuaded Erna to try too, but after two or three puffs she was overcome by a fit of coughing and threw the cigarette away to general merriment. Afterwards they played party games, and Erna found herself having to kiss Karl Greener, of all people, as a penalty. Johann Wolfgang, in yellow pyjamas, joined in the laughter through a crack in the half-open door, until Friedel saw him and sent him back to bed. He obeyed with sulky reluctance. Willy Martin, with his short bull-neck, whispered something in Karl Greener's ear, and they both looked lewdly at Erna.

Erna was seized by a powerful urge to tease Greener. She turned to him. 'So you want to paint me?'

'To kiss you too.'

'Ah!'

'Especially the latter.'

'Wishes that will never be fulfilled.'

'You think so?'

'Yes, I do. So there.'

'I can wait.' Greener laughed self-confidently.

'You'll have to put another head on your shoulders first.'

'No, with my own head.'

'Don't quarrel, children,' Friedel intervened.

[140]

All this time Suzie Martin did not take her eyes off Karl Greener, her protuberant fish eyes in a dull, boring face. She was neither beautiful nor ugly, lacking any charm or particular temperament; when you looked at her the idea of life was instantly diminished in your eyes. It grew narrow, limited, without any point or value. Everything Suzie Martin said and did lacked significance: it failed to move things forward to the slightest degree. From her it was impossible to hope for any surprises; you were doomed to remain in the same place with her forever, as if drowning in a swamp.

Erna turned to look at Fritz Anker, sitting next to her and lost in thought, with a faint, forgotten smile congealed on his lips. For some reason she suddenly remembered her home, her mother, Rost; and her heart contracted. There, now, tonight, the pair of them with no one to disturb them. A surge of hostility towards both of them, especially her mother, rose within her. Now something even more terrible would happen between them when she wasn't there. As if her being there could serve as some sort of supervision, place a limit on their relations, inhibit them to some extent. She felt a pressing need to hurry home at once, but she remained where she was without moving. In the depths of her heart she knew that it would make no difference. The chatter of the people surrounding her, along with the laughter that flared up from time to time, reached her ears from a distance, as if through a curtain, the words making no sense. She felt sad and discouraged. Life stood before her like a blank, insurmountable wall. She was still very young — she did not know yet that behind this wall there was nothing, absolute nothingness. She did not know that the essence of life was in the seeking.

'Is he your friend, that Greener?' she whispered to Fritz Anker.

'My friend? I wouldn't say so. I have no friends.'

'What do you think of him?'

'I don't know. He has qualities that arouse in me a sense of wonder, a kind of humility. Because I don't have them.'

'But he's an empty person, without any substance.'

'It makes no difference. He'll be happy. In his own eyes he's without a flaw. He isn't intelligent enough to be unhappy.'

'That's the reason?'

'He's full of self-confidence because his brains don't stand in the way. Popular, likeable, mediocre: he'll succeed due to this very banality. Sparkling without a spark of inspiration.'

Erna stood up. 'Do you know how to dance?' she asked Anker loudly.

'No, I don't.' He smiled a helpless, bashful smile.

'Come on, I'll teach you.'

'No, I'd rather not … it would be too grotesque.'

'Don't be such an idiot! Friedel, go and play something. A waltz.' She beckoned Karl Greener and began whirling around with him.

'You're beautiful, Erna,' he whispered as they danced.

'Not for you, at any rate.'

'Why not? Are you trying to tell me that you prefer that orangutan Fritz Anker? Would you really rather kiss him than me?'

'Keep your mind on the dance! The rest is none of your business.' She extricated herself from his arms and pounced on Fritz Anker and kissed him quickly on the lips, to his great embarrassment. Then she sank onto the sofa next to him, as if exhausted. A mean, twisted smile crossed Greener's face.

'Please be so good as to pass me a pear, Herr Greener,' said Erna.

Wordlessly he handed her a pear.

'Thank you! You're a real gentleman!' she said mockingly.

Friedel turned to look over her shoulder as she played the piano. 'Isn't anybody dancing?' she said, and stopped in the middle of a chord, which went on echoing in their ears for a few seconds.

People got up to go; it was already half-past eleven. Friedel drew Erna by her side to see them on their way. Outside there was a pleasant coolness in the air. Karlsplatz was deserted, still, and spellbound. The church rose at its side, grey and stern, its columns and crosses silvery in the moonlight. The square itself was suffused with a suppressed, vibrant yearning, not for anything in particular; but the buildings surrounding it were lifeless, and the trees in its little garden were withdrawn and motionless. They seemed to Erna like faithful guardians whose protection would never fail. She could have wept for no particular reason, without even feeling particularly sad, as she walked next to the silent Fritz Anker, smiling his groping, uncertain smile.

To his distress, his never-ending efforts to efface himself and avoid attracting attention usually led to the opposite result, but there was nothing he could do to change the situation. He always felt uncomfortable in his own skin, as if he were suffering from some physical ailment that caused him constant pain. He hated his long, ungainly body, his myopic eyes, his naked face, his glasses. He was ready to admire any empty-headed dandy with easy manners and a smooth, uninhibited, self-confident way of talking, even though he was well aware of who and what they were. But the girls were attracted to them, to these smooth-talking, empty-headed dandies, and not to him, Fritz Anker, who sailed through his courses on philosophy and the history of literature, who was the only son of wealthy parents, and who had plenty of money to spend. True, money could buy things, money made up for a lot, but he did not want to buy. He wanted a freely given gift, love for his own sake, because in spite of his ugliness he was a living, feeling human being, who was himself and nobody else. Someone else could have his philosophy and all the rest of it in exchange for a little bit of simple, earthly, human love. He didn't need anything but that. Not even the vast-fortune he stood to inherit from his father.

When this Erna had kissed him before — was he fool enough to imagine that this kiss was meant for him and not to spite somebody else? Perhaps Karl Greener, or perhaps someone who wasn't even there? What wouldn't he have given to believe that the kiss was meant for him alone, without any ulterior motives. Nevertheless, she was a marvellous girl.

'It's a pity I can't love you,' Erna suddenly blurted out.

'No surprises, a man like me …'

'A man like you more than a thousand others, but not me.'

The possibility had not even occurred to him.

'But I want you to remain my friend. My friend — yes?'

'I'd be delighted.'

'You are permitted to fall in love with me a little too. But only in secret, of course, without making it obvious. All right?'

'Done.'

'Good.'

On the way back with Friedel they bumped into her parents not far from the entrance to their building. Erna greeted them with a little girl's curtsey. Heinrich Kobler removed the aromatic cigar in its amber holder from between his teeth, and said in a paternal tone: 'Ah, good evening, Fräulein Erna, excellent! And at home — is all well? Excellent!'

They did not tarry with her parents and retired at once to Friedel's room.

'You looked so beautiful tonight,' said Friedel as she undressed. 'Didn't you notice how Karl was devouring you with his eyes?'

'No, I didn't notice.'

'I wish I were as beautiful as you.' Friedel gave up her bed for her friend, and lay down on the couch, where a bed had been made up for her. But she soon moved to the bed and stretched out next to Erna. 'Guess what,' she whispered in the dark, with a secret boastfulness in her voice. 'My father has a mistress.'

'How do you know?'

'I once saw them together with my own eyes! A pretty girl. They were coming out of a café. I followed them and I know where she lives.'

'And your mother doesn't know?'

'God forbid! She would claw out his eyes.' After a short silence she pronounced: 'Men are apparently all the same. They all cheat on their wives. How about your father?'

'I don't know.'

'I bet he does too.'

'He loves my mother.'

'So does mine. But that doesn't stop him.'

'And your mother?'

'You mean, does she have a lover too? Not as far as I know.'

For a while they murmured and giggled in the darkness. Friedel nestled against Erna, who made no objections as her friend cupped her breasts in her hands and fondled them. Erna felt a wave of heat sweeping through her; her blood raced, and her heart beat rapidly and loudly. They kissed each other feverishly on their burning, trembling limbs. Friedel's body clung more and more tightly to Erna, a soft, smooth body.

'Oh my sweet, my one and only! How I love you,' whispered Friedel, and a second later: 'How does it feel to embrace a lover? Tell me.'

'I've never tried; I don't have one.'

'I have. Just a little, not properly, you know. But you're better than a boy, a thousand times better.'

The two girls trembled like a flickering flame in the depths of the night as if at the bottom of a deep pit, two pulsating little lives merging into one. The silence hovered over them, covering them like a living thing and making the air vibrate both in the room, where the furniture floated like vague shapes in the darkness, and in the stillness outside. The two girls were suddenly new to each other and to themselves. At that moment they were no longer in their fixed, final forms — they had crossed the boundaries of their beings, stretching into infinity, turning into a blind, alien, abstract force, the hidden force that ceaselessly drives nature into being, becoming nature itself. They mingled with each other. Was there anything, any act that was forbidden to them? Who could take it upon himself to forbid or permit? It was the law of nature, and nothing else existed.

Erna did not feel the touch of the bedclothes on her skin, as if there were a gap between her and the bed, as if she were floating above it. But the memory of home lay deep down in her soul, like a muffled pain, and now, when Friedel fell asleep, it began to rise to the surface and take on a concrete shape. She tried to imagine what was happening between them there at this very moment, and now, in the middle of the night, to her confused, excited senses, it all seemed more terrible, more shocking, like a scene in a nightmare. The betrayal, his as well as her mother's, was directed against her, Erna, and her only.

Suddenly she felt unbearably hot. She threw off the covers, but to no avail. Then she groped her way from the bed to the window and carefully parted the heavy curtains. The little street was deserted, dimly lit by the street lamps. A cat emerged from the darkness, stopped on the verge of the light, and turned its head this way and that, as if seeking something, and then crossed the road at an angle, with unhurried, soundless steps. The whole scene was bathed in the unreality of a dream. It was a little chilly. Cold shivers ran down her spine, but she took no notice. She leaned on the windowsill and looked forlornly into the emptiness. Tears fell from her eyes without her being aware of them. Footsteps rang hollowly in a nearby street, and Erna listened to them unconsciously and followed them with part of her mind until they died away.

She would write him a letter and say:

The world has no value without you. I may be a child but I'm not a child at all. I'll kiss you every morning on the lobe of your ear and on your eyelids and on the tip of your nose.

We'll drink hot chocolate together with the city spread out at our feet. We'll love the city together, and we'll love the winter and we'll love the summer and we'll love the autumn, and I, only I, will love my mother. Everything will proclaim your love for me: the walls, the dishes, the air outside. And if you go away it will only be to see me in your imagination, more beautiful, more desirable, and to taste the sweetness of your return, and I'll quarrel with you a little, to taste the pleasure to making up.

No, she wouldn't write him anything. Not a single word. Now he was lying in bed with her, body to body, and kissing her, and they were laughing. She didn't want him. She would tell Karl Greener, that scoundrel, that he could paint her portrait and kiss her. He was an expert at kissing, that Karl Greener; he had said so himself. She burst out laughing strangely and was horrified by her own laughter. She waited tensely to see if her laughter had woken anyone up. No. Everything was as quiet as before. Even quieter.

10

George Shtift cultivated a thin moustache, composed of wisps of honey-coloured hair on his long face, and smoked short, fat Cuban cigars. All was well with Herr George Shtift. The business — thank God! — was doing well. The rest too. Gertrude and Erna — no complaints. As for the little peccadillo that had given him a few pleasant hours — the painted woman in the Ritz Hotel in Klagenfurt — a harmless distraction, no more. Such things only strengthened the ties between husband and wife. Hadn't someone already said that family life needed to be aired every now and then to prevent it from growing stale, ha ha. George Shtift leaned back at his ease and dwelled pleasantly on the details of that episode in Klagenfurt. He puffed on his cigar.

Her head on her hand, Erna looked down at the book lying unread on the table in front of her. From time to time she cast a penetrating glace at Rost and her mother, who were making conversation in indifferent, insincere tones about some public scandal that had recently been chewed over ad nauseam in the press. The real relations between them were kept under lock and key in another room in the house, and did not infiltrate this banal conversation by so much as a single glance.

George Shtift removed himself from the room in the Ritz Hotel and the arms of the woman in question, and spared a magnanimous thought for Rost. Not a disagreeable young man, and wise beyond his years in the ways of the world.

'What do you have in mind to study, Herr Rost, if I may be permitted to ask?'

'I haven't decided yet.'

'I myself studied law. Five semesters, and then I fell in love, isn't that so, Trudy?' He smiled at his wife. 'I didn't want to wait. I did not have unlimited means at my disposal, and then by a lucky chance I was offered a good job. I can tell you that I have never regretted it. In your case, I take it, the question of means presents no problems.'

'No problems.'

'And you are not about to fall in love.'

'Why do you think that I'm not about to fall in love?'

'In the first place, there is only one Trudy in the world, and she is already taken. Full stop. And secondly, you don't look like someone who loses his head easily. Aren't I right, Trudy?'

'Please stop making tedious jokes.'

'This time you've missed your aim, Herr Shtift,' said Rost, half in earnest and half in jest, looking at the unlit cigarette in his hand, 'because I am already in love, and precisely with that woman who has no equal in the world.'

Herr Shtift laughed loudly and complacently. 'In that case, my dear young man, I pity you, for all your aspirations in that direction are doomed to fail.'

'And I pity myself too.'

'Let me tell you something, my friend — since you have only just started to take your first steps in life, allow a man of some experience to give you a word of advice. There are some women who are wayward by nature, and there are some who aren't. To some extent it depends on the husband. There are some husbands whose wives will never deceive them. Never!' He emphasised the last word with a gesture that dismissed any argument in advance.

'To my regret.'

'That's all there is to say! Aren't I right, Trudy?'

Gertrude gave her husband a contemptuous look, which he failed to notice. In a bored tone of voice she said, 'You're absolutely right.'

Erna no longer pretended to read but took in every word and every glance with a tense expression. What a despicable game! What falsity! Her anger against her mother mounted, against her only, and she had to restrain herself with all her strength from hurling the words at the three of them like bombshells: *Liars! Scoundrels! You're weaving a web of lies! But I know the truth! I know everything!* And she couldn't suppress a feeling of contempt for her father, which contained perhaps a hint of the contempt felt by her mother — contempt for the deceived, the defeated, the weak; for this father whom up to now she had loved with a simple, natural, unquestioning love. He had always been there, a solid, undeniable fact, surrounding her with love and kindness, and she had loved him back. She had never considered him superior to others, better than them. He was her father and she loved him. And now, all of a sudden, he had become small and ridiculous in his complacency, his fatuous self-confidence.

At that moment a void seemed to come into being around her. These two people who had been her parents grew ever more distant, completely strange to her, like figures on a movie screen. There was an unbridgeable gulf between them. She was all by herself, without a refuge. And Rost, the only one who could save her, was together with them in their conspiracy, and he took no notice of her.

In some obscure reluctance to abandon the subject, George Shtift continued, 'And so let me urge you to turn your attention elsewhere, because here, you see, your efforts are in vain. Why waste time on a lost cause!'

Rost said piously: 'But such matters cannot be decided by cold logic. When matters of the heart are at stake, a man has no more control over himself than a sacrificial lamb.'

'You should be pitied, my friend; that's all I can say to you.'

'So there's no hope?' Rost refused to give in.

'Hope! You see that wall across the street?' Shtift pointed at the window. 'It would be like trying to make a hole in it with your fingernails! The same thing exactly!'

Gertrude rang for the maid to serve coffee and various sweet-meats. The Saturday evening crept on. George Shtift slurped his coffee noisily. In a good mood improved even further by the young man's certain failure, he suggested that they all go to a fashionable café with a band — including Erna. Her attempts to excuse herself on the grounds of tiredness were in vain. Her father had just returned home today after an absence of almost a month. Surely she would not de-prive him of the pleasure of spending a delightful evening in the bosom of his family, especially since tomorrow was a Sunday and she would be able to stay in bed as long as she liked. Apart from which, she was already a grown-up girl, 'isn't that so, Herr Rost?' The latter nodded. And she didn't have to go to sleep with the chickens; she was permitted to change her habits and go out once in a while with her parents to a café. Gertrude, on the other hand, responded eagerly to her husband's suggestion and went to get dressed. She could already taste the disagreeable taste of the coming night, when she would be alone with her husband, and she wanted to postpone it and keep it as short as possible, since she could not wipe it out entirely.

Outside, a warm drizzle, fine as dust, was falling. The street lamps were misty; their light seemed sifted through a sieve. Erna was sent back inside to fetch an umbrella while the others waited in the entrance. The pavement grew dark. The light wind brought intermittent gusts of a vague, distant smell of linden trees.

It happened that Erna found herself walking with Rost, at a little distance behind her parents. She took advantage of the moment to whisper to him: 'You're completely shameless!'

'What makes you say so?'

'You know yourself.'

'I don't know anything.'

'And a coward into the bargain.'

'You may be right.'

'Tell me, Herr Rost, won't you be looking for another room soon?'

'I don't think so; my room suits me very well indeed.'

'But you're in the way here. Haven't you realised yet that you're in the way?'

'I must admit that I haven't.'

'And now that you know, what will you do?'

'Nothing.'

'What insufferable impertinence!'

'It's up to your mother.'

'But when you're told to your face that you're not wanted,' she said furiously, 'yes, absolutely unwanted! Don't you have a grain of self-respect?'

'Listen, Fräulein Erna,' said Rost earnestly. He even took her hand, which felt feverishly hot, but Erna immediately withdrew it. 'There's no need to get upset. I'm a little different from the person you imagine. We'll still be real friends, you'll see.' In the meantime they had reached their destination. Rost only said: 'Good. We'll come back to this later.'

In the big, crowded café they threaded their way through the tables until they found a suitable spot. On the stage an ungainly conductor displayed a shining bald pate to his audience. With barely a gesture he coaxed the tempestuous notes of a fashionable operetta from the band. When he turned round to bow to the applause, all that could be seen of his face was a hairy moustache and a monocle. George Shtift, still in high spirits, urged Rost to order kirsch. He held the floor alone. Gertrude hardly spoke, and Rost confined himself to the responses demanded by politeness. All this time Shtift behaved towards Rost with a kind of exaggerated concern, like a person known to be ill who needed to be handled with kid gloves. It seemed that he was grateful to Rost for his lack of success, which confirmed his own sense of self-worth and underlined his happiness. While Rost thought to himself: *What an idiot.*

He was already feeling bored to tears in the family circle; but for the music, which made conversation unnecessary, he would have taken off on some plausible excuse. From time to time he caught a stolen glance, full of desire, from Gertrude. Looking round the room he suddenly saw Peter Dean sitting a few tables away with a man he didn't know. He got up immediately and went over to greet him.

Dean welcomed him gladly. He introduced him to his companion — a man called Shtanz, with a stern, stiff face — and invited him to join them. Rost apologised, saying that he could only stay for a few minutes, since he was there with his landlord's family. To this, Dean said jokingly: 'I see you are getting used to the idea of becoming a family man, and losing no time about it.'

'Soon.' Rost laughed.

'My Franz will be grateful to you. I was going to send him to you with a letter early tomorrow morning. You are invited to my home for lunch. Now that I have met you, he won't have to go.' And after a moment: 'And how are you spending your time?'

'Quite well. Every day has its charms.'

'Yes, it's clear that you're not dying of boredom.'

'Absolutely not. I'm too curious.'

'At your age,' Shtanz opened his mouth for the first time, his voice low, his speech confident, assertive, and brooking no doubt, 'the world is wide and varied. Over the course of the years it grows narrower and its colours grow darker. It's all in the eyes of the beholder.'

The band now began to play a wild czardas, and Rost stood up and took his leave.

'Why, that's Dean, the American you were just talking to,' George Shtift exclaimed admiringly when Rost returned.

'I congratulate you on knowing him. Peter Dean is a million-aire, one of the richest men in the country! Anyone in his good graces has nothing to worry about.'

Rost did not reply. He glanced at Erna, whose fingers were drumming nervously on the table as if of their own accord, and who was looking distractedly into space. What fire! A veritable volcano! She bore no resemblance to her bloodless father, at any rate. Perhaps more to her mother. She would wreak havoc on her surroundings!

Suddenly he felt a wave of affection for this girl, in the turmoil of adolescent upheaval and her tempestuous emotions. His face softened. A quiet smile even crossed his lips. Now he was no longer bored by his company. He even began to feel a certain closeness to George Shtift with his Cuban, humming softly and contentedly to the music through his nose. He picked up the glass in front of him automatically and drank the dregs of the kirsch. The cool, honeyed drink, distilling the essence of a secret world of vivid images, uprooted from ordinary, material reality, and planted in another reality, perhaps more intense and authentic, gave rise in him as if by magic to one certainty: this girl was meant for him, and she would be his.

'The band isn't at all bad,' he said to George Shtift.

'Not at all.'

It was already close to midnight. Shtift called the waiter. It had stopped raining in the meantime. Among the tattered clouds a few stars were even shining here and there, washed clean as new. At the edges of the park, the leaves of the trees arching over the fence scattered belated raindrops. Shtift went on humming to himself the last tune played by the band. He still bore the smell of the café, foreign to the rinsed, fragrant air outside. Gertrude, walking next to Rost, took advantage of an unguarded moment to whisper to him: 'I'm so sad. If only you knew how sad I was.' Rost said nothing. He took hold of her hand in secret and squeezed it. Apart from these whispered words, nobody said anything all the way home. Next to the entrance Rost said goodnight: he wanted to go for a little walk on this glorious night.

In Gertrude's heart, something seemed to be suddenly torn from its place. She felt as if he were leaving her forever, never to return. She was overcome by weakness, as if she were about to faint, and only by an exhausting effort was she able to climb the steps, with the sound of the receding Rost's sure, resolute footsteps echoing relentlessly in her mind. Gertrude was left alone, alone to the point of despair.

11

After the meal, coffee was served in the Oriental-style smoking room. It was decorated with vast dark carpets that muffled every sound; low divans and upholstered stools; copper and bronze filigree ashtrays mounted on slender pedestals, resembling exotic flowers. In one corner sat a Buddha with a very broad, inhuman face, perhaps smiling, perhaps grimacing in indignation, its arms folded and its agate eyes glittering. There were a few little wooden African figures with small bodies and big heads, which had emerged directly from the imagination of their makers like primitive masterpieces. Strange hybrids, half human and half some other bizarre, non-existent creature; and a few African masks, distorted, nightmarish faces against the background of the precious carpets hanging on the walls. In the calm, dim light of the room you felt a thousand miles away from yourself and your private affairs. A doorway led to a large, covered veranda overlooking a garden that lay in the heavy shade of trees hundreds of years old. An intoxicating smell of lavender, detached and dream-like, permeated the air. The material world remained outside the door, very far away, and did not penetrate here.

On a low divan, half reclining, one leg tucked beneath her, Marie Dean sat and smoked. From time to time she let her head fall back, and blew a column of smoke up towards the ceiling. The puppy Waldy lay next to her, a bundle of white fluff, his black eyes staring at some invisible point in the distance, given over to his unfathomable thoughts. The company consisted of Felix von Bronhof, a relation of Frau Dean, a cavalry officer whose eyes were always melancholy, even when he laughed; the stern-faced Herr Shtanz, who kept his eyes on the spiralling smoke of his cigarette and confined his participation in the conversation to brief and, for the most part, obscure remarks that sank into it like in-dissoluble pebbles; and Frau Giselle, or plain Giselle for short, as she was called in the Dean household, a slender, restless red-head dressed in black (her husband Karl Foxthaler had committed suicide six months ago, an event she did not regard as the greatest tragedy in her life), who punctuated every sentence with a loud laugh, called for or not, to show off her pretty teeth and herself in general, because laughter suited her. This laughter was not always appropriate to the content of her words, and it would sometimes give rise to an uneasy feeling of perplexity and inhibit the conversation for a while. Apart from this, she was rich and childless, and she was weaving a secret web around Felix von Bronhof. She could not sit still for a minute; she kept getting up and pacing to and fro, pausing in front of the Buddha or some other statue she had already seen countless times, passing her hand over her hair in a coquettish movement and steal-ing secret looks at the officer. Her nervous restlessness was somewhat out of place here, in this quiet atmosphere, which encouraged contemplation and called for measured, even languid movements. Rost drew enjoyably on the aromatic cigar given to him by Dean. He looked at the cylinder of smouldering reddish-blue ash attached almost in its entirety to his half-smoked cigar.

Dean spoke about unusual, strong-willed people who were not afraid to live their lives in accordance with their inner natures and impulses, without denying themselves to the least degree, in spite of their environment, which did not tolerate any deviation from its norms, and stigmatised anyone who was different as weird, if not mad.

His voice was quiet, warm, addictive, pleasant to listen to, regardless of what it was saying. It held a note of restrained emotion, perhaps even of faint, suppressed melancholy. The more Rost knew him, the more his respect for him grew — there was no room for pettiness in this man; he could never be poor even if he had no money. Suddenly he realised that the fortune that Dean had made was only a pretext for proving his power to himself, like a man setting himself a goal in some game that was insignificant in itself.

Outside, a soft, fresh rain was falling, seeping secretly into the treetops. Through the veranda door, a faint rustle crept hesitantly into the room.

'I'm getting sick and tired of the army,' said Felix von Bronhof, emerging from his long silence. 'It doesn't appeal to me.'

'But the uniform suits you so well!' Giselle placed herself in front of him, and looked him up and down as if she had never seen him before. 'I can't imagine you in civvies.'

'In that case!' the officer retorted dismissively, barely sparing her a glance, and then he said to the room at large: 'It isn't

the place for me. I have no inclination for the whole business.'
He spoke calmly and composedly.

'If you've already reached that point, you should get out,'
advised Peter Dean.

'I'll be resigning shortly.'

'And then we won't see much of you.' Frau Dean ground
her cigarette out on the side of the ashtray.

'I didn't say that.' And a second later: 'I'll take a trip abroad.
To France, to Italy, perhaps somewhere else as well.' He raised
his hand in a vague gesture towards his thin moustache as if
to twirl it — a gesture familiar to those close to him, expressing some last inner hesitation before the final decision.

Rost, who was sitting sideways to the veranda, turned
his head slightly and looked, seeing and not seeing, at the
slanting threads of rain between the leaves, connecting the
treetops to the ground below.

He remembered Gertrude, the despairing, imploring look
she had given him when he ran into her in the passage on his
way out. George Shtift, who had also been present, greeted
him with all the expansiveness of a man satisfied with his
situation and secure in his property. Naturally enough, he
did not notice his wife's look, and Rost himself pretended
not to notice it. Why? Wasn't she an amiable woman after all,
this Gertrude of yesterday and the day before, dear to him in
body and soul? Then why did he let her look rebound from
him as if from a suit of armour? Now he remembered how
at that moment she had provoked in him a fleeting feeling
of annoyance. His stubborn denial must have resulted from
disappointment. For some reason he had envisaged bumping
into Erna, rather than anyone else. Indeed, on a number of
occasions he had stepped into the passage for no reason at

all, in the secret hope of seeing her. But she wasn't there, as if to spite him.

Giselle Foxthaler came to sit down beside him, ready at any moment to get up again. She already had a little scheme in mind. She looked in the mirror attached to the inside of her purse and quickly powdered her nose. The smell of the powder drifting around her was not to Rost's liking.

'And you, young man,' she said as she turned to him, 'don't you have any plans to travel abroad?'

'I have no such plans,' Rost said with an undertone of disdain. This rash, empty-headed woman was already getting on his nerves.

'That's a pity, I know someone you could accompany as a gentleman's companion.'

Rost gave her a hard look. Stressing every word he said: 'I am not a gentleman's companion, *gnädige* Frau.'

A frown of displeasure crossed her face, and she immediately exposed her teeth in an ingratiating laugh. 'I meant no harm, no harm at all.'

'In Italy, don't miss Florence; there's something to see there,' pronounced Herr Shtanz. When Herr Shtanz said there was something to see in a place or a person, he always meant something special that nobody but himself could see. Apart from real estate he possessed a factory in partnership with his brother, managed by the latter. In any case, his way of life, as well as his character, were not well known. He was always careful to deflect conversation from personal matters to general, neutral lines. His wife was confined to a sanatorium for the mentally ill due to a religious mania (she imagined that she was the Virgin Mary, pregnant with the Messiah). This was in contrast to her husband, who was a confirmed atheist and did not believe in either the imaginary saviour in his barren wife's womb or the Messiah from Nazareth. Any tactless question that dared to touch on his private life was doomed in advance to remain open and unanswered. In such cases Herr Shtanz would fix his interlocutor with a look of quiet astonishment, as if he had just said something incredibly stupid. And after a few moments of unpleasant silence, having enjoyed the latter's embarrassment to the full, he would stun him with a remark that had nothing to do with the conversation and was of no interest to anybody, such as, 'His Imperial Majesty will soon pay a visit to the German Kaiser, I have heard from a reliable source …' or some such deliberately fatuous statement, even more insulting to his interlocutor than the preceding silence. But apart from such unusual incidents, Herr Shtanz was always polite, deploying that conventional politeness that serves as a barrier to any unwanted intimacy. He was not, however, a dry stick. He was a man in whom you sensed a solid inner core, a person who could not be ignored.

Waldy roused himself from his complicated musings and rose to his feet. Then he jumped off the divan and sidled up to Dean, wagging his stump of a tail. His attempts to climb onto his master's lap were firmly rejected: 'Go away!'

'Come here, pet, come to me.' Frau Giselle took pity on the pup, but Waldy failed to respond to her invitation and took no notice of her whatsoever. Submissively he lay down at the feet of his master, a white stain on the dark colours of the carpet, no doubt yielding to melancholy canine thoughts.

Marie Dean stood up and took a step into the middle of the room. She stood for a moment between Felix von

Bronhof and her husband; tall, slender, and exquisitely formed. A bright smile crossed her delicate face. She worshipped her husband even though she was aware of his flaws, and after fifteen years of marriage she still found him more interesting than any other man.

From the side the young officer stole admiring looks at her. Marie Dean bent down and picked Waldy up. With one dainty hand she stroked the puppy's back, while he stuck out a tongue as long and narrow as a pink shoelace and tried to lick her fingers. Then she sat down on an upholstered stool and listened enjoyably to the notes of the piano, which had just begun to rain down like muffled hail from the drawing room in the adjacent wing, the strains of a Chopin waltz woven into an exquisite tapestry by the hands of her daughter Martha.

Frau Giselle started to run around the room again as if lashed by an invisible whip. The delicate music, full of melancholy, sweetened the dull rain outside, made it insubstantial, transporting the listener into an ethereal landscape with a mountain and a hillock and a deserted meadow under another, different rain, with a solitary house on the mountainside. And in the meantime a strange red summer appeared, and somewhere horsemen galloped with the manes of their horses standing on end and their mouths foaming, and Frau Giselle flew between them, flapping her wings like a great black bird. Then the piano stopped playing and everything vanished abruptly, although the sounds went on whirling in the air, abstract now and immaterial, existing and not existing at once.

'She plays well,' the officer said to the room, in a different, dreamy voice. He loved music above all things, and played the piano like a virtuoso himself. At that moment, there flashed before his eyes yellow fields of standing wheat and a lone rider, himself.

Marie Dean, the mother, repeated as if from a great distance, like an echo: 'Yes, she plays well.' And little by little the rainy day returned and entered the Oriental room, and everything was scaled down again, took on its ordinary, weekday form, became insignificant.

Except Marie Dean, thought Felix von Bronhof: she alone lost none of her glory even in the light of the ordinary grey day. She alone always remained the same whether she was here, next to him, or not. And he himself, Felix von Bronhof, would shed his uniform and set out on his travels. His mind was made up. But what would he achieve by it? He could not uproot Marie from his heart, and there was nothing to be done about it. And even if Dean wasn't there, even if he should suddenly disappear, even if he should suddenly die, even then, nothing would change — he knew it. There was no remedy. Indeed, he had to admit, Dean was worthy of love. He himself respected him immeasurably. And nevertheless, if only he knew that getting rid of Dean would help, he might well have done something about it. It was a blow of fate. He would go away, yes, definitely he would go away. But on the train he would think of her, in foreign cities he would think of her, in foreign hotel rooms she would be by his side. And wherever he went he would be able to kneel at her feet and kiss the tip of that blue shoe. It would take some time before he received his discharge, and he would have liked to leave right then, at that very moment.

He stood up. The remaining guests were already rather subdued, and Felix von Bronhof registered only unintelligible snatches of speech. Detached, foreign words, slightly muffled as if coming from another room, which seemed to have no relation to him, as if they had been taken at random from a language he did not understand. And suddenly the whole room seemed foreign to him, this Oriental room with its furniture and statues and the Buddha in the corner, which were all so familiar to him that he could have made a precise sketch of it showing the place and shape and colour of everything in it without a single mistake. And the people too, whom he knew so well, they too suddenly seemed completely strange to him, as if set in another world, with no bridge leading from him to them. Felix von Bronhof, the authoritative officer whose subordinates trembled at his glance, who rode his horse in drills or parades like a young Greek god, this same Felix von Bronhof was at that moment lonely to the point of despair, as lonely as at the hour of death. He stood at the veranda door and looked unseeingly at the thin threads of rain, which bore no relation to him, and at the grey dreariness spread by the rain, which bore no relation to him either. None of it had anything to do with him. At the parade tomorrow he would come down hard on his cadets, he already knew, with pointless, unnecessary cruelty. Those innocent young lads from the provinces of upper and lower Austria, he would punish them sternly and harshly, and he would despise himself for it, and nevertheless he would not be able to control himself. This contemptible behaviour was completely incompatible with his character. He was not so weak as to have to disguise his weakness as cruelty or tyranny. The stronger a person was, the greater his sorrow. Sorrow was meted out to a man according to his ability to suffer it.

Standing there by the veranda door, tall, upright, smartly turned out in the uniform closely fitting his manly figure, he seemed to sag in exhaustion. Nobody noticed, apart from Marie Dean, who more or less guessed what he was feeling. Something akin to pity stirred in her for this man, for whom she felt a certain affection. If not for the demanding nature of his unspoken love they could have been the best of friends. But was friendship without ulterior motives possible at all between the sexes? Between a man and a woman the nature of friendship was always different. Pure and simple spiritual friendship was out of the question here. It was the law of nature.

By an unconscious process of association her thoughts passed to Giselle, and her hand unthinkingly stroked Waldy's fluffy back. A good-looking woman, this Giselle, with a passionate temperament too. She shot a quick, sidelong glance at Giselle, who was standing next to Herr Shtanz and pelting him with a hail of words as round and smooth and hard as beans, and came to the definite conclusion: all her efforts were in vain. No, Felix von Bronhof would not be caught in her net. And this certain knowledge caused Marie Dean to feel a certain satisfaction, for which she did not call herself to account.

As if banishing a bad dream, the officer passed his hand over a hard, square brow, expressive of vigour and resolution. His dark-blond hair was neatly combed, with a certain severity, across his head, the parting on the right-hand side as straight as a die. His eyes came to rest on Rost with a slightly surprised look, as if he were seeing him now for the first time. At that moment he seemed to be overcome by inertia — there was something heavy, inflexible, not in the least military, about his person.

All of a sudden the uniform seemed out of place. A thought occurred to Rost, as a result, perhaps, of von Bronhof's expressing his wish to leave the army: a soldier such as this was like a man with part of his body paralysed.

The officer looked back at Rost with his melancholy eyes, and then he seemed to come to a decision, brought up a chair, and sat down next to him. It was evident that he wanted to engage Rost in conversation, but for some reason he held back. Rost looked at him expectantly.

'You are still young, sir; very young, if I may say so. On the very threshold of life. I would like to know how a young man like you sees his life. Please pardon me if this seems to you like idle curiosity; believe me, it isn't simply curiosity.' The officer felt a sudden need to talk, to talk about something else, ostensibly remote from the personal concern that was filling his heart to bursting — to talk precisely to a young man of Rost's age, perhaps in some obscure desire to compensate the youngsters of the same age who were under his command, and towards whom he behaved harshly and strictly, mostly for no good reason.

'I must admit that I haven't thought about it yet,' replied Rost evasively. 'In any case, I have no intention of making plans for the future. There's a time for everything ...'

The officer smoked for a while in silence. 'Everyone, I should think, chooses a certain place for himself, some little island in life. Sets himself a goal.'

'Not everyone.'

Frau Giselle once more decided to circle the officer like a vulture. A frown of annoyance appeared briefly on his face.

'Would you like to go to a café with me?' she said.

The rain was now scattered like a fine, almost invisible dust. Through the half-open glass door a wet smell of vegetation with a whiff of autumn wafted in from the old garden. Rost immediately recognised the smell: it reminded him of the priest's garden in his hometown, next door to his parents' house. A vast, wooded garden surrounded by a high, latticed iron fence painted green, from which the short, hoarse barks, more like coughs than barks, of some hidden dog were constantly hurled like stones at anyone coming near. As a boy he had tried more than once to trick this dog by throwing into the garden a piece of meat with a pin hidden in it, or poisoned with arsenic meant for rats, for no other reason than that its hoarse barks filled the quiet street with unpleasant anger and interrupted the sleepy, sunny summer days stretching indolently along its length. It was in vain: the dog was never harmed. It was probably still barking now, Rost thought, smiling to himself.

In that street on the outskirts of the town, the inhabitants of the uhlan barracks next door, with its perpetual smell of rotten sauerkraut, were often to be seen strolling arm in arm with the neighbourhood maids or on their own, making for Motka Kulick's brothel in the next street. The boys knew where they were going. Sometimes they would follow them from a safe distance and afterwards stand opposite the curtained windows of the three-storeyed house into which the soldiers had disappeared. Sounds of licentious laughter, piano playing, and drunken singing burst from the house non-stop. Sometimes the door was flung open with a loud noise, and Motka Kulick, a short man of uncommon physical strength, his round head set between his broad shoulders without any signs of a neck, would eject some drunken fellow at the speed of lightning, and the latter would fly through the air in a wide arc, fall to the ground with a thud, and lie there like a heavy sack without being able to get up. This Motka was the local hero, working hand in hand with the police, capable of beating people to a pulp as automatically as a machine, with a blind, elemental force. A few years later, during the pogroms, he was stabbed after wreaking havoc with the perpetrators and killing about a dozen of them single-handedly.

Sometimes a window opened on one of the storeys, and a girl with bare arms and breasts would poke her head out, look back and forth as if searching for someone, drop a smouldering cigarette into the street, and immediately close the window again. The 'girls from the boarding house', as they were called in the neighbourhood, smelled of cheap perfume, which hung in the air after they had passed, alien and unpleasant, separate from the mild summer air, making the respectable housewives wrinkle their noses.

These images now rose before Rost's eyes, fragmentary and confused but clear enough, one chasing the next and all at once, as if on a giant canvas. This officer sitting next to him, with his grave demeanour and sad eyes, would no doubt have wooed the Jewish girls like the other officers, if he had been there. And afterwards, when the opportunity arose, with exactly the same sternness and gravity, he would no doubt have ordered his troops, without the slightest hesitation, to shoot their parents, their brothers, and even the girls themselves.

Rost arranged to phone Dean three days later, and left with the officer. It had stopped raining. The air was saturated with cool moisture under a grey sky. The pavement gleamed. The officer strode silently by his side. Rost stopped a passing carriage and ordered the driver to take them to a café on the Ringstrasse.

Sitting opposite the officer, Rost sipped his steaming chocolate, stealing a glance at him from time to time. On this rainy day the café was full of a diverse, leisurely crowd, venerable bald heads next to senior army officers, beautiful and less beautiful women. Splendid carriages and auto-mobiles stopped outside the arched doorway and poured forth new arrivals with every passing moment. Most of their faces expressed genuine or affected satisfaction, all of them apparently pleased to be in the world and here in this café, with the columns of cigarette smoke and the medley of perfumed smells permeating the air.

Finally Felix von Bronhof spoke. 'The believers have some-thing extra, something to fall back on that can't be taken away from them, a kind of life in reserve, so to say. And if their belief is nothing but an illusion, it makes no difference. But what about the others, those who have only all this?' He waved his hand in a dismissive gesture towards the café hall.

'Isn't that enough?' said Rost. 'What else do you need? It seems to me that life itself is good enough, without specu-lating about what lies beyond it.' And after a brief pause: 'You are not an old man yet, Herr von Bronhof.'

'I'm not an old man yet,' the officer echoed absent-mindedly. 'You see, sometimes a man goes down a certain road for ten, eight years, perhaps a road he didn't even choose for himself, but found himself on it as a result of circumstances, of ancestral heritage, and so on, and continued going down it. And all of a sudden he realises that the road is the wrong one, that it leads somewhere he has no desire to go. And that isn't even the main thing. The main thing is that now, even though he has realised his mistake, the waste of his time, he doesn't know any other road to take. Once, if it had been up to him, perhaps he would have known, but now he no longer does.'

All this time he seemed to have been talking to himself rather than to Rost. Now he offered him a cigarette and lit one for himself as well.

Rost looked at his companion's thin, colourless moustache, and all of a sudden he was overcome by boredom. What was the point of this whole conversation? Meaningless prattle. He turned his head to look at the people in the café. Three tables away, a group of four were sitting round a small table: two couples, one middle-aged and one young. Parents and children, decided Rost. He examined each of them more closely. The older of the two men had his profile — a fair, well-scrubbed sphere, crowned by a halo of greying hair; a stubborn, bulbous, snub nose above a heavy handlebar moustache; a round, well-fed, rosy-cheeked face — buried in a newspaper. The father of the family, no doubt with his origins in Hungary or Bohemia, Rost speculated in order to amuse himself. When this man said something, it was carved in stone, there was no gainsaying it! The woman next to him, between forty and fifty years old, apparently attempted to stop the march of time by means of various cosmetics and dressing in the latest fashion. She was leafing through illustrated magazines, a seductive, would-be youthful smile set unchangingly on her face. The young girl at the table resembled her. She must be her daughter. Chestnut-haired, with brown eyes, not ugly but expressionless. A rather banal beauty. Bored, or irritable, she took an occasional sip from one of the glasses of water on the nickel tray, and at lengthy intervals directed a brief remark to the young man sitting next to her, her fiancé or intended, who for his part showered her diligently with words. A desiccated youth, with gold pince-nez perched on the nose of a future scholar, a wispy moustache, and big, blushing ears flaring like giant shells.

She sensed Rost's eyes on her and looked at him questioningly for a moment, immediately looked away, and then looked back again.

That chap obviously bored her, decided Rost with a small smile of unexplained satisfaction, which the girl apparently took to be directed at her and answered with a quick smile of her own, until her intended noticed the wordless game between them and aimed his pince-nez at Rost, thrusting his head forward like a bull ready to butt.

Rost began to take an interest in the situation. He rose slowly to his feet and made for their table, to the girl's astonishment. 'Perhaps you would permit me to borrow that for a moment, madam,' he said, indicating one of the illustrated magazines.

'I haven't read it yet,' the mother answered, instead of her daughter. 'In fifteen minutes' time, sir, if you wish.'

Rost thanked her with a polite bow, smiled meaningfully at her daughter, and returned to his place, accompanied by the looks from the young man, which he felt like daggers in his back. He sat down at ease and crossed his legs complacently.

Felix von Bronhof roused himself from his sombre thoughts and tried to persuade Rost to have a drink with him, and when Rost refused, he ordered three glasses of a green liqueur for himself and swallowed them down one after the other without a pause.

'This rainy day is making me a little gloomy,' he said as if to excuse himself. 'There are some sensitive people who are affected by changes in the weather, like a barometer. This is not always the case with me, only by chance today.'

When he invited Rost to go to the café with him he had entertained the vague hope that he would be able to talk to him, even if not about the matters closest to his heart, and would gain a measure of relief by unburdening himself a little. Now he realised to his despair that there was no chance of that happening. Suddenly he felt a torrent of rage towards himself, towards the young man sitting opposite him, towards some unknown person. His face turned a little red with the force of these inner feelings. Ah, if only he could fight someone now, deliver blows like iron bars and even absorb blows himself, rein in a wild horse, overcome some strong opposing force! In some secret corner of his soul he was insulted at the idea that he, Felix von Bronhof, could unburden himself to some young, upstart stranger, some suspect fly-by-night. The fact that he had come across him in the home of Peter Dean was no guarantee. The latter was liable to rub shoulders with anyone off the street, even the dregs of society. Altogether, his past was shrouded in mystery; there were all kinds of shady rumours about him. It seemed to von Bronhof that he had indeed revealed his innermost secret to Rost, for which he could not forgive himself or Rost. He muttered resentfully: 'I suppose you think you interest me?'

Rost looked at him for a second in surprise. Then a

mocking expression crossed his face. 'Yes, I think I interest you,' he said, and added: 'Why are you drinking so much?'

'None of your business.'

'In my opinion, you are showing a certain disrespect for His Majesty's uniform,' said Rost calmly, with an undertone of derision. His boredom was rapidly evaporating. A thought crossed his mind: *The man is not nearly as bloodless as I imagined. In a minute we'll add more fuel to the fire ...*

'Are you trying to educate me? Who do you think you are?'

'Me? Just a minute!' He stood up and threaded his way between the tables to where the two couples were sitting. The illustrated magazine was now available. The girl handed it to him with a friendly smile, as if he were an old acquaintance.

'And now I am at your service, sir,' he said once he had resumed his seat. 'Would you like me to present myself right away?'

'You're shameless!' fumed the officer.

'That too is possible,' said Rost with a laugh. He began leafing indifferently through the magazine, glancing from to time at the girl's table. Her father had extracted his head from the newspaper: he was puffing on a huge cigar and staring straight ahead, into the hall. Rost glanced at his watch.

'Are you leaving already? And I thought we would have supper and spend the evening together.'

'Like this?'

'Don't take my behaviour amiss. I'm in a bad mood today. It's not directed at you, believe me.'

'I'm sorry, but I have to go. We can meet again some other time.'

The officer wanted to say something else, but he immediately changed his mind. It wasn't worth the effort, and anyway it wouldn't do any good. He summoned the waiter to order another drink. Now he would go on until he was completely drunk and finish the night with some prostitute in a revolting scene of noisy, vulgar debauchery, the memory of which would nag at him throughout the next day, nauseating him and making him sullen, irritable, obnoxious, and cruel in his self-contempt.

12

It was nearly five when Rost left the café and the officer brooding over his drink. It was pleasant to stroll at his leisure along the half-empty, wet Sabbath streets, which smelled of the recent rain. Occasional raindrops fell from the bright green foliage of the trees lining the street onto his bare blond head. Full of a sense of freedom and self-confidence, he felt as if he could conquer the world, attain whatever his heart desired. He regarded the carriages, the automobiles, the people passing by with magnanimity. How good it was that all this existed, free for the taking; existed for him, for his benefit, his enjoyment. And how good that it had rained and that the rain had stopped, and that now it was day, a somewhat elegiac day, soft, hesitant, shy, and that later it would be evening, perhaps more tranquil and subdued than other evenings, and afterwards night, and its smell would be different from the other nights before and after it, the same and different at once, like a new, unfamiliar woman. Every new day demanded a new man, clean as a day-old baby, without the burden of what had come before.

Rost felt a twinge of contempt for the tall officer, who

was apparently fixated on one single day or one single thing, unable to detach himself from it, dead to any other possibility, pouring one drink after the other down his throat to erect a barrier between him and his world. Von Bronhof drank because he was afraid. He, Rost, was not afraid.

He lingered absent-mindedly in front of a window that displayed children's toys. When he caught himself he smiled and walked away. By an unconscious process of thought he found himself thinking of Erna, and all of a sudden he was flooded with joy. He hastened his steps a little and turned into an alley leading to his house.

He had hardly had a chance to put on his dressing-gown before there was a hesitant knock at the door and Gertrude entered the room. Without a word she planted a full, moist mouth on his lips, and pressed her whole body passionately up against him, as if she wanted to get it inside him. Then she sank wearily into a chair. She looked depressed.

'I was waiting for you,' she said after a moment. 'George went with Erna to visit my mother-in-law. I got out of it by pleading a headache.'

Rost brought up a chair and sat down next to her. He took her hand and patted it a number of times as if to mollify her. The windows, with their heavy curtains parted and gathered above the sills by plaited cords, opened onto a grey sky. A dense silence filled the house. No sounds rose from the quiet residential street. Gertrude sat without moving, preoccupied by her thoughts. The flaps of her yellow kimono fell apart to expose her gleaming legs. Her slightly tilted head gazed past Rost into the distance. With a feeling of revulsion she thought of her husband's advances the night before, which she had succeeded in repelling only with difficulty. But how long could she go on refusing without arousing his suspicions? Without causing quarrels and friction? If only she had been of a colder temperament, less sensitive to those hard, angular, clumsy movements that she hated so much. Suddenly the possibility of losing Rost struck her like a lightning bolt, and a shudder ran through her body. Why not? He could vanish as suddenly as he had appeared, an unexpected gift, and then she would be utterly lost. At that moment it seemed to her that it was all a dream, that it wasn't real. She raised her eyes to Rost, as if to make sure that he was still there, in flesh and blood. There was great sadness in her eyes. She put out her hand and felt his arm. Yes, he was there, still there. Two tears came into her eyes, because he was there next to her, and because of the cruel possibility of losing him, without any blame, simply if nature intended it. At that moment she was enveloped in the gnawing loneliness to come. The tears fell from her eyes and trickled down her cheeks without her sensing them.

'Why?' said Rost, coaxingly. Then she smiled, a faint, hesitant smile, stood up absent-mindedly, took a step towards the window, changed her mind, and returned to her seat. The expression on her face was transformed into one of firm decision, despite the traces of the tears still wetting her cheeks. No! She wouldn't allow it; she would fight! She pulled Rost towards her and hugged him tightly, crushing him in a mixture of desire and despair, like someone driven to desperation.

'What does it matter?' she whispered to him. 'The present moment is all that matters, no? Isn't that so?' She drew her head back a little and looked at him as if to etch his face indelibly on her heart.

'You're a grown woman and yet a little child,' said Rost, feeling sorry for her without any particular reason. He sat her on his lap and began to stroke her hair, which gave off a faint, delicate, and at the same time slightly stunning smell. He buried his nose in her hair and breathed in this unique smell, of a woman and of existence itself. Through her he smelled the smell of the earth. Thus the act of creation was ceaselessly renewed, by the eternal Adam and the eternal Eve, by him, Michael Rost, and by this woman, always strange to each other and always close, thrown apart and colliding again. Her smooth skin quivered at his touch, as if recoiling from him. Wildly she showered fierce kisses on his throat, his cheeks, the lobe of his ear, until he picked her up and carried her in his arms to the sofa.

The windows were growing dark in the early evening, and a fine rain had started to beat against the windowpanes like light, solitary flies. The rain struck a single, distinct note in the silence enveloping the house. Rost lay on the sofa and smoked. The smouldering tip of his cigarette flickered like a stray light in the growing darkness. Their faces could no longer be seen, nor their hands, only pale, insubstantial, dissolving reflections and the bright stain of the yellow kimono floating in space. But Gertrude was lying there, her head resting limply across his chest. Suddenly he felt the weight of this head. It became clear to him, in the still dimness of the twilight, that this woman was no longer as important to him as she had once been. Rost became aware of a kind of void in a corner of his soul: the strings stretching from him to her had been torn, like telegraph wires cut in the middle. He even felt faintly sorry for this woman, as full of bursting life as a restrained volcano, who now appeared to him lifeless. The possibility of physical contact, such as that which had just taken place between them, leaving a pleasant languor in their limbs, now seemed remote.

He groped for the ashtray on the shelf next to the sofa and crushed his cigarette against its side. Gertrude stirred and jumped up. She had to go right away: they would be back at any minute. She sought his hand in the darkness, planted a kiss on its back, and left.

Rost lay sprawled on the sofa for a while longer. A few minutes later he heard the sound of footsteps climbing the stairs. He leaped to his feet and switched on the light, which seemed to swallow up the silence. Rost fixed his hair in front of the mirror and straightened his dressing-gown, ready to step out into the passage as soon as the front door opened.

'So, did we spend a pleasant Sunday?' enquired George Shtift in a paternal tone as he took off his raincoat. 'Weather like this is hardly conducive to excursions into the country-side, eh?'

'There are other possibilities,' said Rost, busy trying to catch Erna's eye. When he succeeded at last, she looked eva-sive but not, it seemed to him, hostile.

'True enough,' replied Herr Shtift, and added: 'At your age, oho! Time was too short for me. I would have liked every day to last fifty hours instead of twenty-four.' He hung his hat carefully on the stand.

Erna retired to her room, and Rost accepted his land-lord's invitation to step into the drawing room with him for 'a bit of a chat' before supper. George Shtift ran his fingers over the keys of the open piano, producing a scale of startled sounds that scattered through the air like a handful of beans. Then he slipped into the dining room for a moment, and returned with a bottle of port and two glasses. 'A glass before dinner is an excellent thing,' he said as he poured. 'It gives you an appetite.' Then he said: 'To your health! To the passions of youth! Those were the days.' He wiped the few hairs of his moustache. 'Girls fell into your lap like ripe apples. One after the other! From all sides, I tell you; more than anyone could desire. You had no time left to study. And the hikes in the holidays, bands of four or six boys and virgins. And then came Gertrude — if you had known her then! She was on fire.'

'I can imagine.'

'Oho,' boasted Shtift, 'more than a few got burned by her! My friends were green with envy, believe me, and to this day too. I knew how to choose.'

'You can consider yourself a lucky man.'

'Indeed, a lucky man! You could search far and wide for a woman like her. They don't grow like mushrooms. I know what I'm talking about, believe me. I've seen a few women in my life; I wasn't born yesterday. Another glass? Today, of course, it's different,' Shtift continued, 'not that I'm so old, hee-hee.' He thought again of the painted woman in the hotel in Klagenfurt, and a complacent expression appeared on his face. 'How old do I look to you?'

'Hmm ... thirty-five.'

'Thirty-eight, the prime of manhood, but a man grows more serious, more cautious. No nonsense! Family. Responsibility. You have to keep your eyes wide open. Step by step, carefully does it, right?' He pushed a blue glass ashtray

in Rost's direction and joined him in smoking a cigarette —
in honour of his guest, even though he himself usually only
smoked cigars. He couldn't see any point in cigarettes, he
had to admit. Once, yes, but he had abstained from them
for years. Then he took up the thread of the interrupted
conversation once more, unable for some reason to let it go.
'A woman like her, you see, my Gertrude, in other words,
leaves no room for affairs. She gives everything and takes
everything without measure. Can you imagine a husband
who would cheat on her, on Gertrude?'

Rost gave him the answer he was waiting for: 'I can't
imagine it.'

'That's it! She isn't the kind of woman a man can cheat
on. I see you as an intelligent fellow. And you in particular
can understand me: didn't you yourself admit that you were
in love with her, even if only a little?'

'Are you trying to rub salt into my wounds?'

'God forbid! I wouldn't dream of it. Only to show you
that your senses did not deceive you. Good taste can also be
a source of satisfaction.'

'Very little satisfaction.'

'Agreed, but what can you do? You came too late, you
should have been quicker off the mark and preceded me,
and even then you can't be sure that you would have won
the prize. Perhaps you think there weren't any others besides you? There most certainly were, thick as flies! And you
see the results before you!' He poured himself another glass
and emptied half of it in a single gulp. 'You can never tell
what it is that connects a man and a woman, that particular
man to that particular woman. Here, no observation and no
reasoning will help you. Here, you stand before a mystery,

the secret of nature. I am speaking, of course, of a lasting connection. Temporary liaisons are beside the point.'

A mystery indeed, thought Rost, a dumb ox like him. Why was he sitting here and listening to this drivel? The truth was that he was waiting. An inner ear was constantly focused on a certain door that was liable to open at any moment. His back was facing the door, but no matter, when it opened he would first enjoy the sense of hearing it to the full, and concentrate on listening to the few steps to the table or the window, the piano or the bookcase. He would even close his eyes in order to increase the pleasure, and only open them afterwards, to be surprised by reality. But the door was taking its time to open. He thought he heard soft, muffled steps, swallowed up by the carpet, in the passage, but the door refused to open. Rost began to despair of it — why had he been tempted in his foolishness to believe that it would open precisely now? Just because he wanted it to?

'On the subject of women, you know,' continued Shtift, 'I have some experience in the matter. First of all, you have to understand how to take them; everything depends on that. A firm hand, certainly, but without exaggerating, God forbid! And again: don't generalise. They're not all the same. You have to proceed with caution, find out whom you're dealing with, see which way the wind's blowing. With some women you should come across as weak, small and weak as a sick little mouse — that's what they like. That's the only way you can win their hearts. These are the dreamy kind; for them a man is a doll, a baby — and this is the only way to go with them. They'll give you everything, but only out of pity. If you don't allow them to pour out their pity on you, you won't get a thing out of them. That is their nature. And as soon as they give birth to a baby, in most cases you can pack your bags; they don't need you anymore. And then there are some women who once upon a time heard the words "independent personality" and have never been able to forget them. They have their own opinion about everything under the sun, and the main thing is, it's the opposite of yours. Their personality is sacrosanct — slight them and you've had it! Give them their head, and you're in clover. Cast any doubt — an unforgivable sin! And then there are those who only warm up after you've poured words of love on them by the bagful, never mind how banal and meaningless, taken from cheap romances, reeking of falsity from a thousand miles away — it makes no difference. These are the romantic ones. The more you lie, the more they melt. I promise you success with them. By the way, most women of all types like this kind of thing; they all have a vein of romanticism in them and they are all enamoured of the glittering lie. Perhaps they are all poetesses by nature.

'Some of them harbour an insatiable urge to dominate — these are the dominators. A man who refuses to submit to their authority gets nowhere with them. In order to achieve your aim with them, you have to belittle yourself, even if only for appearances' sake. Always accept their yes and their no without hesitation, as a sentence that cannot be changed, and you will get your reward. There are also combinations, of course: five grams of this type, eight grams of another, three grams of a third, and so on. These are the complicated ones, for the most part hysterical. With them things are more difficult — they're capricious, leaning in one direction and then in another. With them you have to change your technique from one minute to the next, always be on your guard; you need a high degree of diplomacy, and even then your success is not guaranteed. The slightest breeze can turn everything upside down. You're better off keeping away from them, because the best psychologist in the world can't predict their behaviour; you're in for a new surprise every minute of the day.'

'An entire book of rules!' joked Rost. 'You're a real Don Juan!'

'No need to exaggerate,' said George Shtift modestly, with a slight smile. 'A little observation of life, a little personal experience, no more.'

'And what would you do, for example, if you suddenly discovered that your wife was deceiving you?'

'Who, Gertrude? Out of the question!'

'Of course, but in life anything is possible. You can never be sure.'

'In this case it's impossible, not Gertrude and not me! You don't know her, and you don't know the relationship between us. An earthquake would be more possible.'

'I'm not speaking necessarily about Frau Gertrude,' said Rost, retreating. 'Supposing some other woman of yours deceived you.'

'In the first place, on principle, I don't have any truck with women like that. And in the second place, you should know that I am not the kind of man to be deceived. Once a woman has been with me, she will never deceive me. There are some men whom women deceive all the time. And then there are men whom no woman, even the most corrupt, would ever deceive. You should know this, young man, and if something like that were ever to happen to me, I'd show her the door!' He turned his head towards it. 'Without delay! I'm not joking!'

The door leading to the dining room opened a crack, and Gertrude poked her head in to announce that supper was served. On seeing Rost, she pretended to be surprised and greeted him with distant politeness. She took a step into the drawing room and invited him, with the encouragement of her husband, to dine with them. Only a light meal, since it was Mitzi's day off. Through the open door Rost saw Erna leaning against the sideboard and gazing at the windows, and in spite of his eagerness to be by her side, his better instincts told him to let it be. For reasons that were not clear to him, he sensed that if he accepted the invitation he would spoil something. He stood up and took his leave.

In his room he found a white, unaddressed envelope on the floor next to the door. Before tearing it open he hesitated, examined it from all sides, weighed it in the palm of his hand, held it up to his nose and sniffed it. In a secret corner of his soul he guessed whom the letter was from, but he was reluctant to put this knowledge to the test, in case he was disappointed and proved wrong. In the end he opened the envelope and found a page torn out of a high-school exercise book. Erna asked him to meet her the following afternoon: there was something she had to talk to him about. The meeting was to take place on a bench in the Volksgarten, and in case of rain, on the terrace of the café. He was to destroy the letter immediately after reading it.

Her handwriting was big and rounded, full of energy and resolve. She signed with an initial. 'A grown woman in every respect,' said Rost to himself as he folded the note and put it in his wallet.

13

After supper Rost found himself strolling in the city centre, down a steep street that led to the canal. It was a fresh, starry evening in the wake of the rain. The sky arched arrogantly and majestically over the roofs. There was a distant smell of hay in the air. The summer night breathed soundlessly, and the city lay stripped bare before him, imbued with movement, washed shining clean for the Sabbath. From time to time a shiver ran along the skin of the canal, disrupted for a moment by the flames of the street lamps reflected in its waters. Hurrying trams, some empty and some crowded, rattled to and fro along the banks, crossed the bridges with a wooden, slightly hollow sound, and disappeared into the labyrinth of the city. Blue necklaces of electrical sparks occasionally flashed from the network of wires above them, with the explosive sound of dry firewood burning. A dark, pleasant coolness rose from the water below, like that which sometimes bursts forth from a sunless courtyard on a blazing summer day.

With his hands in his trouser pockets and a swaggering air, a cold cigarette dangling from the corner of his mouth,

Rost approached Stock's, from whose open windows and door a roar of laughter rolled down the already deserted alley. It was the baritone voice of Yasha the Odessan: Rost recognised it at once. In the main hall the waiters were clearing the tables. Standing between two tables, Reb Chaim Stock perused the *Neue Freie Presse* with naked, watery eyes, the pince-nez pushed down to the tip of his nose. Not far off, his wife sat idle, small and square, her broad, wrinkled face glistening as usual with the grease of the kitchen. On her little eyes, which resembled burned coffee beans, sat a pair of spectacles, their arms flying through the thickets of the wig spread like a big brown net over her temples. Behind the lenses she stared into space, her hands folded in her lap, a bunch of keys fastened to her apron as inseparably as a limb to her shrivelled body.

It was a holiday. The cooks had taken their allotted leave, the daughter Malvina had gone to the theatre or somewhere else with her poet and his great future, and Reb Chaim Stock and his wife were reluctantly obliged to take a holiday too. Deprived of their contact with the kitchen, which was different for each, they found themselves depleted and superfluous, at a loss. For each, in their own way, the kitchen had provided a point to their existence. Apart from Malvina, the daughter of their old age, their other children were all already married. The sons, short, pious Jews with kosher little beards, engaged in businesses of one kind or another; and one other daughter, also married — Dora Pelz, a woman with a wrinkled, ugly face and a boutique for expensive lingerie, who in her spare time wrote novels that had never been published. Nevertheless, she regarded herself and was regarded by the rest of the family as the most intellectual of them. She was a liberated woman, uninhibited, modern to the tips of her fingers; her big teeth stuck out of her mouth, and her thin lips were unable to stop them. Her novels had two guaranteed readers: herself and Max Karp. Although the latter, to the extent that etiquette permitted, tried to escape, when he failed to do so he would sit with her for hours, read her manuscripts and praise them, argue with her at length about the emancipation of women, and wear her out with his poetry. Afterwards, to Malvina, he would say with a dismissive smile: '*Schund.*'* She did not quarrel with his opinion. If Max Karp said '*Schund*' it was *Schund*.

In the next room a few of the gang were gathered. Rost was welcomed with cheer, and Alfred the waiter was immediately sent to bring him something to drink.

'Misha?' said Marcus Schwartz in reply to Rost's question. 'In the general hospital.'

'Ah! Since when?'

'Two days ago. Did you read in the papers,' Schwartz lowered his voice, 'about a bomb thrown at the Russian ambassador in Schwarzenbergplatz four days ago? An assassination attempt that failed. The press is trying to play the whole thing down, on orders from higher up. In any case, they say Misha had a hand in it. The assassin wasn't caught, of course. In other words, they arrested some innocent man as a smokescreen.'

'Not a word, understand?' warned Yasha. 'We bury it here! Anyone who talks can sell his bones to the rag-and-bone man on the spot. He won't need them anymore, and afterwards he won't get a penny for them.'

---

*   A term in common use at the time for trashy romantic literature.

'Swallow it and it will leave no trace,' said the heroic tenor, coming to his aid in a biblical vein. 'After all, a friend is a friend.'

'Pity it didn't succeed!' blurted Akidos the painter, Marcus Schwartz's roommate. He sat there, long and stiff as a plank with his grey, beardless face, full of suppressed anger, as usual, at the world and everything in it.

'In America,' said Arnold Kroin, 'bless their hands, something like that always succeeds. They know what they're doing over there.'

'Were you ever actually in America, tenor?' Yasha teased him. 'I for one don't believe it.'

'Perhaps you don't believe that I am Arnold Kroin either?'

'That I believe. Who else would agree to inhabit your skin?'

In the meantime Rost questioned Marcus Schwartz in a whisper about the consequences of the assassination attempt, and discovered that only the horses were killed, while the coachman by some miracle escaped with his life. He made up his mind to visit Misha in the hospital. There was no doubt that he had been implicated in the attempt.

He took a sip of his beer and glanced absent-mindedly at the tenor's broad, fat face, which always seemed grubby and in which three gold teeth glittered as if surrounded by mud. A mass of flesh hung from it limply, as if not properly attached to the bones, unseemly and shapeless, with two little eyes buried in its folds. Doughy flesh, mousy hair, gold teeth — these made up the tenor's face and produced his hoarse, smoky voice. He was greedy, his appetite insatiable. Somewhere in a hamlet in Galicia he had abandoned a wife and three children, while he sang like a broken gramophone at Jewish weddings, folk tunes such as 'Shulamith and the Well', *'Hat a Yid a weibeleh'*, and so on, filling his belly to bursting and receiving a few coins into the bargain. He lived in a little room too small for him, suffered from asthma, quarrelled morning and night with his landlady, Frau Feuertzing, over the rent he owed her. From time to time he kept her quiet with two or three florins, and at other times he spent the money he owed her on a prostitute he picked up in the street. Sometimes, when he had too much to drink, he became sentimental and full of self-pity. Then he would curse America for destroying him, that blood-sucking leech which drained a man's blood to the last drop, may the earth swallow it up! He would announce to anyone willing to listen that tomorrow — finished! enough! — he would show the world what he was made of. Caruso, you say? A zero! A chicken! No voice to speak of! But he, Arnold Kroin, his name would be in every mouth; Arnold Kroin was not yet lost! And the next minute he would give way again to the depths of dejection, and promise his audience that the next day he would no longer be among the living. He would give that old witch Frau Feuertzing something to remember him by — he would hang himself in her room! He already had a rope ready. No, no! Don't try to stop him; his mind was made up! The next day he would show up as if nothing had happened, propelling his heavy body, dirty, unshaven, smiling with his gold teeth, and making jokes as usual.

He wore a brightly striped shirt with a celluloid collar to save on laundry costs; a strange suit in the American style,

---

*   Yiddish: 'A Jew has a little wife'.

the jacket with wide padded shoulders and the trousers wide at the top and narrow at the bottom, too short for him; and pale-orange shoes, shabby and scuffed with the heels worn down, but American all the same. For the weddings he would dress in black, the jacket shiny as silk with aged, worn-out striped trousers, and a black bowler hat instead of the reddish one for every day. His outfit was completed by a bamboo cane, a remnant of better days. In general, he looked like a caricature of America.

Arnold Kroin smiled without replying to Yasha's insults. After a moment he turned to Rost and asked if he would treat him to a glass of beer.

Rost said he would.

Reb Chaim Stock stood in the doorway and surveyed the company benevolently, his hat pushed back to expose the high, lined forehead of a Talmudic scholar, the newspaper dangling from his hand. Yasha invited him to join them in a glass, but he declined.

'I'm too old for fun and games,' he said, not without a hint of condescension. A few years ago, oho! Back then he could do anything — none of them could have rivalled him in drinking! But now he was not fit company for them. His voice sounded drained, toneless, choking, as if something were constricting his throat. Then he coughed, a few abrupt little coughs.

'But with the maidservants,' Yasha said with a laugh when the old man left, 'he pretends to be young, the old goat!'

'Wally the little brunette told me,' said Arnold Kroin, 'that he offered her five florins. She laughed in his beard. She gave him an address ...'

'And you, tenor, what kind of business do you have with Wally?'

The tenor drained his beer and puffed silently on his cigar. He came to a decision. He looked at Rost, as if taking his measure.

Marcus Schwartz started telling a boring story in a dull, monotonous voice, about some lawyer in Berlin who seduced young girls with the help of his wife. A good-looking young couple from the upper classes, and suddenly the scandal came to light. He had read all about it in the newspaper. Marcus Schwartz had a peculiar talent for blunting the edge of any stimulating story. Everything that came out of his mouth became banal, dull, and spiritless.

Rost called the waiter and paid. His friends urged him to stay, but to no avail. There was a general feeling of boredom in the air. Everyone stood up to leave. The tenor took the opportunity to ask Rost in a whisper for a loan of two florins. As soon as he got what he asked for, he took off, his stiff, heavy body seeming to croak like his voice as he walked. Yasha accompanied Rost to the end of the road, where he paused to take his leave.

'And Fritzi?' asked Rost.

'I'm sick of her.' And after a moment: 'You want her? She likes you; she'll be glad to have you.'

'No.'

'She's a great girl! You'll enjoy her.'

'You're behaving like a Jewish father with an unmarried daughter.' Rost laughed and shook his hand.

14

The orange-blue afternoon was suffused by a pure, radiant light as it gradually turned into evening, accompanied by the strains of the bands playing in the parks and the noisy bustle of the streets. Patches of verdant green dappled the gardens and the roadsides. The chestnut trees had shed their blossoms. In a brand-new, light suit, bought that very day, with a carnation in his buttonhole, Rost was in a good mood. There was a cheerful, carefree feeling in the air. The world seemed spacious and welcoming. His muscles flexed of their own accord — if he gambled now he would be sure to win; if he wrestled with an enemy he would defeat him.

They both reached the designated spot at exactly the same time, each coming from the opposite direction. They smiled, and at first they did not know what to say to each other, nor was there any need to blemish the pristine feelings in their hearts with words. For a while they walked shoulder to shoulder, circling the round flowerbed, the gravel on the path crunching under their feet. From time to time Rost glanced quickly at his companion, whose pale cheeks were faintly flushed. A trail of soft shadows stretched eastwards from the shrubs bordering the path, and the silhouette of the latticework fence lay slanting and elongated on the ground. Snatches of band music reached them from the other side of the park, interrupted by the noise from the crowded street.

'You see, I even put off an appointment for you,' lied Rost. 'A ... very important meeting with a friend.'

On a side path not frequented by many people, they sat down on an empty bench. She would have liked to look into his eyes, a long, free, direct look; to hide her hand in his forever; to be buried inside him, reduced to a tiny, distant dot at the core of his being — that was how she had secretly, on some unconscious level, imagined this meeting to herself, but now his presence maddened her, made her wild, provocative, spiteful. She could not restrain the resentment in her heart, but even as she lashed out at him with bitter, venomous words, she wanted to lay her head in his lap and weep silent tears, not out of pain but out of a tremulous secret joy: because the day was so beautiful that it made you want to shower it with kisses; because the verdant bush opposite was already deep in shade; because under its branches, once from this side and once from that, a pearly grey pigeon appeared; because a little ant was climbing up her white shoe as if it were a bridge; because the row of box trees pruned like a hedge was half in warm sunshine; and because ... just because.

A passing couple left behind them a faint, pale scent of mimosa, until a barely perceptible breeze came and blew it away. Erna followed the couple with her eyes until they turned into a side path and disappeared from view.

'Next month, the summer break begins,' she said as if to herself. 'Do you like to swim?'

Yes, he liked to swim.

'We'll probably go to the lake like we do every summer.' And after a short pause: 'In any case, you'll have to find another room …'

'Why?'

'Because … You understand … It would be better.' She added: 'Because everyone will be going away.' Erna fiddled crossly with her purse until it slipped from her hands and fell to the ground. Rost bent down and picked it up. 'If you moved somewhere else …'

'Then?'

'Then …' Erna left the sentence unfinished. Apparently she herself didn't know what would happen then.

'Then,' said Rost, 'I wouldn't be able to see you so often, and that would be a shame.'

'Me?'

'Yes, you.'

She gave him a sidelong look accompanied by a slight smile. And suddenly, with a stubborn, childish expression on her face, she burst out: 'I prefer real men, not callow youths!'

'Would you like me to introduce you to a few?'

'I have more than enough.'

'Oho!'

'You don't believe me?'

'Why should I?'

'For starters, there's one who wants to leave his wife for me. Dark-haired …'

'Dark-haired! And do you want him to?'

'We'll see.'

'In any case, I admire his taste.'

'He's a famous musician.'

'Ah.'

'With deep-grey eyes.'

'That too!'

'He's just thirty years old. No more and no less.'

'A wonderful age.'

'You're mocking me.'

'God forbid.'

'I love him very much.'

'Congratulations!'

'When we went for a long drive into the countryside a few weeks ago in his private automobile and stopped at a village inn to drink lemonade, he vowed to end his life if I didn't accept him.'

'And did he end his life?'

'Not yet.'

'Good luck to him.'

Erna burst into mischievous, liberating laughter. Now she was a little girl again, excited and open.

Rost devoured her with his eyes, joining in her laughter. 'So if I were thirty, I would at least have a chance.'

'Not even if you were a hundred!' And at the same time she looked at him with eyes so full of love that it warmed his heart.

'Fine, I'll look for another room.'

'Good idea,' said Erna, 'so you should. Still, you don't have to move right away. You can wait a bit longer, three or four weeks I mean, until the summer vacation starts, let's say.' She bent down and picked up a pebble and threw it in the air. 'And you, won't you take a holiday in the country?'

'I might.'

'In the evenings, you go out and everything is already

asleep. The village, the people, the cows in the cowshed. The night is silent and the stars are silent. The earth breathes, and your heart is full to bursting. And you could roar with happiness and burst into tears and roll on the ground like a wild colt, and stroke your burning body and bite your arm till it bleeds and wake up to the sound of the cattle lowing and the farmer's shouts … I read that in a book,' she concluded with her eyes shining.

Rost smoked his cigarette in silence. His whole being was focused on Erna next to him; he felt that he could sense every movement stirring in her soul. From her side, on his right, he felt a new kind of heat, a primordial heat that had no relation to the weather. That evening in the country which Erna had described to him, how good it would be to run about in it now like an untamed animal, to chase Erna herself up hill and down dale until he lost his senses, to breathe the smell of her soft body like the smell of the warm earth and the dewy grass. Instead he was pursuing her sitting still, without moving a muscle. A short, broken laugh escaped his lips. Erna gave him a puzzled look.

'Why are you laughing like that?'

'I didn't mean to. I just remembered something.'

At that moment Karl Greener and Fritz Anker made their way towards them from another path. Erna saw them in the distance and jumped up to meet them with an exaggerated show of delight. She introduced them to Rost and invited them to sit down for a while, to spite Rost, whose annoyance was obvious to her. For her there was a kind of painful, masochistic pleasure in it. She laughed too loudly, with a coquettishness of which Rost was well aware, and talked with a false, unnatural vivacity.

Fritz Anker hardly spoke, as if the words were being forced out of him, and kept shifting the spectacles on his nose in embarrassment. The unexpected meeting had agitated him profoundly. His spectacles suddenly felt as uncomfortable as tight shoes. In contrast to him, Karl Greener was the very picture of confidence and overweening self-esteem. His free and easy manner of speaking and moving, unforced and unhesitant, annoying in their undisguised conceit, immediately provoked Rost to insult him. On the spur of the moment he pulled the drawing pad from under the boy's arm as if taking a book from a bookshelf, and asked permission only after opening it.

Greener quickly swallowed the insult. A gleam of anger flashed in his eyes and immediately died down. 'Of course. They were done for the whole world.'

Rost briefly turned the pages. 'Hmm ... for the whole world — in other words, the world commissioned them from you,' and he returned the pad. 'So you intend to become a painter.'

'I am one already.'

'Very nice. A kind of minor Rembrandt, I suppose.'

'At the very least!'

'Please sit down,' said Rost, indicating a place on the bench as if it were a seat in his own home, 'here.'

'And you, of course, are not a painter,' Greener challenged him without sitting down, 'and you don't understand anything about painting either.'

'I, of course, am not a painter. But I do understand something about good painting.'

'That was an enjoyable evening we spent at Friedel's.' Greener turned to Erna, with the obvious intention of excluding Rost. 'It was great fun, wasn't it?'

'We should go for a hike together on Sunday, a long hike,' said Erna with affected enthusiasm. 'You could even bring your painting gear with you to paint the beautiful views …'

'Not really,' intervened Rost in a mocking tone, 'painting surely demands a high degree of concentration, seclusion.'

'You're right,' said Greener, not noticing the note of hidden mockery. 'I don't work in front of an audience. It's only when I'm alone in front of the canvas that I see the picture I intend putting on it.'

'Exactly.'

'But we can go for a hike in any case.'

Rost took out his cigarette case and offered it to the boys.

'And are you engaged in some branch of the arts too?' he asked Fritz Anker.

'Me … no.'

Rost liked the look of Fritz Anker. He had some idea of the secret bond uniting the two boys, who were so completely different. 'But you appreciate art, I imagine.'

'You could say so.'

'And you're studying philosophy and history.'

'Mainly philosophy. How did you know?'

'I guessed.'

'You guessed right.'

'I think you lack a certain belief in yourself, a drawback you should overcome. People tend to believe in those who believe in themselves.'

'You're right. But the truth … if you're interested in the truth …'

'Not in the least necessary. It isn't the truth that makes people happy. Relationships between people — are they based on the truth? Even the most intimate friendship is not. Without lies the world would not be able to exist.'

'There's only one scientific truth.'

'So? Outside the laboratory, who cares?'

Greener took Anker's bamboo cane and, with its tip, began to draw invisible shapes on the gravel. He went on to hit stones with it, as if he were playing golf. The sun disappeared behind the treetops and they grew very still. Erna was playing absent-mindedly with her purse, glancing from time to time at Rost. A mild, groundless sadness had descended on her, an enjoyable sadness.

'And when will we start?' Greener turned to Erna.

'Start what?'

'Painting your portrait.'

'I don't want to,' she said, laughing.

'Why not? I feel that it will be my greatest work, a work of genius.'

Erna jumped up without answering; she wanted to go home now. She felt unsatisfied. The meeting with Rost, on which she had unconsciously pinned her hopes for the clarification of something involving change, and the quieting of her inner turmoil, had concluded without any result. Everything remained as complicated as before, both around her and inside her. He would go on making love to her mother whenever the opportunity arose, and she, Erna, would know it for certain. She would sense it through all the walls and barriers; she would sit in the classroom and see them — outside or in her room she would see them, and she wouldn't be able to look away. And as for her, Erna, he would pay her no attention at all. She was only a naive little girl, and perhaps not even pretty, indistinguishable from thousands of others.

They walked down the streets, which were already preparing for a mild, tranquil evening, and filling with a spirit of
liberation at the end of the day's labour, when people wake
as if from an oppressive dream, and crowd the pavements
and the trams and the café terraces, and, as they contemplate
the rooftops still gilded with a film of sunshine, feel a
faint regret for the unheeded passing of another beautiful
summer day. But down below, in the depths of the streets,
a transparent darkness has already descended, and the deep,
dull chimes of church bells pass through it like a shiver of
lamentation, heavy and sombre and calling to mind another,
distant darkness: a mouldy, unhealthy, oppressive darkness
that has nothing to do with that of the conscious, impinging
dark of the evening, and then the sounds fade away while
their echoes go on reverberating in the air.

Erna was filled with sadness. Life was obscure, unfathomable, veil behind veil — you got rid of one and were
confronted by another.

Karl Greener said goodbye and mounted a tram. The
remaining three walked on in silence. They were not far
now from Erna's house. On the corner she suddenly stopped
and impulsively took her leave, overcome by some frantic
need for haste. She looked at Rost as if she wanted to say
something, but she said nothing. She walked quickly down
the quiet street, supple and upright in her slender young
body, with the braid bouncing on the haughty nape of her
neck like a creature with a life of its own.

Despite his eagerness to return to the apartment that was
already so dear to him, Rost intuitively felt that it would be

better not to go home early this evening, and he therefore accepted Fritz Anker's timid invitation to spend a couple of hours in his company. First they went to an expensive restaurant to have supper. After about an hour, when they emerged from the restaurant, warmed by the good meal and the fine, heavy Italian wine, the evening seemed rather chilly, and Fritz Anker succumbed to a mild melancholy concerning the vanity of life, which was destined to turn, over the course of the evening, into a profound and unbearable depression. Anker knew this very well — depression for no particular reason, cruel, crushing, robbing him of breath, turning his bed into a furnace, and keeping him awake till morning. At times like this he would loathe himself boundlessly, loathe his long, lanky, awkward body, his introspective mind, full of inhibitions that destroyed any straightforward, natural relations with other people and with the world, and sentenced him to endless neurotic evasions. At times like these he was liable to drown himself in filth in order to hate himself even more, to provide material reasons for his self-hatred. He was of the age when sensitive souls reach a point of absolute disillusionment with no way out, and the most extreme cases, those incapable of compromise, end their lives. All living beings are doomed to die, everything that exists is doomed to wear out, and in the light of this certain knowledge nothing has any value.

Eating together had created a certain intimacy between the two young men, as if they had known each other for a long time. Anker felt more confident; he waved his bamboo cane in the air and talked desperately. Fear of the approaching night made him frantic, and he wanted to silence the fear by talking, but it peeped out of the cracks between the words and sentences, and even seeped into the words themselves and distorted their meaning. He stopped in front of a café to take out a handkerchief and clean his spectacles. Without them he looked very pitiful, with his strained, staring eyes, the red mark crossing the bridge of his nose like a tattoo, and his bowed head tilted to one side. He pulled Rost into the café, where they drank port. In the middle of one of his cheeks, a faint red spot, the size of a small coin, appeared on Anker's parchment skin.

'You think me a poor creature,' said Anker, 'admit it.'

'No.'

'But I am a poor creature. Without a doubt. Look at my face, at my entire appearance.' He gestured contemptuously towards his body, from top to bottom.

'I can't see anything wrong,' said Rost after a quick appraisal of Anker's appearance.

'You're a polite man.'

'Not at all.'

'Look, I'm a person who likes keeping clear accounts: this is what I have, this is what I lack — there you have it! Everything clear and concise. I don't like playing hide-and-seek with myself.' And after a brief silence: 'Maybe having so much money works against me.'

'You can do something about that,' said Rost, smiling.

'I don't know if I have the strength, I'm spoiled.'

'The money bothers you so much?'

'People can sense it in a second, from miles away, and you can never know if the way they treat you depends on this fact, even if they don't get any benefit from it.'

'What do you care? What do you need them for? Good riddance!'

'And women, will they want me for the sake of my good looks?'

'Never mind that!' Rost smiled with the disdain of the very young, enjoying a far from hard-earned success. 'There are many roads to a woman's heart. Good looks are not crucial. The more you believe in yourself, the faster they fly to you.' As he spoke he felt that he wasn't being entirely truthful, that it wasn't always so easy. 'You should never despair of them. For every man, there's a woman somewhere intended for him alone. Do you really think that in all your life you won't find a single woman who'll love you for what you are?'

Fritz Anker said nothing. He ordered another drink and then suggested going to a brothel. At first Rost was unwilling but, after pressure from his companion, in the end he agreed. When they emerged from the café Anker went up to one of the carriages parked at the side of the road and gave a coachman with a round face and a moustache the address, which turned out to be a house that looked no different from any other. They entered the lobby and went up to the first floor. Anker, who appeared very familiar with the place, pressed a button next to one of the doors with a bronze plate announcing: 'Madame Francie Weisbecher. Masseuse.'

A maid in a white apron led them down a passage into a smallish room with shabby dark-red furniture, dimly illuminated by a pale-red light coming from the ceiling and a lamp standing in the corner. It looked somewhat like a doctor's waiting room. The landlady entered immediately through another door, wearing an evening gown, a well-mannered matron of about forty, who still showed signs of a withered beauty. She greeted Anker warmly like an old acquaintance, addressing him as 'Herr Shtolff', and offered her white ringed fingers to Rost as well. She made a few polite remarks and then said that they would immediately be joined by a few young ladies, and showed them an album with photographs of women. The muffled sounds of a piano came from an adjacent room. A few minutes later four young ladies, resembling cabaret singers, appeared in low-cut evening gowns that exposed their arms, and parts of their breasts and backs. The four of them smiled practised smiles, as if posing for a camera, and walked to and fro with slow, mincing steps in affected modesty.

Fritz Anker adjusted his spectacles. They were far from ugly, each in her own way. In the spacious drawing room next door, prostitutes danced to the strains of the piano. Champagne was imbibed at little tables; riotous drunken laughter broke out; a smell of sweat, mascara, and tobacco floated in the air. Women perched in the laps of men, giggling at their pinches and obscenities. There were about fifty men and women in the room — a variety of women, most of them pretty, none of them over the age of thirty; and a range of men, some young, some old, bald, and paunchy, army officers and civilians.

Fritz Anker ordered champagne. Here his usual shyness dropped away. Here he was not inferior to anyone; here money was what counted, and he did not lack money. There was even a faint note of insolence in his tone, and Rost observed him from the side with a little smile. Anker beckoned two girls who had just walked in, freshly made-up and ready for the next customer, one a blonde and the other a brunette with spiteful green eyes.

'And you, my fine prince, aren't you going to open your mouth tonight?' the green-eyed girl said to Rost. 'You could be a little more friendly to me, my high-and-mighty prince. My name is Caroline and I can be very friendly. Would you like to dance?'

Rost had no desire to dance. He glanced around the room and his attention was caught by a man who looked familiar. The man sensed Rost's eyes on him and stood up, walked over to their table, and greeted him with drunken expansiveness. Now Rost recognised him.

'You took off your uniform; I can't recognise you any-more.' Rost laughed.

'I see you've betrayed me, Caroline; I'll never forgive you,' teased Felix von Bronhof.

'I have to take care of this ignorant youngster. He needs to be instructed and educated.'

'You'll be wasting your time; I'm already educated.'

Felix von Bronhof stood next to them for a while, joking with the girls. He declined their invitation to join them since he was with friends, and promised to come back later. Rost sensed a forced gaiety in the man. Anker shifted his spectacles to and fro. Rost had forgotten to introduce him to the officer. The idea of introducing two people to each other in a place like this seemed very strange to him. The place itself united strangers in an alliance like that of a prison, where there was no need to introduce people as dictated by etiquette.

The blonde was already drinking from the same glass as Anker and stroking his hairless jaw and chin. Her name was Yetti and she came from Linz. 'All right, if you buy me a diamond ring,' she said in a wheedling voice.

'Sure, I'll buy you a diamond ring.' Anker laughed drunk-enly for no particular reason. Then they got up and left the room together.

Rost took small sips of his champagne; he felt no desire to drink. Caroline's prompting was of no avail, even though she was by no means ugly. He was suddenly overcome by boredom. The dim lights; the music; the dancing; the excessive, noisy merriment — he was suddenly struck by the falsity and artificiality of it all. It was all intended for one purpose only. Fritz Anker, with his beardless parchment skin and his feelings of inferiority, who was supposedly interested only in the pursuit of universal truth, he of all people was caught up in this noisy illusion of life. And Felix von Bronhof, the arrogant, tyrannical officer, he too. But Michael Rost himself was in no need of it; the time for compromise was thankfully still a long way off.

'What a boring customer you are,' complained Caroline, 'as lifeless as a stuffed animal.'

'How right you are, my dear.'

'You should be ashamed of yourself! Call yourself a young man? You're not a man at all.'

'How much do you usually earn? You won't lose anything; I'll give it to you in full.'

'I spit on it!' And then: 'Perhaps you think I'm not good enough for you? I can give you money; I earn enough! If I wanted to I could be rich, with the finest carriage in town. Gowns from the top boutiques, a villa — understand? It depends on me and me only! The day after tomorrow, my old baron will come. I just have to say the word, and he'll be only too happy to waste his money on me. You understand?'

'I understand.'

'Do you want to meet me tomorrow in town? A private meeting. I like you. If you like, you can come to the café opposite the museum at four o'clock tomorrow. I often go there.'

Rost replied evasively that he couldn't promise to be there.

'With me you'll live like a prince,' continued Caroline, her green eyes flashing. 'I'll accept my baron's proposal. He's extremely rich, a Hungarian tycoon. He always leaves me a few hundred when he comes here, in secret of course, behind the madam's back. Take a look at this ring.' She displayed the large sapphire ring on her finger. 'That's a present from him too.'

'A fine ring.'

'Well, what do you say?'

'Another time, perhaps; right now I can't.'

Fritz Anker returned, his embarrassment leading to a moment of strain and unease. He downed a few glasses, one after another, in an attempt to overcome his embarrassment, but his introspective nature, constantly probing into himself and his inner life with a kind of neurotic self-awareness, made it difficult for him to dull his mind with alcohol. As always, after escapades of this kind he loathed himself. He felt dirty, degraded, decadent; and the distance between himself and the other, ostensibly pure world, inhabited by love and relationships that were free from ulterior motives, now seemed immeasurable. He drank steadily. And in the end, in order to increase his self-loathing, or perhaps to forget it, if only for a moment, he left the room with Caroline.

It was getting late, and Rost was bored. But since he had some idea of Anker's state of mind and felt sorry for him, he sat and waited patiently. Felix von Bronhof approached him again.

'My friends have left,' he said, and added after a moment: 'Yesterday perhaps I was a little too … Please forgive me.' There was a melancholy look in his eyes again, and he now appeared to be perfectly sober. 'The most conspicuous feature of places like this is boredom,' he said, 'don't you agree? The frantic attempt to overcome it makes it even more obvious. If war broke out, I would be only too glad to … You know, in peacetime a soldier is a completely superfluous man. Your life is as lacking in purpose as that of a resident in an old-age home, until in the end it all becomes meaningless, and you don't know what the point is anymore.'

Rost smoked in silence, while the officer became increasingly garrulous.

'We, you see, an ancient nation at the peak of civilisation, are doomed to decadence — by we I mean the aristocracy. Among the simple folk, of course, there is still plenty of vitality. You see, the entire structure, the structure of the monarchy, will inevitably collapse. The foundations are weak; in the upper echelons everything is rotten and corrupt. There you have it.'

Anker returned, and the three of them left. It was after midnight, and outside everything was still. The coachmen at the sides of the Ringstrasse sat huddled mutely on their perches. The horses bowed their heads as if in resignation. A kind of quiet sadness, not painful, pervaded the air. A sickle moon appeared and disappeared behind the buildings, only to return, suspended in the void. Life seemed to be shrouded in a thin, transparent veil. Looking through the veil of the night at the day to come and all the days endlessly following it, you felt your heart thrill in anticipation of all the changes and surprises they held for you.

But not so Fritz Anker. He was afraid to look at the days to come; to him they appeared as a black, threatening void. He was afraid of the pain he was liable to cause himself without wishing to do so, of the changes that would certainly not be to his advantage; he saw everything negatively, as if afflicted by some mental deformity. Tall and lanky, he strode down the hollow streets, full of despair. He imagined that he could hear the echo of his steps separately, isolated, distinct from those of his companions. The fresh night air dissipated his drunkenness. A strange vision flashed before his eyes: the three of them were walking to his grave. He saw himself lying in an open coffin, dead, stiff, with his spectacles on his parchment face, which was still exactly the same. The coffin floated at a little distance before them, not borne by human hands, not on a hearse, but floating slowly in the air, with the three of them walking behind it. It only lasted a moment, like a fleeting vision dispelled with the blink of an eye. No, there was nothing to be seen but for a solitary policeman pacing to and fro along the pavement, and in the distance two prostitutes turning unhurriedly into an alley.

He gave vent to a little cough, to prove to himself that he was still all there, unchanged. And nevertheless at that moment he seemed utterly foreign to himself, and the two people with him were closer and more sympathetic to him than he was to himself. This Rost, this strong, blond youth whom he had only known for a few hours, already seemed to him like a sturdy support for his own tenuous existence. He felt that from now on it would be hard for him to do without his friendship; he needed him as a kind of psychological crutch to lean on. He was not yet aware of this truth: that every man was doomed to bear himself, by himself, to the end of his days, and that if he lacked the necessary strength to do so, nobody else could do it for him.

They went into a café on the Ring for a coffee. The place was almost empty, suffused with a strange sense of solitude. A handful of customers sat here and there, nursing glasses of water. Two girls were sitting at one of the tables, one of them busy applying rouge to her cheeks. A certain desolation and the nervous wakefulness of after midnight filled the air.

Rost sipped his coffee mechanically, and a warm feeling rose in him as he imagined the pure, virginal darkness in Erna's room, a room that he had never seen but that nevertheless felt as familiar to him as if he had known it forever. He pictured her lying on her white bed, warm and smooth, her soft limbs relaxed, one arm dangling over the side of the bed, her even breath filling the still room. A torrent of warmth flooded him.

'All this,' said Fritz Anker to nobody in particular, 'is very little. I ask where the crux of the matter is, the essence.'

A faint smell of face powder, vague and fleeting, wafted towards them from the two girls. Felix von Bronhof looked at Anker. 'The crux of the matter: we pursue it all our lives long, but when we already have it in our grasp we realise immediately that it was only an illusion, and once more we pursue this will-o'-the-wisp.'

'In that case, perhaps you can tell me what it's all for?' With a practised, automatic movement, Anker adjusted his spectacles and narrowed his eyes at the officer.

The officer said indifferently: 'Perhaps for the sake of the pursuit itself.'

'I'm not interested.'

'Life,' continued von Bronhof without paying any attention to Anker, 'isn't about attaining, but about endlessly pursuing. A hunger that is never satisfied — that's life. Once you're satisfied you might as well be dead.'

Rost felt a little bored. What was there to philosophise about here? Every moment had a beauty of its own, every day, every night, every drop of rain, every breath of wind. Movement was full of vibrant life, and so was stillness. An immovable mountain too was full of life. And if he ever reached a point when he did not feel the beauty, the eternal pulsing — he would end it. In any case, he would not sit and philosophise. But he would never reach that point. It was simply out of the question.

He watched the rings of reddish-blue smoke rising from his cigarette. It was pleasant to think, at this hour after midnight, with his feelings stirred and his senses aroused, that the world was vast and varied and full of change, and that it could fill a man's short life, with no room for boredom or gloom. There in a dark room Erna slept, warm, pure, flawless; and from her a stream of bliss flowed down the night streets and straight into his heart. Apart from that, there was her mother, Gertrude, who was probably lying there now on fire, her eyes staring into the darkness, consumed by vain expectations. She might still do something foolish: her temperament was too passionate.

No, Rost reflected, life was not a matter of sober calculation; what counted here was temperament and the raging of the blood.

'In certain situations,' continued Felix von Bronhof, 'travel can also help. Simply going somewhere else. When you change your location you leave behind your attachment to the things that poisoned your life there. In the new place they lose all their significance, and you wonder how such things could have had the power to upset you.' More than persuading others, he wanted to convince himself. But even as he spoke he felt that his words were not absolutely true. He knew there was one thing that the journey he was about to take would not make him forget. He would run away from it, and it would pursue him wherever he went, more cruelly than ever.

His head in his hands, Fritz Anker sat, hunched and silent. His future life weighed on him like a heavy burden. Already he felt tired. He would always have to pay for everything with money. In himself, as a human being, he would never obtain anything. He was worthless. He himself, from top to toe, was nothing but an illusion, an empty void. His value was measured by that of the money in his pocket. And soon he would have to go home, to the room screaming so loudly of its emptiness that it could drive a man insane. All alone, with no way out.

He looked distractedly at his companions, registering their presence as if from a great distance. They were strangers, like everyone else in the world. There was no relation between him and them. He remained alone, alone to the point of madness. He would have to suffer his life alone, without succour, without anything in common with his peers. Suddenly he stood up, threw a coin onto the table, and made for the door without saying goodbye, with slow, faltering steps. He looked like an old man taking his last steps.

Rost quickly made his excuses to the officer and hurried after Anker. For some reason he was afraid to leave Fritz

Anker on his own now. He felt sorry for him.

At the entrance he looked up and down the deserted street, and made out Anker's stumbling silhouette not far off. With a few quick strides he caught up with him, and began to walk next to him in silence. Fritz Anker took no notice of him — perhaps he didn't even know he was there. When they reached the corner of the street, facing a broad square with a monument looming in its centre, Anker hesitated, and then crossed into the square, walking in the middle of the road.

'Are you going home?'

Anker turned his head slightly in his direction and went on walking without replying.

'It's possible for a man to put an end to his life too,' whispered Rost.

'What? Yes, of course. I haven't thought about it yet. I haven't found a way.'

'It's not so difficult.'

The square was empty and brightly lit. A deep-blue, almost black sky arched over it, studded with moist stars. The treetops whose branches overhung the high latticed fence of the big gardens to one side of the square did not stir. The coolness of the night welled up from the depths of the garden as if from a cellar. The windows in the row of buildings opposite were blank. In the muteness of the night, a man was closer to death than to life. Death blunted its sting to a considerable degree; it became simple, self-evident, not terrifying. It was real, and the rest — life in all its manifold activities — seemed like a dream whose reality could be denied.

'There is another possibility,' said Rost. 'A man can absorb himself in some kind of activity, if he is unable to enjoy idleness.'

'Activity? Which? What for? What would that change? My father never raised a finger. Nor did my grandfather. The fortune passes from father to son. The business runs itself, and the capital increases of its own accord. You want money? A thousand, five thousand, ten thousand? My father knew how to enjoy himself, and he still knows now, at the age of sixty-six.'

He sat down on a bench outside the park that they were now passing. 'I've never lacked for anything in my life — all my wishes were fulfilled even before they took shape. Wealth diminished me; I had nothing left to wish for. All the things that money can buy have no value in my eyes — all they bring is loathing and remorse. As for the rest, I don't know if really exists, and if it does, I am unable to obtain it.'

'You haven't tried yet. You have to try and try again. Keep on trying, once from this direction and once from that. Persistence is what counts.'

'But what if it all seems pointless?'

'That will pass. You can never know what surprises life holds in store for you; all you know of life is one limited social circle. One day I'll take you someplace where you'll meet a different type of person. You need to get out of those four walls, where you never stop thinking about yourself, for a change.'

Anker lit a cigarette and puffed on it for a while, staring ahead of him at the wide empty street. 'You know, I've never had a friend, a real bosom friend … When I was small it was impossible. At the kindergarten I wasn't allowed to play with the other children; my nanny wouldn't let me, I don't know why. Yes, I remember, so I wouldn't get some infantile disease. I had no brothers or sisters and I always played by myself. I never went to school: when I reached school-going age I was taught by private tutors at home. Only on my birthday and a couple of other occasions, a few of my parents' relatives and friends who had children were invited, and after the official reception we were allowed to play. They all played and kicked up a row, and I always stayed on the sidelines. I stood and watched. The same thing happened when I was invited to their homes. When I grew up and started attending high school, I made friends from time to time, but it didn't take long for the friendships to cool off. I think they didn't like me. Our coachman Johan always brought me to school in the carriage, and he was always waiting to take me home at the end of the day. I was always like a prisoner. When I turned sixteen and the supervision grew a little more lax, I no longer found a way to connect with boys of my age — I was already sunk into myself, completely withdrawn, and unable to open up. Later on I tried to make friends, but to no avail. Whenever anyone approaches me, I immediately begin to analyse him, criticise, find fault, dissect his attitude to me and mine to him, until in the end I'm left with nothing. The affliction of introspection, if you like. No one's perfect, me less so than others, and nevertheless I would like a friend to be perfect, and his relationship with me to be pure and strong. All this is, of course, beyond the bounds of possibility, I know.'

'Don't demand too much. People aren't entirely good or entirely bad, they're both — all depending on the situation and the circumstances. Maybe more than bad they're foolish. In any case, they're not simple, and however much you probe you'll never fully understand them.' Rost glanced at his watch and stood up. 'It's late.'

At the end of the street Anker stopped a passing carriage and accompanied Rost to his front door.

15

Misha the anarchist lay on his back, pale and thin. His long legs reached the end of the hospital bed. A faint smile crossed his face when he spotted Rost from a distance. He held out a weary, emaciated hand, somewhat damp and feverish. 'I'm feeling a little better,' he answered the as-yet-unasked question, 'but I spit on everything.'

Rost drew a chair up to the head of the bed and sat down. It was a long room lined with two rows of beds and two rows of windows opposite each other, with the curtains drawn on the windows facing the sun. The air was saturated with the smell of medicines, carbolic acid, and sickness.

Misha took a cube of ice from the square black basin on his bedside locker and put it in his mouth. His Adam's apple rose and fell as he swallowed it. With the days-old stubble on his cheeks, and the wisps of hair stuck to his forehead by dried sweat, he made Rost think of an abandoned ruin overgrown with weeds.

'Did you hear about the assassination?' whispered Rost.

'I heard. A pity it missed the target. Next time the job will be cleaner.'

'Lower your voice.'

'I'm not afraid. What can they do to me?' After a brief pause: 'This time I won't die, I know. Not this time. My time has not yet come.'

Rost looked at the patient in the next bed, who had a round, bald head, a heavy moustache, and beady little eyes. He was busy sucking on segments of an orange offered to him by the clumsy working-class woman sitting next to him.

'I'm not afraid of death, believe me,' said Misha, 'but not now and not here. I won't reach a ripe old age; they've already seen to that. And who needs it anyway, tell me? Twenty-eight, thirty, thirty-five at the most — isn't that enough? But I won't go alone, I can promise you that.' With a weak gesture he smoothed back his hair, and the coarse cotton of the hospital pyjama sleeve fell back a little, exposing his thin, hairy forearm to the elbow.

Through the window patients could be seen walking in the hospital grounds with their visitors, or sitting on the green benches dotted about. The sun coming from behind the building advanced over the mown lawn. In the ward the visitors spoke in low voices to the patients; from time to time a brief, hollow cough was heard. There was a feeling of solemnity in the air, restrained and oppressive. In this place you suddenly realised that death was not a fiction but a relentless fact, waiting for you at every turn. Not the heroic, glorious death of which poets in their innocence sang, but the mean, sordid, ugly death — the real, naked death, which had nothing poetic about it. There was no escaping it; it was always there, ready to harm, whether you paid attention to it or not. In its light life took on a different meaning; in its light the laws men made for themselves were of no value at all.

'That's one way of looking at it,' said Rost, as if in con-clusion to some hidden train of thought.

'And you, of course, see the years stretching out before you, until eighty, maybe even ninety or more, right?'

'I don't think about it. It's all the same to me.'

'A quiet life, everything weighed and measured. A kilo of wife, a kilo of children, a kilo of happiness — I spit on it!'

'Are you talking about me?' Rost smiled.

'I'm speaking in general. I'm in favour of high tempera-tures, you understand, the boiling point! A long, drawn-out death — that's not for me. Full steam ahead — march! Open a savings account, and from time to time deposit a kilogram of health, save half a year of life for your old age? Not for me. An old-age home — I don't need it! As far as I'm con-cerned they should all be finished off. I've heard there is some savage tribe that provides its old folks with food for two days and sends them into the forest to die. Good idea. Old age is ugly, a disfigurement of the human image.' A faint flush appeared on his wide cheekbones, between the stubble of his beard. The talk was wearing him out, and Rost said so. Misha swallowed another ice cube.

'It makes no difference to me. Death depends on fear; it comes to those who fear it. I am not afraid. I'll be up again in a week.'

'If you'd like to convalesce — stay somewhere in the countryside, for example — it could be arranged.'

'Not now. I can't spare the time to see myself as a sick man.'

A young girl entered the ward. Rost, who was facing the door, immediately guessed that she was coming to see Misha. He introduced her as Liova. She was dressed with deliberate sloppiness. Her black hair was cropped, and she narrowed her short-sighted eyes when she looked at Rost. She was as swarthy as a gypsy; her teeth glittered. If she had taken better care of herself she might even have been pretty.

Rost got up and was about to leave out of politeness, but both of them dissuaded him: he was not in the way at all; in any case visiting hours would soon be over. He remained standing and looked out of the window.

The two exchanged a few words in whispers. Then Liova sat in silence for a while, occasionally stroking the back of Misha's hand, which lay exhausted on the blanket.

He was lost: the thought flashed through Rost's mind. It was the law of nature, and there was nothing to be done about it. Thus he passed sentence on Misha without any regrets. There was no one in the world who should be mourned simply for the sake of politeness or convention. No sooner did one person die than another was born somewhere to take his place. There was no point in dwelling for too long on the fate of this or that individual.

In the meantime the end of visiting hours was announced, and Rost left the hospital with Liova. They stepped into a crowded, bustling street, full of sunshine, which left no room for illness and dismal thoughts. Greedily he breathed in a lungful of this vibrant life. His back straightened of its own accord, and his chest swelled. Everything was before him; everything was made for him, for his enjoyment; everything was there for the taking by anyone who knew how to take it. He threw back his head and tossed his blond locks off his forehead. 'And you are studying …?'

'Chemistry.'

'Why?'

'What?'

'I asked why?'

'A woman is not inferior to a man.'

'And the proof is — studying chemistry?'

'Women can achieve anything that men can.'

'Pity!'

'Why?'

'Because then the world would be all male, and boring.'

'You prefer ignorant dolls, who think of nothing but their looks.'

'Definitely.'

'From now on, you will have to change your tastes. Those days are over; a new era is beginning.'

'I hope not. A few thousand real women will remain to make the world go round.'

They went into a little park opposite the university. It was bathed in sunshine, and small children were playing there under the supervision of their nursemaids or mothers.

Liova said: 'For generations you've imprisoned us in harems, in kitchens, in nurseries. You did everything in your power to prevent us from coming anywhere near your lofty male preserve. You preferred to run things on your own, shutting out one half of the human race. That's all over! Now it's the turn of us women. Where you failed, we'll have a chance to succeed. You'll see that we are your equals.'

'Excellent, but at the end of the day, who will take on the burden of childbirth? After all, this is one job men can't perform, even with all the goodwill in the world. And the human race needs children, no?'

'You're taking things to the point of absurdity. That's

what you men have always done, for lack of serious arguments. Much easier, of course.'

'Perish the thought! In all sincerity, I really want to know.'

Liova's gait was awkward and stiff, like that of a manual labourer. And Rost, observing her from the side, even though he suspected her of deliberately adopting this unnatural way of walking, found himself thinking that she was probably not intended to bear children. Every movement she made seemed to speak of barrenness.

When she remained silent, he went on: 'And if women are to run the world, science and culture and all the rest, and bear children as well — I ask how? And when? Between one pregnancy and the next? They won't have the time.'

She sat down on an unoccupied bench. 'With a man like you it's impossible to discuss such matters.'

'Why not with a man like me?'

'Because you radiate frivolity from miles away. I bet all you can think of is chasing skirts.'

'You've hit the nail on the head, only I don't see it as frivolity.' He lit himself a cigarette and continued. 'Let me tell you something, but don't be offended. According to your views and theories, we are both almost the same sex, equals in all respects, so I can speak to you frankly. You should go to bed with a man, as simple as that, and do what comes naturally — and that will rid you of all these false notions.'

The furious blush spreading over the girl's cheeks, although not readily perceptible under her swarthy skin, did not escape Rost's eyes. She said only: 'You are very rude.'

Rost was secretly delighted to have succeeded in embarrassing her. 'Please forgive me. Since you aspire to be the equal of men in every way, I permitted myself to speak to you without disguises and hypocrisy, man to man, so to say.'

'Who asked for your advice? I know what to do without you telling me. In any case, you won't be the man in question.'

The outrageous possibility hinted at in her words gave rise in Rost to physical distress. He hastened to say: 'Perish the thought! I wasn't speaking for myself. I would never consider myself worthy,' and, in order to put an end to the conversation, he turned to a little girl with golden curls, who was playing with a big doll nearby, and asked her what her name was in a coaxing, ingratiating tone of voice.

Her name was Lena and her doll's name was Clara, said the child without a trace of shyness, and went back to playing with her doll.

Rost ran his hand over her silken curls, which were decked with a blue bow, and turned to Liova. 'Do you like little children?' But Liova was already full of hostility towards the conceited fellow sitting next to her. Every word and gesture of his was calculated to negate her opinions, her chosen path in life, her very right to exist. She felt this obscurely and hated him for it.

She said irrelevantly, simply to quarrel: 'Your tone is so patronising, so ex-cathedra! I suppose you think you're cleverer than anyone else.'

'Quite right,' said Rost with an ironic little smile.

'You're making a big mistake. The truth is that you're nothing but a cheeky boy still wet behind the ears.'

Now she wants to quarrel, thought Rost with satisfaction, *but she won't get her way, not with me.* He looked at the church looming up behind the park, its whiteness turning pale orange in the dazzling sunshine.

'Misha is mortally ill, you know,' he said after a while.

[231]

'I suggested he go somewhere to convalesce when he gets out of hospital. I would have no difficulty arranging it, but he refused. If you have any influence over him …'

'Nobody has any influence over Misha. If he refused, he probably has his reasons.'

'I suppose so,' said Rost resignedly, and he stood up, parted from the girl, and left the park.

The girls in his town, when they graduated from high school, cut their hair short and smoked cigarettes. Some of them travelled to take courses in the country or abroad, wore pince-nez on an ugly nose, took trips with boys to the Alps, pored over Karl Marx, Nietzsche, and the like, brewed tea on Primus stoves in small rooms, and waited every month for their allowance from Daddy; some embraced ideals of changing the world order, of 'returning to the people', of eliminating the class struggle, and so forth; others sat bored at home waiting for their intended, read books and were bored, strummed on the piano and were bored, brooded over their resentment of their conservative parents and were bored, and came to the conclusion that it wasn't worth it … until they too escaped to the courses or the 'people'. They had been cheerful and pretty at high school, their hair long, their cheeks full and rosy, and their smiles aimed winningly at the strutting officers. Sometimes they agreed to go for a sleigh ride with these officers, and to drink schnapps afterwards and dance to the strains of the harmonica, and a few of them were tempted to embrace 'free love' and were obliged in the course of time to travel to the provincial capital to have an operation for a 'blocked intestine'. At home there were clandestine dramas. The mother wept, the father pounded his fist on the table, and the daughter rebelled: 'The world has changed! You belong to the old generation! We understand more!' All this went on in secret, and the whole town knew the truth.

He turned into the Ring, where trams and carriages clattered to and fro in the joie de vivre of a mild summer's day. In the secret hope of meeting Erna, he directed his steps towards the Volksgarten, but not far from the entrance he bumped into one-eyed Jan, who was making straight for him and thus impossible to avoid. They approached each other and stopped.

Jan twisted his bony face into a vicious expression. 'I have a small score to settle with you.' He pierced him with his one eye.

'You are mistaken. There are no scores to settle between us.' Rost kept both eyes on his enemy's movements.

'If your memory is failing, I can help you.'

'My memory isn't failing, and I'm warning you to get out of my way.'

Jan was shorter than him, but sturdy and broad-shouldered. He could have been about thirty years old.

'Look here,' said Jan, suddenly changing his tone. 'I'm for peace not war. I like you.'

'And so?'

'Let's go and have a drink. What's past is wiped out. My treat.'

Rost smelled a hidden agenda. In any case he would not have taken up Jan's invitation.

'I don't want to,' he said firmly.

'So you reject my outstretched hand. Good. We'll meet again.'

'*We won't meet again.*' Rost stressed every word. 'If you have anything to say to me, say it now.'

'I'll say it in a dark corner.'

'You're a coward.'

'We'll see,' Jan spat through clenched teeth, his one eye smouldering with primitive rage.

'In any case, if we do meet again you'll regret it.' Rost concluded the conversation and set off at a brisk pace, all his senses on the alert for any sound behind his back. But there were no footsteps following him: apparently the one-eyed man had given up on him for the time being. Nevertheless, after entering the park, instead of continuing straight down the main avenue, he turned right onto a side path, in case his enemy decided to attack him from the rear. After taking a few steps, he stood still and, through the iron grille of the fence, looked at the broad square facing the entrance of the park, which a few people were busy crossing. In the distance he caught sight of Jan in his hat, walking away in the opposite direction, and he relaxed. Now he retraced his steps to the main avenue.

It was half-past four in the afternoon. Rost walked slowly down the avenue, contemplating the people strolling along the criss-crossing paths or sitting on the chairs and benches. In the park café the musicians were already tuning their instruments for the afternoon's performance. No, if she were going to come, at this hour she would already have been here.

He had no desire to remain in the park, and he turned back and left through another gate facing the Ringstrasse, not far from the museum. He walked towards the Opera, feeling rather disappointed. Even though he had not made an appointment with her, for some reason he had been sure that she would be there, and now all at once he felt aimless. The day ahead of him suddenly seemed empty. True, it was still a beautiful day, warm and fine — the chestnut trees lining the broad street were in full leaf, and when you passed you could sometimes breathe a fresh, reviving scent of cool forests, and when you raised your eyes to the leafy boughs above, you could hardly see a patch of blue sky through the foliage — and nevertheless there was something missing; now, all this was no longer enough. Up to an hour, or even half an hour ago — but not now.

The glory of the things in themselves was no longer enough to make them beautiful. They needed someone to come and embellish them with a glory of her own. But that someone had not come, had not sensed that she needed to come, and Rost was disappointed. A feeling of profound apathy overcame him. This feeling was completely new to him, but it did not last long. He quickly caught himself and a smile rose to his lips. 'Come on,' he said to himself, 'it's not the end of the world. You need to pull yourself together.'

And then she appeared. Not far from the elegant café opposite the Opera. She came towards him with Friedel Kobler, apparently on their way to the Volksgarten after all. They certainly didn't need Friedel Kobler, he thought, but for lack of any alternative …

Erna's face began to beam as soon as she set eyes on him. But after he greeted them she blurted out, whether in annoyance or secret delight: 'You always pop up where nobody planted you.'

Rost said with a smirk: 'Perhaps you would prefer it if I were lying stabbed in the street now?'

'Oho, as far as I'm concerned!'

'What do you mean, stabbed?'

'What I say, stabbed with a knife.'

'Don't be so naive, he's only bluffing.'

Partly in earnest, partly joking, he said: 'Only three-quarters of an hour ago I was about to be stabbed. I was a hair's breadth from death.'

'Trying to make yourself interesting!' Erna threw at him.

They were standing in the middle of the pavement, blocking the way. Rost invited them to enter the café. After a moment's hesitation Erna agreed. They sat down next to the wall, in the corner of the terrace running along the façade of the café, somewhat sheltered, by the row of occupied tables in front of them, from the eyes of the passers-by. In a cream-coloured summer jacket and a broad-brimmed straw hat, Erna looked very pretty indeed. The delicate lines of her face still hovered between girlhood and maturity, that mixture of child and woman which added to her charm. But her full red mouth already held a definite hint of the obstinacy and capriciousness that would make more than one man wish they had never met her.

Rost stole stealthy glances at her as she sipped her steaming chocolate, and Erna, who felt his eyes on her, blushed. In a few months, Rost noted, an evident change had taken place in her: she was no longer the same little schoolgirl. A distance had opened up between her and her friend, he thought as he contemplated the heavy lines of Friedel Kobler's face with her long, fleshy nose and expressionless calf's eyes. Truth be told, you couldn't say that Friedel was ugly. She wasn't ugly. There was nothing wrong with her hair, for example: dark blonde, soft, and fine. But still there

was something missing, that essential spark, whose true
nature was elusive and could not be defined in words, which
gave things a point and determined their value. As in the
case of certain works of art — ostensibly perfect, executed
in accordance with all the rules and theories of aesthetics —
you could find no flaw in them, and yet they left you feeling
empty; they did not thrill your soul.

'I like sitting in cafés,' announced Friedel contentedly, after
drinking her raspberry cordial to the dregs. 'Daddy doesn't
mind, but Mother forbids it. Young girls have nothing to look
for in cafés, she says. She's probably afraid I'll be seduced, ha
ha, but I'm not a little girl anymore. I'm sixteen and a half!'

'And therefore you can be seduced with impunity.' Rost
laughed.

'That's not what I meant.' Friedel giggled and blushed.

Erna gazed absent-mindedly at the people passing in
front of the terrace. How anxiously she had awaited this
hour! All morning in school she could think of nothing but
her overwhelming desire to see him. She paid no attention
to her teachers, until her distraction became so obvious that
they asked her if she was ill. And at home she hardly touched
her lunch; her appetite had vanished. To her parents she
made the excuse of an upset stomach. Then she waited. The
slightest noise made her jump. He did not spend much time
in his room and not on a regular basis. She did not expect
him to come home, but she waited in any case. And when
Friedel came in the end and persuaded her to go out, she only
agreed in the hope that she might come across him in the
Volksgarten. And now she found herself sitting opposite him,
and it was all perfectly natural and simple and self-evident,
and she couldn't even look at him or say a single word.

She simply sat there, bathed in a great happiness, like a pure stream, which left no room to wish for anything else. She completely forgot about the presence of Friedel, and perhaps even the presence of Rost himself. That is to say, she felt it inside her, in every organ of her body, like the blood coursing through her veins, rather than outside her as an independent, clearly delineated entity — a feeling indefinable in concepts or even in images. She could have gone on sitting there like that forever, until the day she died. As if from a vast distance she heard the conversation between Rost and Friedel, and the talk at the neighbouring tables, only the voices and not the words themselves. Life was so beautiful, so very beautiful — and she had never known it. Beautiful and sad too, sad enough to make you cry, or scream.

'Why are you so silent, Erna?' Friedel roused her from her trance. Erna looked from Friedel to Rost, and then she smiled at Rost, a light, pure smile that remained fixed on her lips for a moment. *Here he is, sitting in front of you*, she thought, *flesh and blood. All you have to do is reach out your hand a little and you can touch him, and at the same time you long for him as if he were far away in another town.*

'The dreams of a young girl, who can know them?' said Rost.

'Would you like to know?'

'Very much.'

'Perhaps one day I'll tell you.' Erna laughed.

'When you're already old?'

'Of course, when I'm already old.'

'By then you'll have forgotten everything. You shouldn't wait so long.'

'By the way, I won't grow old, I don't want to. I'll always

stay young. And afterwards —'

'We have to live full, rich lives,' said Friedel, 'so that we can relive them in our minds when we're old, enjoy them again in our memories. Otherwise old age is empty, boring, a burden.'

Rost looked at her in surprise. Where did Friedel get all that from? He would never have guessed that she had it in her to say such things.

'Where did you read that?'

'Oh, I know it for myself. It's not hard.'

'I don't know if you can choose,' said Erna. 'I imagine that most people live the lives they have to, not the ones they would have chosen to live. Isn't that so?'

'I suppose it is; not many people are able to live according to their heart's desire.'

Suddenly Erna said, without any transition: 'I ask myself, for example, a young man like you, what goal have you set yourself in life; what do you aspire to? You aren't studying; you don't do anything else. Nothing. Don't see my question as indiscreet, I really want to know.'

'Perhaps one day I'll tell you,' replied Rost in her own words. And after a moment: 'A question like that would be appropriate to my aunt, if I had an aunt.'

Erna pulled a face. 'In any case, one could say that you are what people call a shady character.'

Rost burst out laughing. 'Quite right — a shady character.'

They all laughed. Then Rost said: 'But you are not in the least a shady character; you're a sweet, pretty girl.' Erna sent him a quick, grateful look.

'I agree,' Friedel chimed in.

A breeze began to blow and ruffled Rost's hair. Opposite them a shaft of sunlight fell halfway down the entrance to the Opera, while in the lower half, between the mighty pillars, the shadows had already gathered, like the forerunners of the evening. Friedel stood up to leave. She had a piano lesson from six to seven.

For a while Rost smoked in silence, watching the smoke rings snatched from his mouth by the wind and blown away.

'Before we met I looked in the Volksgarten. I thought I'd find you there.'

'And I —' Erna began and left the sentence unfinished. Rost suggested going for a ride in a carriage, but Erna said that she couldn't. It was getting late: she had to go home soon for supper. They agreed to meet the next day.

Erna had been nice to him today, not aggressive as usual, and Rost had enjoyed every minute of it to the full. The electric current running from her to him filled him with happiness. Suddenly he knew with an unshakable inner certainty, the intuitive certainty that needs no proof, that this Erna, this supple, upright girl with all the capriciousness and fire of her youth, was not indifferent to him at all. He gave her a look full of tenderness, and Erna responded immediately with a sweet smile, as if confirming his hidden thoughts. No, they had nothing to say to each other. It was as if they had both been surprised by the same feeling, whose beauty would only be dulled and diminished by words. The life around them seemed to recede into the distance; its ceaseless bustle and clamour registered only vaguely, as if through a ghostly veil of mist.

A tram stopped nearby, people hurried in and out, and it set off again, bell ringing and wheels rattling; and it all seemed strange and unreal. At a table close to them a man with a moustache and a mole next to his nose was energetically haranguing his companion, a youth with a snub nose and a blank look — their eyes registered the scene unthinkingly, as if of their own accord.

Rost dared to stroke the back of her hand, which lay abandoned on the table, and Erna did not protest. Soon it was time to leave. They took a roundabout way, through dim, narrow alleys already filled with the smells of cooking for the evening meal, and the fitful, somewhat sickly rays of the rapidly setting sun. Children with flushed faces hurried to finish their games before going home for their supper; maids in white aprons crossed the street, carrying jars of foaming beer from the nearby taverns. The calm of the approaching evening after the day's work gradually settled on the streets of the city. Rost and Erna walked slowly along the narrow pavements without speaking. On the corner of their street he parted from her and retraced his steps.

Straight after supper in a nearby restaurant, where he ate from time to time, he went home. He only wanted to see if there was any mail for him before going out again. He intended telephoning Dean to ask if he was free to meet him this evening. There were no letters awaiting him, and he sat down to rest for a moment in an armchair. The house was quiet: it seemed that they had all gone out on this mild, pleasant evening. But after a couple of minutes there was a soft knock on the door, and Gertrude came in. She fell on him immediately with a moan of abandonment, and began showering him with kisses all over his face and neck without saying a word. When she calmed down a little she complained: 'I can't stand it anymore. I don't know what will become of me. I haven't got the strength to go on.'

The electric light was not switched on. The darkness in the room was relieved only by a long, slanting shaft of light shining into the window from the opposite building and stretching down the wall to the edge of the floor. Rost could not see Gertrude's distraught face.

'What happened?' he asked with a hint of impatience.

'Nothing happened; to my regret nothing happened.'

'Then why are you upset?'

'Don't you understand,' whispered Gertrude, breathing hotly on his face, 'don't you understand that I love you?'

'Good, that's not new. So where's the tragedy here?' His tone was chilly, dismissive, but Gertrude was too upset to notice. She took his hand in both of hers and buried it in her lap, and whispered as if to herself: 'They went out a little while ago, he and Erna, and I waited; I didn't know if I was waiting in vain like so many times before, like I'm always waiting, every hour and every minute of the day. Perhaps it's a bad idea to confide something like this in a man. No good ever comes of it. It's better for a man not to know, but I can't stand it anymore. You're never here; I never see you. There has to be an end to it. I can't go on.' Again she fell on him, kissing and biting him with a passion so fierce and violent that it seemed as if she wanted to annihilate him. Then she started again: 'And you, all I want to hear from you is one word. Do you love me? Only one word.'

'Of course,' Rost replied, lighting a cigarette.

No, he thought to himself, all this was already a little too much, definitely too much. Then he said: 'We should be careful. They could suddenly return.'

'I don't care; I don't care about anything. I just want to know, just tell me this: why don't I ever see you?'

'How can you not see me? I stay here; I'm here every day.'

'You stay here but you're not here. You're never here. It must be because you don't love me anymore, because if you did you'd be here. I can't take it anymore,' she repeated vehemently in a stubborn whisper, as if by these means she hoped to find a solution to her gnawing pain.

Rost said in a tone of mild rebuke: 'You were different at first — playful, relaxed. I don't understand. You've completely changed.'

'I haven't changed at all. What can I do? I love you too much. It's wrong to love so much. It's a crime to love so much. I don't know how I could bear it if — I don't know, if something happened to you.'

Suddenly he felt sorry for her. At that moment she seemed pitiful to him. Obscurely he perceived the full extent of her feelings for him, which bordered on the grotesque. To mollify her a little, he stroked her hair, and then her downy nape and her back wrapped in a silk dressing-gown. Then he stood up and went to switch on the light, and for a moment it dazzled his eyes.

'Why?' asked Gertrude. He saw that her eyes were wet with tears.

'I have to go. I have an appointment to meet a friend.'

'You're going again.' Her voice was steeped in sadness.

With his back to her, Rost stood in front of the wardrobe mirror and combed his hair. In the mirror he could see part of the room and its furniture reflected, but not the sofa on which Gertrude was sitting. He lingered a little too long over his grooming, as if hesitant to leave her. Abruptly he thrust the comb into his pocket and turned round to face the room.

Gertrude went on sitting, withdrawn into herself, her head drooping towards her bosom, gleaming between the flaps of her gown, which had fallen open. At that moment there was a sound of voices and footsteps coming closer in the hallway.

Gertrude started from her place in a panic. 'When?' she threw the question at him and stole out without waiting for an answer. He waited for a minute until George Shtift and Erna disappeared into the sitting room, and then he left his room.

16

Kärntner Strasse was brightly lit and crowded with people, and Rost strolled along it at his leisure. The café was not far off. and he had plenty of time. He thought about the earlier scene with Gertrude, which had left an unpleasant taste. The whole affair was taking on a form that was not at all to his liking. Such relationships, without any obligation on either side, were not meant to turn into foolish tragedies. He would not allow the reins to slip out of his hands. Soon he would have to put an end to it.

In the meantime he reached the café. He sat down on the balcony, next to a large bay window open to the street. On the other side of the street was an illuminated shop window displaying a number of pairs of elegant ladies' shoes. Rost enjoyed looking at the passers-by, examining the faces of the women who appeared in his field of vision and disappeared again forever, thinking how Erna outshone them in her charms and how superior she was to them in every respect. He felt the mild evening breeze on his skin, soft and fragrant with the smell of women's perfumes and perhaps a hint of lilac in the distance.

There, in the town of his birth, at this hour of the evening, the priest's garden and the other gardens of the neighbourhood were heady with the pale-mauve scent of real lilac blossoms, and the young boys would hide behind woodpiles and throw love notes at the giggling groups of girls, the Sonyas, the Wandas, the Tzilas, and the girls would let out peals of pure, ringing laughter and shout 'yes' or 'no' across the street. They would squabble over nothing and make up again, and so it would go on. And the evening would flow gently down the street, slow, scented, and a little tired too, and the priest's dog would hurl his hoarse staccato barks into the clear laughter, and into the twinkling of the stars, which would sometimes fall like burning embers or sparks of electricity. Afterwards they would walk down the street in pairs and take the opportunity to hide in the shadows of the treetops arching over the garden fences, and the sounds of laughter would flare up and break out again here and there, quick and muffled, this time due to tickling and playfulness. But he, Rost, was not there now, and it was good to be here, in the midst of the tumult of the city, among the hurrying crowds, and to keep that street in his heart with all its shades and smells, like someone keeping a precious object in his pocket, from which he could take it out and feast his eyes on it whenever he wanted to.

Erna arrived promptly at the meeting place. They made for the main street, where Rost stopped a carriage and told the coachman to drive them to the main avenue of the Prater. A golden summer's day unrolled before their eyes, and a light breeze caressed their faces. The streets were very beautiful; glowing in the sunshine, they seemed renewed, revealed to the eye as if being seen for the first time. Erna was silent. She was full of a quiet joy, which nonetheless held in its depths a tremor of fearful curiosity, the expectation of something strange and unknown, which perhaps hid within it the most important secret of life. She let Rost take her hand. He stroked it tenderly several times and then raised it to his lips.

The streets retreated on either side, and from time to time the horses' hooves struck the paving stones with a shower of sparks, the sound slightly muffled by the noise of the city. Erna felt like an important, grown-up woman, free to do whatever her heart desired. It was as if she had only just become truly grown up, only this minute become a woman. All at once the hesitations of the transition years disappeared. No, she was no longer the naive little girl of yesterday, of an hour ago. Now she was sitting on the soft seat of a splendid carriage, shoulder to shoulder with a young man, with this Rost, who filled every corner of her soul. For the first time in her life she was riding in a carriage like this. All the previous carriage rides of her life counted for nothing in comparison. Behind them ran the canal, in whose calm waters the trees and buildings were reflected upside down. From time to time Erna sent an unintentional sidelong glance at her companion. Soon they were trundling down the main avenue of the Prater, dappled with patches of sunshine. The carriage wheels turned soundlessly, and on either side, from among the trees and bushes, a pleasant, somewhat moist breeze blew, bringing with it a smell of hay.

When they reached the middle of the avenue, they got off, and Rost dismissed the coachman. At first they could hardly stand on their legs, which had fallen asleep during the ride and seemed to be made of cotton wool. They felt pleasantly tired and as if their insides were swarming with ants. Erna suddenly burst out into loud, mischievous laughter, and began hopping on one leg away from Rost. After a moment she ran back towards him and seized his arm. 'Come on, let's run for a bit and stretch our sleepy legs!' She let go of his arm and said: 'You wait here. I'll go first and you catch me, what do you say?'

The avenue here was almost empty. Occasionally a carriage went by, or a pair of pedestrians. Rost let Erna advance for twenty steps or so, and then he ran after her and caught her. Erna gasped for breath and laughed, displaying a mouthful of gleaming white, even teeth. Rost held her in his arms, pressed her to him, and felt the firm little breasts under her dress. She rested her head on his shoulder as if she were tired, and her broad-brimmed hat slipped to the side. The delicate smell of her hair rose in his nostrils, and he had to restrain himself by force from pressing his lips to it. He knew that he could not afford to be hasty here and risk ruining everything. Suddenly she pulled away from him.

Through a narrow, shady path, between the trees lining the avenue, they arrived at a sunny lawn, the grass trampled here and there by holidaymakers who had left behind bottle caps and crumpled yellowing newspapers used to wrap picnic foods. The whole place spoke of idyllic family outings, petty clerks and honest workers with their bulky wives, who did not forget to lift the skirts of their Sunday dresses before sitting on the grass, and dirty children stubbornly growing out of their clothes, like flowers out of their pots. Three pigeons pecked at invisible seeds.

Rost and Erna crossed the lawn at a slant and entered the woods surrounding it. They walked in silence along a narrow unpaved path, the undergrowth brushing against their clothes. After a few minutes they arrived at a small clearing, and Rost suggested sitting down to rest. A dense, almost tangible silence reigned here, underlined by the buzzing of a single stray bee. The city was far away, unseen, unheard, non-existent. Rost took off his jacket and spread it out for Erna to sit on. He lay down next to her.

'It's as if we weren't here,' remarked Erna after a short silence, 'not in this city and not even in this world. We're very far away, aren't we?'

'We're far from the world, but close to each other.'

Erna pretended not to hear him. She took off her hat and threw it down on the grass.

Rost stroked her leg once or twice, from the ankle to the knee. 'You don't still bear a grudge against me, do you, Erna?'

'A grudge? Why?' Erna appeared embarrassed, but she thought: *To stay like this forever, just like this, next to him, with the high blue sky above and the wall of woods all around and that little ant crawling up to the tip of that blade of grass, like this forever.* And then Rost bent over her, and before she knew it he was pressing his lips to her mouth in a long kiss, kneeling and locking his arms around her neck. When he let go of her in the end, he saw that there was a deep blush on her cheeks. She appeared to be smiling, but there were tears in her eyes, and now it was she who pulled him to her and covered his face, his eyes, his hair, with endless kisses. She held his face close to hers and gazed at it intently, as if imprinting its features deep in her heart so that she would never forget them. Then she laid his head in her lap, and ran her long, slender, outspread fingers through his blond forelock.

'And I thought you couldn't stand me, my wonderful little Erna.' He looked up at her gaze, intent on his; at the deep-blue eyes glittering in her pale face.

'I can't stand you and I love you. I could kill you with love.'

Nothing moved. The city's din was inaudible in the distance. The summer twilight covered them and them alone. Apart from them there was no one in the world; apart from them nothing existed. They did not speak.

With his arm around her waist, Rost sat next to Erna and looked in front of him. Now, he thought, perhaps it would really be best to move out of the room in their house, for a number of reasons. He turned to look at Erna, and feasted his eyes on her pure, radiant, joyful face. Erna suddenly roused herself and remembered that it was time to go home.

After accompanying Erna to the entrance to the building, he went into a nearby café and phoned Fritz Anker, who turned out to be home and free for the evening. Ten minutes later Anker appeared at the appointed spot. They crossed the Ringstrasse and continued walking along Kärntner Strasse. Rost declined the carriage proposed by Anker. He was brimming with energy now and in no mood to sit in a carriage — he needed to release his energy in movement. Fritz Anker, his cane in his hand and a cigarette between his lips, was in a mood of resignation and secret renunciation, affording him a measure of relief from his nagging introspection and self-torment. He strode shoulder to shoulder with Rost, long and skinny, his myopic eyes groping to his right and left. His suit of expensive cloth, custom-made by a tailor of the first rank, nevertheless seemed not to fit him due to his shuffling gait and his faltering, awkward movements. Everything about him seemed out of place. He himself was constantly aware of this, and others felt it too. For the most part he would elicit, in everyone he met for the first time, a feeling of unexplained uneasiness, a feeling that lingered in some hidden corner for a good while afterwards. Yet you couldn't say that he was unlikeable — there was even something benign and friendly in his face.

There were already rosy tints of sunset in the air, and a pale crescent moon was hanging in the transparent azure heights. Rost was fizzing with a huge, breathless happiness, without any channels to let it out and restore his inner equilibrium. He felt capable of all kinds of wild, irrational acts. He could still sense Erna's soft, full lips on his, smell the modest, delicate scent of her sixteen years. The touch of her hair, the firm apples of her breasts still lingered on his hands. He sensed all this as if it were stamped on his skin, but he refrained from dwelling on it now. He stored his happiness in a corner of his soul for later, like a precious treasure.

There were not many diners at Stock's today. With un-disguised curiosity Fritz Anker scanned the strange faces, some of which had square beards plastered to their jaws, and little yarmulkes stuck like black patches to their shaven heads. Reb Chaim Stock circulated among the guests with his usual measured tread, his hands behind his back and his pince-nez perched on his nose. Max Karp leaned on the bar, whispering to Malvina as she poured jars of beer and glasses of plum wine. In the next room, where Rost took Anker, none of the usual gang was present except for Marcus Schwartz, busy eating a stuffed chicken neck, and Arnold

Kroin, the heroic tenor, avidly watching his every bite.

'Ah,' the heroic tenor greeted Rost hoarsely, 'we haven't seen you for ages. You are neglecting us, sir.'

'Today we're going to have a party! Are there only the two of you? Where's everybody else?' He went to the doorway leading to the main room and called Max Karp to join them. 'Where's Yasha? I've brought a new friend with me. His name is Fritz Anker, believe it or not, and he wears spectacles — that's beyond a doubt.' Anker smiled shyly. 'And you, tenor, haven't you dined yet? All in good time. We'll start at the beginning.'

Through the open window came the sound of a baby crying, as usual. Fat Fritzi stuck her head between the window bars and looked in.

'Ah, Fritzi, please come in,' called Rost. He ordered food and drinks for everyone. 'Where's Yasha?' he asked Fritzi.

'We're not together anymore,' she replied, with a trace of suppressed resentment.

'So, you're available now.'

'Not to you, little Rost,' she said, not without a hint of lewdness.

'Thank you. Luckily I didn't wait for you, or I would have ended up an old bachelor.'

Afterwards they were joined by a short, broad-shouldered young man of about twenty-six, with a very large cropped head and an open-necked shirt displaying a chest as hairy as a monkey's. Max Karp introduced him: 'Herr Shor, a student from Belgium on holiday in our city. He finds the girls here more appetising than the Belgian girls. They don't smell of onions.'

'Enough compliments,' said Shor, laughing. His broad

face was open, with a bold, intelligent expression. He was dressed casually and even sloppily, more like a peasant than a student. His whole appearance was expressive of a generous spirit, totally lacking in pettiness and small-mindedness. His disproportionately broad, high forehead was already creased with deep horizontal lines.

Rost liked him on first sight. He invited him to join them, and Shor immediately agreed with a frank laugh, without the niceties of false manners, as if they were old friends. Rost raised his glass in a toast: 'Here's to girls who don't smell of onions!' and everyone laughed.

'And you,' he turned to Max Karp, 'has it come out already?'

'Has what come out?'

'The literary journal for young people, of course.'

Karp twisted his lips in a smile that was both embarrassed and bitter. 'No, it hasn't,' he said between his teeth.

'All for the best. So, here's to the literary journal that will never come out!'

'It will come out!' cried Karp in alarm.

Fritz Anker didn't open his mouth. He sat next to Rost and nibbled without appetite at the white meat of his chicken. From time to time he shot a glance at one or another of the people at the table, and he felt out of place. There was no connection between him and these people. There was no truth in their faces. Each face had its own falsity. Each of them was trying to present a certain image. Each of them was trying to act a part, to appear to be someone else, just not himself. They didn't have the courage to show their true faces, only putting on mask upon mask. Take this girl Fritzi, for example, with a smile permanently fixed on her face for no reason; or the fellow with the tie and the hair and the mutton-chop whiskers, looking as if he had stepped straight out of a comic opera; or the hoarse one with the gigantic belly and the flabby unshaven face, who kept clearing his throat as if about to burst into song; and this Max Karp, with his self-important expression, as if he were doing them all a big favour by sitting at the same table as people so inferior to him — what a joke! Yes, the only one with a human face here was this Shor. And Rost.

The sky outside had turned dark grey. Evening was here, and somewhere or other someone had started playing a new couplet on a harmonica. Someone laughed in a deep voice that turned into a high, shrill one, and someone else shouted down the length of the street: 'Two and a half, Karl, I'm telling you: two and a half, no more!'

And nevertheless a secret tremor of sweet sadness arose in Fritz Anker, a snatched memory of fragmentary sights and things that had been completely obliterated, drawn up from the depths of his soul, where he had never been aware of their existence. The true, deep reality was there, eternal as the universe, while these faces next to him — their reality was exaggerated out of all proportion. He went on mechanically chewing and taking occasional sips of beer, without tasting anything. Anchored in himself like all lonely people, it was hard for him to come out of his shell, to forget himself. The cheerful, argumentative words bandied about around the table reached him from a distance, like empty shells.

Anker pushed his plate away, having left most of the rice and chicken on it. He raised his eyes and looked distantly at the people sitting around him, who were still eating with lively appetites. A murky feeling arose in him that while he was sitting here he was missing something somewhere else. If he had had the courage he would have stood up and left. These people, however distant from him and indifferent to him, protected him from himself, even though their presence felt to him like a heavy burden on his back. It was growing harder and harder for him to bear their noisy talk and laughter, the clatter of the tableware, the smell of the food. He looked around him as if seeking salvation. His eyes came to rest on Shor, to his left, who was at that moment wiping his mouth with a napkin.

'Nonsense!' he thought out loud, without being conscious of it. 'It's all nerves; you have to pull yourself together or else —'

Shor turned to face him. 'Nerves? Did you say nerves?'

In his confusion, the embarrassed Anker picked up his half-full mug of beer and took a few sips.

'You aren't used to mixing with people, it seems,' said Shor.

'Not really … The young people of our generation aren't very sociable. Decadence due to affluence — in western Europe, that is; in Russia it's different. And you yourself, do you like the masses?'

'I can't say. I might not like them, but I am capable of joining them, at any rate, fighting side by side with them to improve the situation.'

'The material situation, and after that?'

'After that, the spiritual.'

'So that in the end, they too will become decadent from too much culture. A diabolical revenge indeed.'

'Until we reach that stage! The people are still fundamentally healthy. And again: if this is indeed the only way, there is no need to delay it.'

'But neither is there any need to assist and expedite it.'

'That, of course, depends on your temperament. Between you and me, it's not the end so much that appeals to me, but the means of attaining it — the war. I long to see in the masses the awakening of a terrible, blind force, like the sudden eruption of a volcano in a stream of boiling lava.'

'In other words, you like to delude yourself with fantasies.'

'Not exactly, no. What I imagine to myself is thousands, tens of thousands of people marching down the high road to conquer a city — a terrible elemental force with thousands of heads, a grandiose spectacle!'

'Not very human, I must say.'

'Human! Are you trying to be funny? There's no such thing in the pure, idealistic form imagined by fools. By his very nature a human being is motivated by self-interest, direct or indirect, momentary outbursts, impulses — he has no god and needs no god. And the goal? Speaking for myself I prefer to see the day when the savage beast inside all of us awakens, to some imperialistic goal. Yes, I want to help in reaching the heights of passion beyond which there is nothing. Annihilation.'

Reb Chaim Stock stood in the doorway and supervised the work with a satisfied smile. Alfred the waiter rushed busily to and fro, clearing away the empty dishes and replacing them with full ones, his face flushed and sweaty and his yarmulke slipping sideways on his cropped head. As if he had a knife to his throat he screamed: 'Two litres of wine! Five trout! Three cognac!' The heroic tenor sagged in his chair like a shapeless lump, stuffed to the neck with food and drink. His face was the colour of dirty lead. 'You understand,' he croaked, 'after the performance, which was a great success — five litres down my throat! It was in Boston with a troupe of actors. And what a wine! And what do you think,' he turned to them all triumphantly, 'no effect at all! As if it were nothing but soda water!'

Marcus Schwartz tried to pinch Fritzi next to him, and she cried, half protesting, half pleased: 'Get your hands off me!'

'My treat, tenor,' said Rost, 'as much as you can drink, even ten litres!'

'This isn't America, sir.' The heroic tenor gestured towards his throat. 'My voice …'

Rost laughed. 'Your voice won't come to any harm, I guarantee!'

'No, not today.'

'And you, Karp? I'll make you an offer — if you drink five litres, no, only three, I'll give you a hundred kronen for your literary journal. You're all my witnesses! What do you say?'

Malvina, who had left the bar for a moment to stand next to their table, shook her head at Karp, but he refused to catch her eye. He was already a little drunk, and the challenge did not seem too difficult.

'Good, give the hundred to' — he looked round the table — 'to Shor, he'll be the adjudicator.'

'First we have to set the time,' said Shor. 'How much time?'

'One hour.'

'No, that's not enough.'

In the end they agreed on an hour and a half. Rost had two more conditions: that they put all three bottles on the table at once, and that he himself would taste them first to make sure they were not diluted with water. After that he whispered to Anker, who handed him a one-hundred-kronen bill, which he then passed to Shor in full view of the company. In addition, Karp was forbidden to eat anything while he drank. And Karp began. First of all he emptied two glasses down his gullet, one after the other with his eyes closed, like someone throwing himself off a cliff. He opened his eyes, set the empty glass down on the table with a thud, and looked around with a foolish smile. The heroic tenor scrutinised him with an expert eye. Then he looked at the first bottle, which was still two-thirds full.

'I'm betting a krone on Karp,' he said.

'And me a krone against him,' called Marcus Schwartz.

'Cash on the table!'

In the meantime Karp emptied another glass. His face was already as red as if it had been flayed.

'Another krone on Karp! That makes two!' cried the tenor enthusiastically.

'Another krone against him!'

The tenor poured him another glass and egged him on in English: 'Come on, boy!'

Schwartz protested. 'Nobody's allowed to help him in any way whatsoever!' And Shor judged that there was nothing in the rules against it, since no such condition had been specified.

A mocking little smile never left Rost's face. From time to time he glanced at Malvina, who remained standing where she was, flushed and agitated, crushing a handkerchief in her hands. Her Max already had a boastful, victorious expression on his face, as if showing his true colours at last.

It was ten o'clock. The main hall was already deserted.

More than half an hour had already passed since Karp began drinking, and there were still two full bottles to go. The tenor never stopped urging him on: 'Drink! Time's passing! It's costing me two kronen!' until Karp collected whatever was left of his senses to protest in a slurred voice: 'Shut your mouth, you rattletrap!'

Sweat oozed from Karp's red forehead. He looked around in confusion, and poured himself another glass, from which he took small sips. In his dazed mind a last, dim spark of clarity remained, propelling him towards the wine, some vague yet insistent inner impulse urging him in the direction of the full bottles without his knowing why or wherefore. Fritz Anker contemplated the spectacle with a combination of indifference and disgust.

Akidos appeared with his tall, skinny body and beardless, ageless face, and sat down stiffly next to his roommate, Marcus Schwartz, without saying a word. He gave the impression of a man who has been insulted but considers it beneath his dignity to return insult for insult, and his expression seemed to say: *Everything that's happening here is child's play. You won't succeed in surprising me — we've already seen it all before.*

The tenor kept at it without pause. 'Time's passing!' he shouted, his voice rising above the commotion. 'Two kronen! Water he can't even drink, and he puts himself forward to drink wine …' But Max Karp, his head drooping on his shoulder, his face flushed and sweating, took no notice of him. With a forgotten smile fixed on his lips he began to sing to himself in a barely intelligible grunt:

Only twenty-two
The battle survived

Go and get brides —
We took the order in our strides
Tra-la-la-la-la

Only twenty-two
We beat them in the street
Go blow the bugles
Stamp your feet!
Tir-la-tira-boom!

By the skin of our teeth
We beat them in the street.
Tie them in a bow
Give them to the rhino!
Tir-la-tira-boom!

Tie them in a bow
Give them to the rhino!

With boot polish smear
The boils on your rear
When the enemy draws nigh
Raise your tails high!

When the enemy draws nigh
Raise your tails high!

'Sing, children!' he cried in a failing voice. 'It's obvious you're not poets!'

In any case, it was now clear that he was out of the game. Someone else would drink the remaining litre and a half.

In the meantime Yasha appeared in the company of a red-headed girl with a cheeky snub nose. With a loud hail-fellow-well-met and a slap on the shoulder he greeted Rost. Then he laughed cheerfully in his deep baritone and turned to Fritzi with a 'Servus, Fritzi,' to which she responded by pulling a face.

'And who's this red flag?' She jerked her chin at the ginger girl.

'Shut your trap, slut!'

And before anyone could stop her, Fritzi landed a ringing slap on the red-head's cheek. A moment later the two women were tangled together, shrieking and pulling each other's hair, kicking with their feet and knees. Everyone fell silent. Yasha watched the fight for a couple of minutes before calling out: 'That's enough!' He went up to them and in one swift movement pulled them apart. After that, in an innovative form of peace-making, he dealt each of them a slap: 'Take that, the pair of you! And now keep quiet!'

The two women remained dumbfounded for a moment, as if astonished by what had happened. From the red-head's torn blouse, a very white breast peeped out with an aggrieved, insulted air, while her flushed face merged with her dishevelled hair into a single flame. She stood there at a loss, not knowing what to do next, like someone who had been absorbed in some very important work, demanding all her attention, and then suddenly torn away from it and cast into an alien world. Fritzi, still clinging to a lock of red hair uprooted from her rival's head, shouted, 'I'll get you in the end! I'll pay you back!' and repaired to the kitchen to wash her bloody nose.

The tenor took advantage of the general uproar to pour

one glass of Karp's wine for himself and one for Akidos, but the latter, who had been ejected from his seat by the fight raging next to him, went on standing, long and thin as a nail, and staring at the red-head. She tidied her hair and straightened her dress, at the same time hurling in the direction of the absent Fritzi sharp denunciations of her looks and her immoral way of life, while not omitting the sins of her father and her father's father, and especially her mother and her mother's mother, who had been filthy whores themselves, rolling in the gutters with any dirty drunk. She made these accusations with a certainty that brooked no doubt, as if she had witnessed all these misdeeds with her own eyes, until in the end Yasha blocked the stream of words with a firm 'That's enough! Enough! You hear me?'

The red-head heard him and fell silent on the spot. She drew up a chair next to Shor at the table, and sank into it as if overcome by exhaustion. Now that the tension had eased, she became aware of all the sore spots in her body, and her head burned like fire.

Fritzi, washed and tidied up, returned to her place. Akidos chivalrously offered her the glass of wine in front of him, but Fritzi shot him an annihilating look and rejected the wine together with his signs of concern. All at once, everyone seemed perfectly sober, except for Max Karp, who had been oblivious to what was happening behind his back, and who now went on mumbling his song unintelligibly to himself, his body caved in on itself like a shapeless heap of ruins.

The tenor, worried about his two kronen, was the first to interrupt the uneasy silence. 'Are you going to drink or not?' he said right into Karp's ear, as if he were deaf. Karp shook his drooping head, as if to rid himself of a pesky fly.

'It's useless!' exclaimed the tenor in despair. 'What a good-for-nothing. Only twenty minutes left.'

Karp's big head sank further and further into his shoulders, like a lead weight. His eyelids drooped; his eyes were almost closed. He seemed to be asleep, but he was only in a stupor. He had stopped singing.

Rost suddenly laughed out loud. The whole thing was grotesque. He remembered the afternoon, and his heart swelled with joy. What a distance between here and there. A good thing that life had so many facets, a guaranteed remedy against boredom.

He told Yasha about the bet, and the latter pronounced: 'It's over! He's lost the bet!'

'Well, now you've seen the savage beast in action,' said Anker to Shor, referring to the catfight. 'Do you find it uplifting? I find it repulsive.'

'Being uplifted isn't the issue here. We can leave that to the past generation.'

Rost called the waiter and paid. His enjoyment of the situation suddenly deserted him. He rose to his feet, followed by Anker and Shor. For a while they wandered the quiet streets under the dark, distant, star-strewn sky. From the dense bushes at the sides of the avenue, the fresh, cool night air blew, drawing the soul unconsciously to the stirring of a mysterious, minute, ongoing life, eternal as the universe.

Shor strode with broad, sturdy steps, swaying slightly like a sailor as he shifted the weight of his heavy body from foot to foot. Suddenly he lifted his voice in a song that throbbed with a profound hidden sadness. His voice was rich and somehow discordant, and it was precisely this discordance which gave it a modest, restrained grief, stemming from the depths of the many generations that had come before him.

Here you are, reflected Fritz Anker, *walking side by side with these two people, who are very far from being the worst or the most boring of your fellow men, and who are even in a certain sense close to your heart — and nevertheless! nevertheless you are walking alone, in absolute solitude, and all the world stands empty before you, and it holds nothing capable of connecting you to it. And who is to blame? Whose is the deformity?* He came to the conclusion: *There is no remedy, none at all.*

In Rotenturmstrasse, prostitutes idled on the corner, pacing to and fro in the garish light of the empty street. Rost exchanged a few sharp-tongued witticisms with them, and his laughter echoed hollowly and nakedly in the air.

There's no difference between me and these women, concluded Anker to himself, *I'm just like them, alone and at the end of my tether, alone and emptied out.* And now he would have to go home, soon or at the break of dawn, and he would find no refuge there.

'Let's take a carriage and go for a drive,' he found himself saying without intending to, 'to the Prater, for example.'

Rost agreed, but not to the Prater, not just now: first they should go to a café and have something to drink; he was parched.

But then Anker changed his mind. Whether now or in two hours' time, it made no difference — in any case there was no escape. He had to live with himself. Putting it off didn't help; it only made it harder to go home in the end.

'Let's leave it for another time,' he said, 'I want to go home now.' And he parted from them abruptly and walked away, dragging his feet.

His head slightly bowed, he walked down the street without looking right or left at the unlit shop windows, where the clothes and objects on display, fitfully illuminated by the street lamps, seemed huddled in a deep sleep. At the corner of an alleyway he was accosted by a girl with a heavily made-up face. At first he recoiled and stared at her stupidly. Then he nodded and followed her in silence. When they passed a small café, he invited her in. At this late hour there were only a few customers. In a corner two men were playing dominoes and smoking cheap cigars. One of them kept repeating in a rusty voice, 'You won't get away this time — I've got you this time,' turning the dominoes over and slapping them down triumphantly.

Anker ordered cognac. The girl was in her twenties, with rather sad, beautiful eyes. Otherwise she was neither beautiful nor ugly, like thousands of others. She sipped the cognac carefully, pausing between sips, and holding her hand under the glass in case of any spilled drops.

'On the one hand,' said Anker to nobody in particular, 'it's true, that's the way of nature. You get what you pay for, money on the table. In other words, such and such for such and such a sum, but on the other hand …'

'What on earth are you talking about?' His companion looked at him uncomprehendingly.

'Never mind, it doesn't concern you.' He drank his cognac to the dregs, lit a cigarette, and after a short silence said: 'I won't ask you about your history. I already know the answer; it's always the same old story, as if they read it in a book and learned it off by heart: deserted by an officer, pregnant and destitute, thrown out by their parents, et cetera, et cetera … All this is nauseatingly familiar. They all lie, just as they lie about the rest, the main thing. But since the lie is known in advance, there's no deceit here. From the outset you knowingly buy fake merchandise. Fine! Only one side acts in good faith: the buyer. Here, there's no room for lies, otherwise the transaction would never succeed.'

The hotel room into which they were conducted, by a servant asleep on his feet, was square, with wallpaper that featured gigantic pink roses on a pale-green background. A smell of soap and cheap cosmetics hung in the air.

Anker quickly opened half the window, which overlooked an unlit courtyard where all the surrounding windows except for one, with the curtain closed, were already in darkness. The girl removed her hat and started to take off her clothes, while Anker, sitting on a chair opposite her, followed her movements with exaggerated interest, and smoked without saying a word. The girl in front of him was no longer two steps away from him, but seemed to have receded into the distance, as if she were situated in another apartment, viewed through windows, not real. Now she was already naked, and she went up to the bed and lay down on top of the covers without bothering to remove them. 'Well?' she threw at Anker, who had not yet moved. He rose to his feet and sat on the edge of the bed.

'Wouldn't you like to smoke?' he said, and stroked her thigh.

'Aren't you going to come to bed?' said the girl impatiently. 'Take off your clothes and lie down next to me.'

'Good, I'll take off my coat. As for the rest, I don't know. Maybe not today. I'm not ready — that is to say, I'm not in the mood.'

In an instant the girl took in the true state of affairs, and she sat up abruptly as if she had been stung. All of a sudden her nakedness seemed wretched, superfluous, pointless, and exposed. Her immodesty proclaimed itself loudly.

'What!' she spat furiously between her teeth. 'You dishrag! You're not a man at all: I ask myself what you are ready for, if you're not even ready to go to bed with a woman! You useless little bastard!'

'Shut your mouth!'

'And if I don't? What will you do to me? Perhaps I'm not pretty enough for you? Too good for the likes of you! Where did you grow up, I'd like to know! Not among normal civilised people, at any rate. Finish your business and go, you miserable sourpuss!'

Anker turned around deliberately, as if preparing to reply, but before he knew what was happening, his hand suddenly rose and came down on the girl's cheek in a loud slap. This act took Anker himself by surprise. As if it had happened of its own accord, without his willing it. And not only that: he felt no anger or hatred towards the girl. On the contrary, after the event, as soon as he realised what had happened, he even felt rather ashamed.

With her hand covering her cheek, the girl sat on the bed and wept silently and tearlessly. Anker stood limply in front of the bed, not knowing what to do. He couldn't see the girl's face, which was turned away from him, but he saw her body shudder slightly from time to time. She slowly turned to face him with damp eyes. Her expression was now imploring, fawning, like that of a beaten dog. Suddenly she leaned forward and took his hand and pressed her lips to it. Softly, timidly, she murmured to no one in particular: 'There's no need to hit me …' and then, in a tone of suppressed but impassioned appeal, without letting go of his hand: 'Don't you want to? Tell me, really, don't you want to?'

Anker sank back onto the bed. 'I didn't mean it,' he blurted out in a kind of apology. 'There's something vicious deep inside me that suddenly comes out and does things I never meant to do.' He took off his glasses and began rubbing the lenses with his handkerchief in embarrassment, his naked eyes looking lost and miserable.

The frightened girl lay on her back, breathing unevenly and stroking her round, firm breasts. Together with the shame at his strange behaviour, Anker also felt a certain satisfaction — one might even say of self-acceptance — because what he had done showed clearly that there was still a healthy, animalistic element in his make-up, that he was still capable in certain situations of acting on impulse, without the long road of hesitation, doubt, and nagging introspection separating impulse from action. This realisation shed new light on his nature and its possibilities. He felt grateful to this girl, who was a stranger to him, who lived her life in the gutter, cut off from respectable society. At that moment he might even have recognised a deeper bond between them, a sense of closeness, or rather a similarity between lives lived on the margins of society — rebels whether they wanted to be or not. They were both outsiders, free from the fetters of society.

This was not the first time he had spent the night with a girl like her. He had always dimly sensed that he had something in common with them, and needless to say he had never felt revulsion towards these women, but now for the first time he became fully aware of the kinship between them. Suddenly he felt a wave of compassion, compassion for himself, whose existence seemed to revolve around nothing, and compassion for the naked girl next to him, waiting for a kind, loving word from anyone at all, even from him — he who had nothing to give, nothing but the money to pay for a false, imaginary happiness. And despite that, he bent down and kissed her on the mouth.

She wrapped her arms around his neck and pressed him to her, whispering with her hot breath words of clumsy, fawning desire, words pathetic in their nakedness, which nevertheless contained true feeling. No wonder — Anker extricated himself — when the loneliness is so absolute and extreme that it drives you mad and robs you of your breath, and you see into the heart of things in their final nakedness, without a fig leaf to cover them. And as if he suddenly realised that he wasn't on his own, that there was another living creature in the room with him, he said: 'You wouldn't understand. And perhaps you don't need to; it's better for you not to. Because there's only one way out. One and one only.'

The girl sat up. 'Perhaps I should go now, if you don't —'

'No, why? There's still time. The night is less empty with two.' And after a moment: 'On the contrary, I think you're a very nice girl.' He lit another cigarette. 'You know, there was someone, a writer, who invented something new, a kind of instrument, if you will, to measure the male substance in a woman and the female substance in a man. No more and no less. So and so many grams of the female substance in a man — disqualified! An inferior specimen! Because according to him, needless to say, women are base creatures, afflicted by every shortcoming, incapable of genius. Genius!

And after coming up with this invention, he killed himself. He went and killed himself! As if it weren't all the same in the end. A man, a woman — a ren't they both poor wretched creatures, always deserving of pity, in every situation and circumstance? And genius, creativity, what use are they in the end? With or without them, the situation is hopeless. As for suicide — that's a completely different matter. It has to be examined. At any rate, not for reasons such as these. Imagine a man afflicted by cancer, suffering from agonising pain for which he knows there is no remedy — what will it help him to know that such a thing as genius exists in the world, in the form of Spinoza or Kant or Goethe or whoever you will? Will that relieve his pain? Save him from death? All this is no more than an amusement, a means of evading the void, the unbearable fear of facing the absolute nothingness that is the very essence and end of all existence.'

All this time he spoke in a whisper, without any exaggerated show of pathos, but in a tone that went straight to the heart, full of restrained sorrow, that final sorrow which lacks all hope. He seemed to have forgotten all about the naked woman at his side. Now he fell silent, the room fell silent, and the city fell silent.

After a while the girl said: 'The things you are saying are sad, and your voice is sad too, your voice most of all. Why are you so full of sadness?' As if she felt a sudden chill, she reached out for the chair where she had left her clothes, took her blouse, and slipped it over her head. 'Listening to you talk like that makes a person feel like crying, crying inconsolably.'

'And you, what's your name?'

Her name was Gretel, and the other girls called her 'the

nun' because she was unhappy and depressed.

'A difficult childhood, I imagine. And then the cruelty of the big city, extreme poverty, hunger, a seductive man, and then another, and so on and so forth.'

'It started at home,' said Gretel. 'I had a stepfather. I was only ten. Once, he came back from the bar drunk. My mother wasn't at home. For a minute he looked at me with a mean, crooked smile. I was busy making a dress for a broken doll I'd found. Suddenly he grabbed me and threw me onto the couch. I thought he was going to beat me, like he often did for his pleasure, but this time he didn't hit me. The smell of alcohol from his mouth took my breath away, and he hurt me. I cried a lot. Afterwards he said to me: "Now keep your mouth shut! One word from you and I'll cut out your tongue!" And he would have done it too. From then on I did whatever he asked. In the course of time I got used to it, and I even began to enjoy it, since it didn't hurt anymore. It turned into a kind of game. I did it with the neighbourhood boys too. But him, my stepfather, I couldn't stand. As time went by he stopped hiding it from my mother. She knew and she didn't protest. She was afraid of him. Sometimes he beat her until she bled. Now he had no shame at all. More than once he threw me onto the couch before her very eyes, and she went on with the housework without taking any notice. But afterwards, when she caught me in a corner, she would hit me and call me a little slut, a pile of garbage! As for her, once he caught her with Johan the cripple. He beat her senseless; she lay in bed for two weeks. But he came to a bad end too. Once, when he was drunk, he started a fight with Poldy the blacksmith — and he got what was coming to him. Poldy beat him to a pulp. When they brought him home he was unrecognisable, and three days later he died. My mother wept inconsolably for him, and I wasn't in the least bit sorry — on the contrary. By then I was already fourteen.' She asked Anker for a cigarette, and after lighting it she went on: 'I didn't stay at home for long after that. My stepfather was a carpenter, and even though he spent most of what he earned on drink, there was enough left for household expenses; but after he died we were destitute. That was when I took off.'

Anker glanced at his watch. It was a quarter to two. A woman's voice rose from the next room: 'No, that's not what we agreed on! I don't want it that way! Another krone, or you can forget it.' Then the silence returned.

He gives her another krone, said Anker to himself, *because that's the way he wants it, and it's worth another krone to him. And she* — his thoughts skipped to Gretel — *recounts all this without a drop of bitterness, resigned to her fate, as if it's all quite natural. By the age of twenty or twenty-three, she has already tasted life to the dregs.*

He turned to look at her. She was sitting in a pink blouse that came down to below her navel, with her long, shapely legs stretched out on the bed, their white skin, the skin of a true blonde, gleaming palely against the background of the green satin eiderdown whose colour matched that of the wallpaper. On a sudden impulse, not untouched by compassion, he bent down and kissed her thighs, one after the other. It was as if he were asking for forgiveness from her, and from all living creatures, for the insult of life, for its absolute futility, for the fraud at its foundation. Even if he could not be blamed for it, and nor could anyone else, he knew it with utter clarity, without any illusions; knew it for himself and for the others who were incapable of knowing — and because of this knowledge, perhaps he could, to some extent, be blamed …

'You're a strange man,' said Gretel, 'not like other men.' She took his hand and stroked it gently. 'What wonderful hands you have!' she exclaimed. 'I've never seen anything like them before.'

Anker smiled faintly to himself for no evident reason. Not so long ago someone else had admired his hands. He was sure it was also a woman, but who was she? Oh, yes — it was little Erna, Erna Shtift. His heart was flooded with warmth at the memory. What a marvellous girl. If only he had been allowed to love her! For her sake he would have cut his veins before her eyes. But he had to put such thoughts behind him, for once and for all. She was not made for the likes of him. Suddenly he thought of Rost. And the suspicion that there was something between them came to him with the illumination of a lightning bolt. But if this were the case she was bound to suffer — Rost was unlikely to stay tied down for long.

He felt a sudden, piercing pain for this little Erna, who was destined without the shadow of a doubt to suffer.

Anker's nerves were already a little on edge, both because of his emotional state and because of the late hour of night, which exaggerated things out of all proportion and magnified them in the imagination a hundredfold, until they took on the dimensions of a catastrophe. And as if with the need to protect someone, he turned to Gretel and began to stroke her back gently through her blouse — long, slow strokes, over and over, until a shudder ran down her spine. Then he raised his feet from the floor, stretched out on the bed, and drew Gretel to him.

Leaning on her elbow, her face close to his, she looked at him for a moment with something like gratitude in her damp eyes. 'You can be very sweet,' she whispered huskily, 'very sweet.' And she pressed her body tightly to his. Soon she fell asleep with her head resting on Anker's arm. There was a faint, contented smile on her face, a kind of released tension. As if sleep had ironed out the strains that life had engraved on her face, and it was now perfectly calm, and even as innocent as a baby's.

Carefully Anker removed his arm from under her head. For a moment she opened her dazed, unseeing eyes, her lips slack, and then she closed them again. Anker felt a certain languor in his limbs and a pleasant kind of warmth, which gradually evaporated, but he wasn't sleepy. He sat up.

He looked at the girl lying naked by his side, at her parted legs, shameless in her abandonment, as authentic as nature itself, without any wiles, capable of straightforward, uncalculated enjoyment, breathing calmly next to him in all the pores of her relaxed body, like a satisfied animal.

The brief moment of envy passed, leaving him with a sense of satisfaction — not the physical satisfaction of gratified appetite, but a spiritual satisfaction at the kinship that had come into being between him and this strange woman. Only two hours ago her existence had been beyond the bounds of his own existence, completely unreal to him, and now she had broken into his life and he had to carry her with him, even if not always consciously, until the end of his days.

He thought that nothing was ever lost in the world: the slightest, briefest contact with another being was etched deeply in the soul, irrevocably as the grooves in a gramophone record, never to be effaced. And this strange woman, whether he loved her or not, had now come to settle in his soul forever, and this fact, far from vexing him, even caused him to feel a kind of satisfaction. All of a sudden the night became less terrifying. Now he could face going home without his usual dread. But nevertheless he went on sitting where he was without moving.

The night was quiet, but he could hear it. The sleeping woman's breath was calm and even. The night was ostensibly empty, but it was full to the brim. Every scrap of it was full of seething, passionate, secret life. It seemed that all you had to do was switch on the light, and all the life ceaselessly swarming within you and without would be revealed before your eyes, surprised in the middle of its never-ending clandestine activity. It was a long time since Anker had felt so full of life. The night seemed as smooth and caressing as dark velvet. Perhaps it was worth it, in spite of everything. Moments like these could sweeten the bitter pill. No, he made up his mind, he would not go home yet.

He lay down next to the sleeping girl again. In the distance a shrill siren pierced the stillness of the night, rose and fell without repeating itself. The night closed in again, more densely than before. At that moment Anker sunk into a dark, fathomless pit.

It was not clear to Anker whether he had fallen asleep or not. He could have sworn that it was only a moment ago that he had closed his eyes, that he had not been unconscious for more than a minute. But now that his mind slowly began to clear, he became aware of a quiet rustling sound, almost imperceptible, very close to him. With his eyes closed he lay still, pricked up his ears, and concentrated all his senses in the direction of the sound. Now there was silence. Perhaps his senses had misled him, but no — there was no doubt. The sense of a foreign presence did not leave him.

With extreme caution he opened his eyes a slit. Immediately the window loomed opposite him, its previous darkness already tinged with a hesitant shade of blue. Without changing his position he turned his eyes to the right. Not far from the bed, next to the chair on whose back he had hung his jacket, stood Gretel, still as naked as before, rummaging through the wallet she was holding in her hand. So that was it!

Anker went on lying there without moving. For some reason the whole thing seemed ridiculous and childish to him, but at the same time he was curious to know how it would end, as if it had nothing to do with him. Gretel took a bundle of one-hundred-kronen notes out of the wallet. She tucked the wallet between her thighs and began to count the notes. Anker counted them with her. There were eight notes in the bundle. She counted them twice to make sure, then she picked out two notes and held them between her lips, intending to replace the rest in the wallet.

'Are you sure you only need two?' said Anker quietly.

Gretel started. In her shock and horror, the wallet slipped out of her hand and fell onto the chair with a rattle of coins; and the notes, including the two between her lips, scattered around the room. At first she made an instinctive movement as if to bend down and pick them up, but she did not. With lowered eyes she stood still, completely at a loss, shrinking, naked, terrified, as if waiting for her sentence to be passed.

Anker too waited in silence, for some reason apparently

amused by the whole affair. Gradually the silence grew increasingly tense, until it seemed about to burst and became unbearable.

Without raising her eyes, her fingers mechanically scratching her belly in a kind of dumb, stubborn embarrassment, Gretel stammered: 'I didn't mean to, truly … This is the first time … truly … I'm not like that …' and a second later, in a spurt of courage: 'My summer jacket is already worn out and I only meant …' Timidly she raised her eyes and looked at him.

'Pick them up and give them to me!' ordered Anker.

Gretel made haste to obey, picking up the notes one by one and handing them to Anker, who counted them carefully, folded them in half, and slipped them into his trouser pocket. 'All you had to do was ask. I might not have refused.'

Now she had completely regained her courage. 'I wasn't thinking. When I woke up and found you asleep, the idea suddenly popped into my head. No, that's not how it happened. The truth is that I was simply curious, I only wanted to see what was in your pockets, that's all; and when I saw all that money I couldn't resist. But don't think that's how I usually behave — I swear that this was the first time ever!'

'Fine!' he said. 'The slate's wiped clean. We won't speak of it again.'

Gretel went on standing where she was, not knowing what she should do next. When all was said and done, she regretted the two fine notes. She cursed her luck.

'Come and sit next to me,' said Anker, making room for her. When she sat down, he put his arm around her waist and drew her closer. Her breast was now next to his face, a round, firm breast. Eagerly he breathed in the sharp, stunning smell of her flesh, which inflamed his senses. He pressed his cheek to the smooth, cool breast, and remained like that for a moment. How good it was to feel the pulse of a living being so close to him, to listen to its rhythmic breathing, its heartbeat.

Outside, the sky grew paler. The light breeze of a summer morning blew gently through the open window. The electric light, which was still on, shone with a superfluous orange glow that suddenly seemed rather mean and sordid. All the warped distortions of the heart were ironed out with the dawning of this morning, and with the closeness of this living, breathing presence trembling between his arms. They had disappeared without a trace. Nothing existed in the world but for this fresh morning, pulsing and stirring with life; and this smooth-skinned, ardent woman, burning him with her breath; and Fritz Anker himself, only a small part of him, as if his whole being had shrunk to a single point, still flickering somewhere out there.

After that, everything merged — the morning, the woman, Anker himself — into one pulsating whole. For a while he lost consciousness. Only heavy, broken breathing interrupted the silence in the room. Afterwards they lay calmly side by side, their limbs languid with contentment.

Gretel raised one of his hands to her lips and kissed it in sudden wakefulness. 'Do you want us to see each other again? Not for the money, believe me; I don't want money from you.'

Anker reached for the electricity switch above the bed and turned off the light. It was already daybreak. For a while he smoked in silence, watching the spiral of orange-blue smoke as it rose to the fly-spotted, whitewashed ceiling and dissolved into the air, caught by the almost imperceptible breeze and blown away. It was four o'clock. The sound of a window opening somewhere reached their ears, and then the heavy creaking of wheels, coming closer before receding into the distance again, swallowed up by the dense silence. Suddenly Anker was seized by a frantic haste. As if afraid of being late for something important, he jumped out of bed and began to quickly put on his clothes and comb his hair. Then he handed the girl the two hundred kronen. 'More than enough for a handsome summer coat — what do you say?'

He parted from her in haste and left the room.

17

When Rost woke up it was already ten o'clock. Through the crack in the curtains the sun drew stripes of heat that slanted across the floor and onto the soft, colourful rug in the middle of the room, a good imitation of a Persian carpet. The house was silent. Erna was at school, and she, Gertrude, had probably gone out with the maid to shop for lunch. This suited him very well. An hour ago a faint, timid scratching at the door had penetrated the agreeable drowsiness in which he lay wrapped. He kept still and pretended to be asleep. He knew at once who it was. The tragic expression that Gertrude had been wearing lately was not at all to his liking. He was getting sick and tired of the whole thing. Thank goodness the summer break was fast approaching: in a week or two the family would leave town on their vacation, and the problem would resolve itself naturally, without drama, without the unnecessary clarifications that were so hateful to him. He would have to move out of his room, since he could not go on staying in the empty house, and there would be no room for resentment and reproaches and tragedies. Later on, perhaps, he would visit their vacation spot for a week or two, where he would be a free agent, while she would be under the constant supervision of her husband.

With these thoughts in mind, he finished shaving and completed his toilet. It must be said that in some corner of his soul he felt a little sorry for her, for Gertrude, but could anyone actually expect him to tie his life to hers forever? She had become obsessed — was it his fault? Relations that were never intended to be anything but carefree and light-hearted, entered into simply out of joie de vivre, and that by their very nature were transient, since there was no basis in the external circumstances for anything else — the investment in such relations should not exceed what they were able to contain. There was no need to give all of himself where even half was more than enough: it would be a waste of his resources. As far as he was concerned, the affair was over.

When he was ready to go out, he heard the passage door opening, and the sound of Gertrude's voice. He waited in his room to avoid bumping into her, but before long there was a knock at his door, and without waiting for an invitation Gertrude came in, still in her hat and overcoat.

'I was afraid I would miss you,' she said, sinking wearily onto the sofa. 'I hurried back as fast as I could.'

Rost remained standing next to the table and looked at her.

Gertrude breathed heavily, her face rather red. 'You're going out again,' she said with a note of resentment in her voice. 'Aren't you going to give me a kiss?'

'Is there something you want to say to me?' His impatience was lost on Gertrude. 'I haven't had my breakfast yet.'

Gertrude took off her dark-red straw hat and put it down on the sofa next to her. Passing her hand over her curly hair she suggested: 'We can make you coffee here, or anything else you fancy.'

Rost did not reply. The room was now bathed in the sunshine coming through the open windows.

'Would you mind closing the curtains a little? It's too hot in here and, besides, the sun ruins the furniture.'

Reluctantly Rost went over to the windows and drew the curtains. At once, Gertrude's presence became more pronounced, as if she had just entered the room. The room was now in semi-darkness. Rost stationed himself next to the table again. There was a faint smell of naphthalene in the air.

'I don't have much time now,' said Gertrude without moving. 'I have to make lunch.' And after a moment: 'This afternoon, Erna's going to Friedel Kobler's; she already told me so.' When Rost said nothing, she added after a slight hesitation: 'Perhaps you're free this afternoon?'

No, this afternoon he would definitely not be free.

'I could have sworn that that would be your answer,' she said in a rather mocking tone, and went on absent-mindedly smoothing her hair. 'Lately you've been neglecting me. One might say that you've been avoiding me.' And as if in an attempt to awaken his appetite: 'The maid won't be here either. I gave her the afternoon off. It made me so happy, the idea of a whole afternoon together with nobody to disturb us.'

'Today it's impossible,' Rost repeated firmly.

'Today's impossible, and yesterday and tomorrow too — it's always impossible for you!'

'Are you trying to make a scene?'

'No,' said Gertrude in mounting agitation, 'where do you see a scene here? I was only happy about this afternoon, and now I'm no longer happy, I have nothing to be happy about.' She took a handkerchief out of her purse and wiped her face. For a moment she looked at him in silence, her eyes glittering. 'In two weeks' time we'll already be leaving for our summer vacation,' she said as if to herself. 'I don't know how I'll be able to.'

'So I'll have to look for another room,' said Rost, pretending not to understand her meaning.

'Why don't you come with us? We can rent a bigger apartment. It's a beautiful spot.' She looked at him pleadingly.

'Maybe I'll come to stay for a week or two. I can't come for the whole summer break.'

There was a silence. Gertrude lowered her eyes, lost in thought. She kept stroking her purse compulsively. Rost felt increasingly impatient. *I have to put an end to it*, he repeated to himself. But he went on standing there. He was overcome by boredom. It came to him in a flash that he no longer had any feelings for this woman. She was a stranger to him, a total stranger.

Gertrude stood up and advanced with slow steps. She crossed the shaft of sunlight, full of tiny motes of dust, slanting from the window to the middle of the room, and stood facing him. She was a little shorter than he was. In a voice full of suppressed emotion she whispered, 'In the last few months I've lost everything. Suddenly it's become clear to me that I have nothing left; my hands are empty. Everything is repulsive to me. Nothing attracts me, nothing appeals to me, I go on performing all my tasks as before — on the face of it nothing has changed, but the truth is that everything I do is simply out of habit. I don't know where it will all lead.' She took a breath. 'I'm speaking to you frankly, without reservations, as if I were talking to myself. There are moments in life that leave no room for silly pride. Great sorrow is naked.' And then she addressed Rost directly: 'And you? Don't you have anything to say to me? Why are you silent?'

'I can't save you.'

He knew very well that this was not the answer Gertrude had been waiting for. She had hoped for entirely different words, but these were words he could not say, not now and not to her. Perhaps it would have been better to lie, to put off the decision and wait for it all to gradually work itself out in the natural course of events. Now he stood there silently, and all he wanted was to be outside already, far away from this woman and her sorrow, which was beginning to be a burden on him.

Gertrude sank into an armchair standing nearby. 'Yes,' she said with a sigh, as if overcoming an inner obstacle, 'perhaps you aren't to blame, and nor is anyone else.' She covered her face with her hands and sat for a while without moving.

Rost was beginning to see the whole thing as ridiculous, ridiculous and annoying at once. Hoping mistakenly to bring the oppressive situation more quickly to a close, and also perhaps stirred by a certain unacknowledged pity, he took a step towards Gertrude and put a hand on her shoulder as if to wake her up. She recoiled and pushed his hand away. She looked at him distantly, and there were tears in her eyes.

'What is it?' Rost's patience snapped. 'What for God's sake is the matter?'

'I can't go on, I can't go on.'

Rost tried to placate her. 'What's the great calamity? You have a husband, you have a daughter; you're healthy, beautiful, in the prime of life, leading a comfortable, prosperous life; and you even have a lover — where's the tragedy here?'

'I have nothing,' Gertrude repeated stubbornly. 'I have nothing. I don't need a husband; I don't need a daughter. I'm not dead yet ...' And then she blurted out: 'I'm ready to leave everything right now, at this very minute! All you have to do is say the word; all I need is one little hint from you, and I'll go with you wherever you like, just one little word —'

'Stop it!' Rost cut her off sharply. 'What on earth are you talking about?' He stared at her in astonishment. For a moment he thought that she had lost her mind. He couldn't believe that her words were meant for him — the whole idea seemed so preposterous. And as if he had only just grasped how ridiculous it was, he burst out laughing.

Gertrude jumped up. 'You think it's a joke?'

'I'm going to have breakfast. See you later!' And he left the room.

At four o'clock that afternoon he met Erna as arranged. First he looked for a room, and he had already seen one, not far from where he was living now, that more or less suited him. He promised to give them an answer the next day, and went to keep his appointment with Erna in the Karlsplatz gardens. After a few minutes she appeared. Her vivacious schoolgirl's face, always lively and capricious, began to beam as soon as she set eyes on Rost, who was standing in the shade of an ancient leafy chestnut tree. At first, in her breathless haste or inner excitement, she was unable to utter a word, and she stood still and looked at him with her eyes glittering like smouldering coals. Rost too was silent. He took her slender hand in both of his and gazed at her in wonder, as if seeing her for the first time. Her broad-brimmed white hat haloed her long, pale face with its delicate features. Her stubborn, rebellious mouth, with its full, sensuous lines, riveted his attention. There was something adult and knowing about this mouth, in contrast to the girlish face, something that promised unknown pleasures of a completely new kind. A strange, spell-binding mouth, impossible to overlook.

'I'm so happy, so happy,' said Rost, unable to restrain the joy that filled his whole being to bursting. 'How lovely you are, my little Erna! I can't stop looking at you.'

Erna blushed deeply.

In the end they uprooted themselves and began to walk slowly along the manicured lawns and the flowerbeds, among the children running about or building crumbling sandcastles; the nannies bent over their handwork or their book; the feeble old men and women enjoying what might be their last dazed, sweltering summer, an enjoyment that was already dimmed by senses dulled through long use. They walked silently, their fingers interlaced, flooded by a deep, inexpressible joy that made their hearts beat faster and the blood race in their veins. Every banal word took on a special meaning, a simple, innocent meaning. The summer day seemed boundlessly, breathtakingly beautiful, unlike any other day before or after it. An orange sun weighed down on the city, making people's movements lax and heavy, some-how muffled, vague, and dim. But here, between the two lovers, everything was clear, deep, and transparent at once. Delicate threads stretched from one to the other, vibrating almost visibly in the heat. They saw everything that was happening before their eyes; they took in everything and nothing. Their eyes were clear, their senses sharp enough to register the faintest movement, but at the same time they were blind and deaf. Perhaps one day, many years later, some detail of that strange hour would surface in their minds, some hint of a smell or sound registered unwittingly by their stunned senses, and this detail would bring in its wake, would raise from oblivion, the state of mind that they were experiencing now, whose smell was the smell of ripe grain and hay, mingled with the red smell of poppies.

Yes, thought Rost — *this is the point of everything. This is what makes it all worthwhile. Even fifty years of suffering. You could give your life for a moment like this.*

They found themselves close to the street, and he suggested going to a café and having something to drink, because they both suddenly realised that their throats were parched. The street was full of the ceaseless hubbub of trams clattering on their rails and ringing their bells, the creaking of heavy horse-drawn wagons, carriages for hire and stylish private ones, of people crowding the pavements. A hot smell of fresh horse manure, dry dust, and melting asphalt filled the air. An insipid smell of vanilla rose from the sweet shops. The newspaper sellers shouted the headlines of the evening editions. The ice-cream vendors, selling their wares from the polished vats on their barrows, cried in hoarse, drawn-out voices: 'Ice—cream! Ice—cream!'

They sat down on the awning-shaded veranda of a café on a side street. Erna took little sips from the tall, narrow glass of cold, refreshing soda mixed with raspberry cordial. From time to time she gave Rost a long, close look.

'Weren't you with Friedel Kobler?'

'I was.' And after a moment: 'I don't know, my mother seems strange lately. She's always irritable. Especially to me, it seems.'

Rost changed the subject. 'I went to look for a room today. I saw one that might suit me.'

Erna cried in a disappointed voice: 'What, are you thinking of moving?' And then she added: 'Yes, of course, that would be best.' She felt a brief instant of regret. Her parents' home suddenly appeared empty and dull.

'You're going on vacation soon.'

'And you won't come?'

'Yes, I will.'

'Anyway it doesn't matter,' snapped Erna.

'What doesn't matter?'

'Nothing.'

Erna fell silent. She felt a secret pain that she could not explain. For some reason she felt uncomfortable. Across the road, workers were repairing the pavement, arranging square paving stones on the ground and knocking them into place with brisk strokes of their hammers. Some of them were naked from the waist up, their bodies tanned, their chests hairy. Most of them were wearing bell-bottomed corduroy trousers. She kept her eyes on them for a while with an air of distraction, although she wasn't actually thinking of anything. She was in a kind of daze, a state of pleasant, animal contentment, together with the dull pain that did not leave her.

In the meantime the sun had been sliding down in the sky and stealing little by little under the veranda awning, where it had reached the edge of their table, which was covered with a grey oilcloth, now tinged with orange.

Erna raised her eyes to Rost as if tearing herself from a distant dream, and she gave him a long look with an amenable, childish smile on her face, at the sight of which Rost's heart was flooded with warmth. The whole of this young life was now directed at him, streaming thrillingly towards him.

'I could go on singing your praises all day long, telling you how beautiful you are, how sweet you are, my dear little Erna,' he whispered, leaning towards her. 'Without the certainty of your existence nothing has any importance. Not the sun, not the summer — nothing matters without you. Do you understand? There would be no point to anything. The days, the years up to now, until I met you, are empty to me. My life only begins with you.'

Erna put her hand on the back of Rost's hand, which was lying on the table, and stroked it gently once or twice with her eyes lowered. The sun was now climbing up her bare arm and into the short sleeve of her blue summer dress without her noticing.

With her eyes still downcast she said: 'In a minute I'll start to see myself as a very important person, equal to a cabinet minister at least.'

'You are very important! There's nobody more important than you.'

'And yet I often feel like a little girl, a naive, ignorant child.'

'Your body is full of wisdom. These arms, legs, this hair, this nose, these eyes — they're all full of wisdom. I'll still convince you of the wisdom of your sweet body. There is more than one kind of wisdom in the world, and the foolishness of youth is wiser than all the systems of philosophy put together. The two of us, you and I, are immeasurably wise because we're young, full of life to the tips of the hair on our heads!'

They stood up and walked in the direction of the nearby Volksgarten. Unconsciously they chose side alleys for fear of bumping into anyone they knew. These were quiet alleys surrounded by high walls, drowsing in the sweltering heat, with children playing in them undisturbed, secluded from the city's roar. An old woman's ancient head peeped out of an open window, a cat next to her. From an upper storey the hurried notes of a piano tumbled down. In another alley there was nothing to be seen except for a carriage parked outside a doorway, the coachman huddled on his seat with his head bowed as if he were sleeping, and the horse wagging its cropped tail to chase away the flies. After crossing the busy Ringstrasse, they found themselves at one of the entrances to the Volksgarten. They strolled along quiet side paths at a leisurely pace in silence, afraid to mar with a superfluous word or a hasty movement the tremulous joy filling their hearts. A refreshing coolness wafted from the clustered bushes and the ancient trees with their heavy boughs. The noise of the city was faint here, and the only other people they encountered were solitary walkers or couples seeking seclusion. From time to time a burst of music from the park band reached them as if from another world, strange and distant, and suddenly disappeared again as if swept away by an invisible hand. The snatch of a tune was left lingering in the air, not at all melancholy, but secretly piercing the heart nevertheless, and bringing with it a sense of summer and youthful high spirits. From time to time Rost glanced at Erna walking beside him with her hat in her hand, and a stray lock of blue-black hair falling onto her fair cheek, which was blooming with a faint, almost imperceptible blush.

They found a bench and sat down. The bench was deep in the shade, with only a few rays of sunlight dappling the ground a little way off. Rost took advantage of a moment when the path was deserted to kiss her quickly on her mouth and neck.

'Please don't, darling,' Erna protested weakly, blushing bright red. 'Someone might pass.'

'And if someone does? We're not doing anything wrong.'

'I don't know. My mother would certainly think so,' Erna said with a smile.

'Oh, your mother! In her eyes you're probably still six years old.'

'I'm only sixteen,' said Erna, 'but I often feel like a grown woman in every respect. I feel that I'm able to love, allowed to love like a woman, and I don't need to ask for anyone's permission but my own!' She said this in a confident and decisive tone that brooked no question, and as if to reinforce her words she seized hold of Rost boldly and kissed him on his mouth, his eyes, and his hair with passionate, reckless abandon. She bit his lip until it bled, and she didn't let go until he extricated himself gently from her embrace.

'You don't have to eat me alive!'

They looked into each other's eyes and burst into peals of liberating laughter, which lasted for some moments.

Two young men appeared, coming towards them on the path. Rost recognised them from a distance and burst out: 'Damn it all! You can't hide anywhere in this town,' and to

Erna: 'We can't get out of it now.'

Fritz Anker drew closer with Shor, and Rost introduced the latter to Erna.

'We're not intruding?' said Shor.

'Since I forgot to order the gatekeeper to lock the gates against intruders ...' Rost joked in a forced tone.

Anker remained standing, stealing embarrassed looks at Erna.

'Anyone seeking seclusion should go somewhere else,' remarked Shor. 'Speaking for myself, I have no such desires; on the contrary, I'm delighted to meet you.' And smiling frankly at Erna, he added: 'Especially in the company of such a charming young lady!'

He sat down on the bench, on the other side of Erna.

'And you, aren't you going to sit down?' she said to Anker. 'You're invited to sit down too.'

Anker had no desire to sit. Leaning on his cane, stooping slightly and staring through the thick lenses of his glasses, he regretted having approached them. His sharpened senses told him that he had made a mistake, that they shouldn't have intruded. But at the same time he couldn't take his eyes off Erna. How joyfully her eyes were sparkling: he noted this without a trace of jealousy, but with a secret pang in his heart, and felt acutely aware of his own extreme loneliness. 'Why don't we take a carriage,' the words escaped him unwillingly, 'and have supper in the fresh air?'

But Erna had to be back home at seven o'clock sharp.

'What a shame you have to leave us so soon,' said Shor. 'Perhaps we'll be luckier next time.' They said goodbye and walked away.

'Poor Anker,' said Erna. 'I don't know, for some reason

I feel sorry for him. A young boy who seems like an old man. He's a person without any talent for living.'

When they left the park, the Ringstrasse was already full of people hurrying home after the day's work. The covetous looks that passing men directed at Erna did not escape Rost's notice, and they added to his satisfaction. He felt destined for good fortune, and full of extraordinary strength, both physical and spiritual.

The sun was now shining a reddish light on the upper storeys of the buildings, while the streets below were dim and shadowy. The walls and pavements, which had sweltered during the day, now gave off their imprisoned heat, and only in the open space of Karlsplatz was the air fresher. But Rost and Erna were out of luck: when they approached their street and were about to take leave of each other, Gertrude suddenly popped up and confronted them.

'Where are you coming from?' she asked with affected nonchalance.

Rost conquered his momentary embarrassment and said casually: 'I bumped into Erna in the street and saw her home.'

'You think she couldn't find her way on her own? She isn't a baby anymore.'

'I couldn't agree more,' said Rost, with a hint of irony.

Gertrude turned to Erna. 'Were you at Friedel's place?'

'Yes, of course. Why do you ask? You know I went to visit her.'

'I just thought that this wasn't necessarily the way back from there.'

'What, am I only allowed to take one way home?' Erna demanded, and then added quickly: 'It isn't seven o'clock yet.'

'Have it your own way,' said Gertrude. 'Go upstairs, I'll be along in a minute.'

Erna stayed where she was.

'Well, what are you waiting for?' Gertrude was vexed. 'I told you I'd be along in a minute. I need to get something at the shops.'

'I'll come with you.'

'What a pest!' Gertrude was losing her temper. 'I didn't ask you to come with me, did I?'

'Calm down, Mother,' said Erna, 'I'm going. I just thought you would like the company, but if you don't want me to …' She nodded at Rost and walked away.

'So it's her!' Gertrude looked in her daughter's direction.

'What's her?' Rost feigned ignorance.

'Don't pretend. You know exactly what I mean.'

'I don't know what you're talking about,' stated Rost firmly. He started walking away, and Gertrude followed him.

'You can say what you like,' said Gertrude furiously. 'I won't allow it. Do you hear? I won't allow it!' And after a moment: 'She's only sixteen!'

'Nobody says she isn't.'

'Stop joking! You know I love you.'

'And so?'

'I won't let anybody take you away from me, you hear? Nobody in the world!'

'Nobody's tried.'

Without paying any attention to him Gertrude continued: 'You meet Erna too often; I won't have it!'

'Coincidence.'

'When it happens all the time, it stops looking like a coincidence.'

'You're making yourself ridiculous. I can't see any harm in accompanying Erna for a few steps when I happen to meet her, simply because I have an intimate relationship with you.'

'That's not what we're talking about! I'm certain that you're courting her.'

'You're mistaken.'

'In any case I won't allow it. I'll take whatever steps are necessary.'

They were walking next to the park, and Rost stood still and leaned against the black iron grille of the fence.

Better to end it peaceably, without unnecessary complications, thought Rost to himself. This whole quarrel, however disagreeable, could not darken the happiness filling his being. His heart sang joyfully within him, and he was inclined at that moment to be merciful towards Gertrude and the whole world. The church bell rang briskly seven times, as if delivering an irrevocable sentence. Gertrude stood before him in silence, as if waiting for something to happen. For the first time Rost noticed a rather deep line next to her mouth, and a few small, barely perceptible wrinkles around her eyes. Suddenly she seemed to him pathetic, pitiful, even though — apart from these slight signs of ageing — the lines of her face were still firm and definite, without any sagging or slackening, and her eyes shone with a bright, youthful gleam. Her lips parted slightly as if she were about to speak, but she said nothing. She went on standing in front of him and looking as if through him and beyond him to somewhere very far away.

Rost waited. He picked a leaf from a branch overhanging the fence and played with it absent-mindedly. Suddenly he was overcome by a burst of impatience — what was he standing there like an idiot for? He'd had enough. More than enough. He held out his hand to take his leave.

Gertrude came to her senses and shook his hand in silence. Then she hurried away without looking back.

18

As soon as they finished eating, George Shtift folded his napkin and stood up. He had to see a man on business and didn't know when he would be able to get away. In any case, he didn't want them to wait up for him — Gertrude and Erna could spend the evening as they pleased. The daylight streaming through the open windows into the shaded room was already tinged with the faint grey of approaching dusk. Mitzi the maid cleared the table with a familiar domestic clatter. Erna moved her chair to the window and took up the novel she had been reading before supper. She looked out at the row of windows in the building across the street. In one of the windows a young blonde girl appeared and disappeared again.

He was there somewhere, mused Erna, there for her, sitting or walking or eating or talking to his friends, but there, in the flesh. His friends too were dear to her, whoever came into contact with him was dear to her, because they had been touched by his presence, had absorbed something of his being. Without thinking she rose to her feet and went over to the piano in the corner and ran her fingers over the keys. Then she turned on her heel and faced the interior of the room, standing behind her mother, who had not moved from her chair at the dining table. In a sudden excess of love she threw her arms around her mother's neck, raised her face, and showered her cheeks and brow with kisses, just as she had done not long before in the Volksgarten with Rost.

'Stop it!' cried her mother in annoyance and pushed her away.

'You're a beautiful woman, Mother,' exclaimed Erna admiringly, 'a great beauty.'

But Gertrude was in no mood now for playing games with her daughter. Suddenly she felt estranged from this girl. She turned herself around and examined Erna in silence, not without a hint of hostility in her regard. Unable at that moment to give herself a clear account of this new feeling towards her daughter, she obscurely sensed the hostility growing inside her. At the same time she had to admit that Erna was a beautiful girl, extraordinarily beautiful. With a charm that was impossible to resist. No, she was no longer a little girl, her own sweet little girl; before her stood a grown woman, a beautiful stranger armed with dangerous weapons. A rival not to be made light of. Waging war against her would not be easy, and victory was not assured. Right then, Gertrude would have preferred Erna to be ugly, crippled, afflicted by some disease.

By nature Gertrude was not a bad woman or a cruel one, but now she began to feel a gnawing sense of inferiority eating away at her. She was only thirty-seven, in the prime of life, without any obvious signs of getting old, but fear had already begun to steal into her heart, the fear of inevitable ageing, from which there was no escape. This fear was not yet frank and explicit. It came upon her quite rarely, a slight tremor of apprehension, sometimes in the wake of a feeling of exhaustion after meals, or a hint of fatigue after walking, even though they were not necessarily signs of ageing. She was still full of energy; she still had an unquenchable thirst for life. The certainty of years lost without profit, without pleasure — dull, monotonous years by the side of her boring, mediocre husband, who did not even know how to make her feel like a woman; years that were gone forever — preyed on her mind. For apart from a few insignificant little flings, which served only as an amusement to relieve the day-to-day boredom of her life, the years had gone by like one long desert. At the time she had not been fully aware of how empty they were, except perhaps for an obscure sense of discontent, a kind of hunger for something not known. The true nature of her past life had only become evident to her when she met Rost and saw what a wealth of sensations — despair, apprehension, endless joy — could be contained in one day, even one hour: a richness beyond measure. And now, when she had only begun to feel all this, to taste the wonders of this life to the full, she sensed that he was already tired of her, that he was slipping out of her hands. No! She would not permit it — even if it cost her her life. That Erna, flesh of her flesh, would do this to her! They would see who was the stronger! For she knew, with an intuitive certainty that needed no proof, that something was going on between Erna and Rost, and she was determined to put an end to it, whatever it took. In the meantime she had even managed to blur her real motive, jealously, and suggest others to take its place. A jumble of disjointed thoughts and feelings struggled within her, without any order or logic, the most conspicuous among them being a new and overpowering animosity.

'I would like to know how you came to meet Rost on the way to Friedel's?' she demanded with suppressed fury, fixing her daughter with a penetrating look.

'A coincidence,' lied Erna in almost the same tone as Rost, without being aware of it. But this detail did not escape the sharpened senses of her mother. *She's already talking like him,* the thought pierced her.

'In any case,' said Gertrude, trying to keep her voice calm and measured, 'I'm asking you not to meet him again.'

'Why not?' asked Erna.

'Because I don't want you to. I'm asking you not to associate with him.'

'Not with him in particular?' said Erna in a tone of affected indifference.

'He's not suitable company for you.'

'And for you?'

'What do you mean?'

'You talk to him too, and you don't see anything wrong with it.'

'There's no comparison,' snapped Gertrude, at a loss for a retort, 'you're still a little girl.'

'First of all, I'm not a little girl anymore. And second, I'm your daughter. Company that's suitable for the mother is also suitable for the daughter, no?'

Gertrude flared up. 'Stop being so cheeky. I don't even know you anymore.'

'I'm not being cheeky at all,' said Erna, maintaining her composure. She sensed obscurely that she was the stronger of the two, and she felt completely calm. 'It's simply common sense. If you forbid me to associate with someone, you need to explain yourself.'

'I don't need to explain anything. You're just a girl and you don't understand. I'm telling you that I don't want you to — and that's enough!'

'Fine! But it's not enough for me at all,' said Erna, and she returned to her previous place by the window.

The room was already half in darkness. Gertrude stood up and went to switch on the electric light next to the door. The orange light suddenly flooded the room and hurt their eyes. Gertrude came to stand next to Erna. 'You should pay more attention to your studies and not take them lightly, especially now before the exams. That's your job now, not occupying your mind with frivolities.'

'I don't take my studies lightly and I'm not going to fail my exams, don't worry. But you still haven't explained to me why I have to run away like an uncivilised savage without a word of greeting when I meet Rost!'

'I have nothing to explain and I don't want to explain. I don't want you associating with him, do you understand?'

Erna made no reply. She turned her head and looked out of the window. A moth flew around and beat itself against the electric light globe, which was made of opaque glass. She had no wish to continue the argument: her mother was unjust. Unjust! The real reason for this sudden prohibition wasn't hard to guess. The whole argument made her uneasy, as if clumsy hands were being laid on something fragile and infinitely precious to her. From now on she would be more careful; she would not allow it to be besmirched. In any case, Gertrude had succeeded in somewhat spoiling her good mood and making her feel indignant and resentful. And when after a few minutes her mother told her to get dressed and come out for a walk, she excused herself on the pretext of a headache, and Gertrude did not press her.

Erna retired to her room. It was still early. For a while she sat idly at her desk. The fresh, quiet evening gradually calmed her. But deep within her, in some hidden corner of her heart, a feeling glowed like a light dimmed by her hand, a feeling directed towards the room at the end of the corridor, towards the streets of the city in general, in one of which he was now to be found.

She took a blank sheet of paper and began to write rapidly:

I always knew that one day you would come. I was always ready to welcome you; I just didn't know that you would come now, and in this shape. From now on, there is nothing in my body or my soul that is mine or anyone else's but yours. Yours, yours, and yours alone. All you have to do is come and take it. Whenever you come and command me I will obey. Whenever you come to take all of me or part of me, I am ready and willing; I will never obey anyone but you. My mother wants to separate us. She won't be able to. Nobody will. And if you ever leave me, I'll always go on loving you. I won't cry, but I'll be sad; I'll call you and wait for you, I'll always wait for you, I'll never be able to have enough of you. I'll want you and love you, and I won't stop calling you to come back. Now I'm here in my room, and at the same time I'm in other places, wherever you are, in any one of the streets where I have been or will be with you.

Take this room: I've known it since I was born. I grew up in it. But only from the day I met you has it become dear to me, its white walls and ceiling and furniture and every corner of it. You have never seen my room. You don't know that my bed has brass knobs, that one of the chairs has a broken leg, and that the closet door sometimes refuses to close. But nevertheless you are always here, sitting opposite me or walking around the room, smoking, laughing; and when I take off my dress you stand and watch and smile. I'm not in the least shy of you. You stroke my breasts and my stomach and my thighs and back, and you kiss me all over my body and under my armpit and behind my ear. I'd like to take off all my clothes to be completely naked for you, for you to see me just as I am, just as I love you. I have no shame because you can see no fault in me; after all, I'm a part of you, of your being — and are you ashamed of yourself? I wish it would come quickly, the hour when I can love you as a woman, as a lover, with all this body of mine, which burns for the touch of your hand, which trembles in anticipation of your body.

Erna's face was flushed with excitement, and her heart was beating rapidly. She read over what she had written in her large, rather loopy handwriting, which was energetic and decisive and still had something childish, a hint of the schoolgirl, about it. A gleeful smile spread over her face as she read her daring confession. When she had finished, she leaned back in her chair and sat for a while without moving. Then she stood up and tore the page to shreds and threw them out of the window. She watched the scraps of paper blowing in all directions, floating slowly through the air as they scattered, some of them disappearing into the foliage of the tree under the window. She returned to her desk and scribbled a note, without an address or a signature, on a piece of paper:

> Tomorrow, four o'clock. Wait for me in the café where we
> sat today. I'll try to come if my mother doesn't stop me.

She put the note into an envelope and stepped cautiously into the passage, stole down its length, and opened the door to Rost's room. Without switching on the light, she slipped inside, quick and light-footed as a cat, put the note on the table, and left the room.

The summer holidays arrived: parched yellow days, clear and still as water without the slightest breeze ruffling their surface. Erna graduated to the top form. Preparations were afoot in the Shtift household for the trip to the summer resort in two days' time. Gertrude was now almost constantly irritable, ordering Erna about and scolding her with and without reason, watching her every move, criticising and condemning everything she did, as if she were under some supreme obligation to supervise her daughter ceaselessly and correct the way she sat and stood and ate and spoke or didn't speak. Nothing about Erna was to her satisfaction. Everything she did annoyed her, until even George Shtift, who was not particularly perceptive, remarked to his wife, not in Erna's presence, that she was behaving strangely towards their daughter. But Gertrude dismissed his attempts to defend the girl with a few short sentences about the change for the worse that had taken place in Erna lately, without going into the matter any further.

In fact Gertrude secretly sensed that she was wrong, that she was being cruel to her daughter for no fault of hers, but she was unable to overcome her inner need to torment her. By now she was full of bitterness and open hostility towards her daughter. And the sense of her own injustice only made her abuse the girl even more, incited by her feelings of weakness and inferiority towards this baby who was still wet behind the ears, and who nevertheless possessed the advantage over her — the complete and absolute advantage in all respects.

And Erna showed no signs of anger towards her mother. It was impossible to make her lose her temper. She refused to be provoked by her mother's jibes, as if it were all perfectly natural; and her composure only fuelled the older woman's wrath. Sometimes, when Gertrude's stings were blunted by Erna's steely armour, and her rage broke all bounds and erupted in shameless, unrestrained outbursts, her daughter would try to pacify her as if she were a child or a sick woman, and do her best to change the subject. She dealt with her mother's rages as if they were of no account, as if they had no effect on her at all. Since she encountered no resistance, Gertrude felt like someone butting against a featherbed — she was made to appear ridiculous, and for this she could not forgive her daughter. She lost all control of herself, and needless to say she no longer had any control over her daughter. Erna seemed to have slipped through her fingers; she no longer knew her; she did not recognise this unbowed girl who suddenly showed signs of such strength of character and self-control.

Rost had left his room in the Shtift residence and was now living not far from the home of Friedel's parents. He now had two rooms, a bedchamber and a sitting room, whose windows overlooked a small square where pigeons often pecked at the swept paving stones, or boys played with a football. He was very pleased with his new quarters. His landlady, Frau Stengelberg, a respectable matron with white hair and a youngish face, lived alone in the large apartment with her maid, where she was only occasionally visited, mainly on Sundays and holidays, by her sons and daughters. She had been left a widow by her second husband a year before, and was not yet thinking of getting married again.

She was already an old woman, she would say, not without a trace of flirtatiousness, and who would want her? She still showed signs of a vanished beauty, and it was not difficult to imagine her as a young woman when you saw her daughter, who looked a lot like her.

Rost was happy in this quiet, spacious apartment.

EPILOGUE

Marie-Anne's restless, irritable sleep was invaded by the sound of the passage door opening. She reached out her hand and turned on the table lamp on the little bedside shelf. A cloudy pink light spilled into the large room, not enough to banish the shadows huddling in the corners. The clock said a quarter to five.

Semi-recumbent in the wide bed, Marie-Anne rested on her elbow without moving. In the heavy silence she made out the muffled steps of Michael Rost in the next room. Then came the sound of water splashing into the bathtub. In the end she couldn't wait any longer. She got up and wrapped herself in her dressing-gown and opened the door into the next room.

'Did you go there again?' She remained standing in the doorway.

'You're not asleep?'

'I couldn't sleep.' And after a second she said it again: 'I couldn't sleep.'

'I lost,' said Rost indifferently, putting on grey silk pyjamas.

'I asked you not to go there. Lately you've been losing all

the time. You've lost a lot.'

'I don't care. I'm sick of the whole situation.'

'And me?'

He stood facing her, drawn up to his full height, rubbing his cigarette lighter with his thumb. 'You want me to be honest with you?'

'I couldn't sleep,' she said as if to herself. 'Bad thoughts all night long, and now …'

'I want to start all over again. I can't stay in the same situation for long.'

'Meaning?'

'You're a grown woman,' continued Rost, 'and apart from that I've lost all my money. All of it.'

'Do I need your money?' Her voice quivered slightly. She came closer to him and wrapped her bare arms around his neck. Her dressing-gown slipped off her shoulders and fell to the floor. She remained in a blue nightgown that was ruffled at the edges of the neck and sleeves. She threw her head back and her rust-coloured hair fell onto her shoulders.

'So this is the end?'

He led her to a stuffed armchair. 'Sit down, and let's talk calmly and quietly.'

Marie-Anne repeated: 'Michael, is this the end?'

'What did you think? For our time together to end in a marriage certificate — is that what you wanted? And then to have children out of boredom and habit, or to look for new lovers all the time? You should know at least fifty men before you deserve that. You're only twenty years old.'

'I thought … You're certainly not twenty anymore … What's a marriage certificate got to do with it? I wouldn't want to marry you! What an idea!'

'Quite right. I always considered you an intelligent, un-sentimental woman.'

Marie-Anne tossed her head with the arrogance of a spoiled rich girl. And after a brief silence: 'And so you're going back to your shady business deals.'

'Shady? A bit of self-righteousness to see me on my way? By the way, you can stay on in the apartment if you want to.'

'Thank you! I don't want to.' She stood up, walked towards the bedroom door, and changed her mind halfway. Suddenly she turned on her heel and went straight up to him and slapped him on the cheek. 'You bastard!'

Michael Rost pushed her away, and she fell back and landed on the carpet. 'Go to bed, Marie-Anne! I don't like tragic scenes.'

Naked to the waist, Marie-Anne lay on the floor, sobbing softly. Outside, under the windows, a car drove past. Then all was quiet again, except for the sound of Marie-Anne's broken sobs.

After a while she dragged herself over the carpet to where Rost was sitting and smoking, and seized hold of his knees. Raising her face, wet with tears, she said to him: 'Forgive me, my love … you know how much …'

Rost picked her up and carried her to the bedroom and laid her down on the bed.

Then he retired to the bathroom.

NOTE ON
THE TEXT

Youval Shimoni and Lilach Nethanel

There were a number of dilemmas to be solved during the process of transferring the text from manuscript to print, whether in the choice between several linguistic possibilities proposed by Vogel, in confronting the raw and only partially edited form of the text, or in stitching together the Viennese story and the Parisian frame.

For the language, we were helped considerably by the decisions taken by Menahem Peri, as explained in his afterword to *Married Life* (Hakibbutz Hameuchad/Keter, 1986), choosing between the high, archaic language and the relatively modern Hebrew that served Vogel in other places. In his linguistic choices, Vogel sometimes left alternatives, with the accompanying note 'Re-appraisal needed', and sometimes we have restored his original choice or blended versions together.

More difficult decisions had to be taken in everything

regarding the state of the text and the order of the events related in it. Vogel brought the heart of the novel — the triangular relationship between Rost, Gertrude, and Erna — to a conclusion in most respects, but the episodes accompanying the central plot were very often left in their original, raw state. There are clear signs of groping for expression, groping for characterisation, reconsiderations intended to establish what had not yet been developed and granted life of its own; and there are also glaring contradictions, often on one page and from one paragraph to the next.

Vogel scholars may find here fertile ground for contemplating his programmatic and stylistic struggles, but our sympathies here are for lovers of literature in general, who would certainly prefer a single, focused version to the kind of problems that arise from the uneven level of textual development. For this reason we have chosen to condense repetitive or contradictory statements on the part of background characters, and we had difficulties with more-important secondary characters such as Peter Dean, who posed a problem of another kind — there is virtually no follow-up to Dean's act of exceptional generosity in the first part of the book, and there is no way of knowing if Vogel intended to develop this strand of the story any further. One way or the other, judging by the plethora of erasures and the absence of any follow-up, it is clear that Dean was sketched in a preliminary and rudimentary fashion, and the author seemed to be doing everything in his power to boost the man's profile: millionaire status, which began with washing dishes; going on to trade in hashish and opium, guns and knives; taking control of oil companies and railways; depositing huge sums in the banks; buying an old palace. We have chosen to abridge some such characterisations, though it is heart-breaking to imagine the young Vogel, in his poverty and hunger, inventing for himself a patron and mentor as rich as Croesus, who would turn to him and rescue him from all the hardships of this life.

Some passages that seemed strange in their first, unedited positions have been moved to places where they are better suited to the plot and the tone. For example, after the first sexual encounter between Rost and Gertrude, Gertrude asks Rost about his life and he begins to answer her, but what begins as the reply of a character in a post-coital bed changes abruptly into the expansive and eloquent voice of Vogel himself — but apparently still spoken by his protagonist, a protagonist not capable of such insight or descriptive flair, certainly not in bed, moments after intercourse. These exquisite descriptions, most certainly the author's voice, have been relocated to where the style and the content of the material are more appropriate.

Another difficult decision had to be made regarding the framing story. Admittedly, it differed from the rest of the text in that there were no unedited sections in it, but because it was not complete, there remained a worrying gap between on the one hand the continuity of Rost's night-wandering in the streets of Paris, from the café to the bridge and from there to a prostitute's room, and on the other the last scene, which takes place in Rost's apartment, with a female partner who has not been mentioned before, where he tells her he is leaving her. Because of this gap, and in the interest of making the whole text comprehensible, it seemed that if this scene were moved to the end of the manuscript, it would conclude the framing narrative, and would more effectively recall the distance between the younger, Viennese Rost and the older, Parisian Rost. In this Parisian opening we find a kind of foretaste of the core of the novel, a story told in a distorted way by a stammering actor, who describes to Rost his love affair with a mother and her daughter before the war. On the following page Rost feels the flicker of a faint memory of a similar night, 'buried beneath the rubble of the years and their events': for this reason too it seemed appropriate to end the Parisian opening at this stage and not with the later, relatively distant scene, in order to foreground once again the older Rost's process of remembering, through which the crux of the novel emerges, portraying him at the beginning of his time in Vienna.

If a minority of readers denounce us for not reproducing the manuscript in its unfinished state, they may rest assured that these issues will remain open to discussion and criticism at all levels. We took these decisions to enable today's reader to read something that has been hidden for many decades, and is long overdue for attention — and not only with a magnifying glass. The man who wrote in his diary in March 1913, 'I am suspended between two fires: I don't want to die, and I'm not equipped to live as others do', and in August 1916 wrote, 'And you are as empty as you were before the war. Empty, empty, and there's nothing to hope for. Just to walk towards death, to walk slowly, with a prolonged yawn' — this man had the artistic talent to build, on this very earth, a vibrant, colourful world driven by powerful emotions, where the characters — whether depictions of Vogel or of his acquaintances, or creatures of his imagination — fill this world to overflowing with their commotion, their passions and desires, with the whispering of their hearts, and with their meditation on the meaning of life, such that all of them, even the most desperate and gloomy among them, are very far from causing yawns.

(Translated by Philip Simpson)